KU-202-538

THE BOUNDARY LINE

Eager to escape the heat of London in July, Terry Manstone goes on a hiking trip in Sussex — only to find herself lost, with darkness and a storm approaching. Hoping to make it to the next village, she sprains her ankle, and becomes a guest in a nearby house. Here she meets the handsome Dr. Blaise Farlong and his bitter, scheming wife Ruth. Terry never thought she'd fall in love with a married man; and when Ruth's machinations push her into Blaise's arms, their problems are only just beginning . . .

Books by Denise Robins
in the Linford Romance Library:

GYPSY LOVER
KISS OF YOUTH
THE ENDURING FLAME
FAMILY HOLIDAY
BRIEF ECSTASY
THE TIGER IN MEN
LIGHT THE CANDLES
THE PRICE OF FOLLY

DENISE ROBINS

THE BOUNDARY LINE

Complete and Unabridged

LINFORD
Leicester

First published in Great Britain in 1932

First Linford Edition
published 2017

Copyright © 1931 by Denise Robins
All rights reserved

A catalogue record for this book is available
from the British Library.

ISBN 978–1–4448–3129–0

Published by
F. A. Thorpe (Publishing)
Anstey, Leicestershire

Set by Words & Graphics Ltd.
Anstey, Leicestershire
Printed and bound in Great Britain by
T. J. International Ltd., Padstow, Cornwall

This book is printed on acid-free paper

Part One

Monte Carlo

1

The storm broke suddenly and with unexpected violence over Rossdown Forest, and it was only then that Terry Manstone realised three very important things: firstly, that it was growing very late; secondly, that she had lost her way; and thirdly, that she had no idea where she was going to sleep tonight.

Ten minutes ago she had been sitting under an old and beautiful beech-tree, her back against the broad trunk that was grey with lichen and scarred with many initials, extremely weary but quite content. Above her the leaves were spread like green lace through which only now and then, when the wind stirred the branches, she glimpsed blue skies. All around her stood other beeches, as big, as beautiful, as serene. The rich gloom of the forest was pregnant with peace.

Here was tranquillity and dim enchantment; a silence broken only by the twitter and chirp of many birds.

The girl resting alone had found what she had wanted so badly. Peace, relief from the heat, the rush, the stifling atmosphere of London in July. The joy of being alone — with time in which to think her thoughts and dream her dreams undisturbed.

Then this sudden, treacherous change in the weather. The muffled boom of thunder, sudden darkness, and big drops of rain spattering through the leaves on to her upturned face.

She picked up the rucksack which contained her entire travelling-kit, slung it over her back, brushed a few twigs and dry leaves from her grey flannel suit, put on a mackintosh, and pulled her scarlet beret firmly over her head. She was not particularly afraid of storms. She rather liked to see the lightning flash and play in the heavens. But she did not relish being in a forest

4

during a storm. It was a little dangerous. Besides which, her wrist-watch told her that it was half past eight. She had had nothing to eat since that heavenly tea in a Sussex farmhouse at four o'clock. She was hungry. And she had tramped fifteen miles today. That was enough.

She was loving this first day of her solitary walking-tour. She had had to fight for it, too — defy her mother and sister who had done their best to prevent her from going away.

Her mother — a conventional, narrow-minded woman — considered it dreadful for a girl of twenty-one · to roam round the countryside alone. Her sister, Barbara, who would never have dreamed of doing such a thing, felt the same about it. But Terry had broken loose — sick to death of the restrictions, the boredom, the waste of time of the social round at home in Wimbledon.

The storm rather spoiled things this evening, however, and Terry's heart beat a little nervously as she walked quickly through the forest. It was not the way which she had come. She had no 'bump of locality,' and she had lost her bearings completely.

She looked anxiously around her. She was on a moor — Rossdown Moor — famous in Sussex for its wild and unspoiled beauty. Magnificent now, with the lightning flashing over it, but the sky was black with storm-clouds and the thunder crashed with deafening peals, crackled like the sound of calico being ripped down in pieces. It was rather nerve-racking even for Terry, who was young and had very few nerves in her healthy body.

Where on earth was she?

The rain pelted upon her, soaking through the red beret set so jauntily on the small brown head, through the thin silky mackintosh and flannel suit and white silk blouse — soaking her to the skin. Her tan brogues squelched with water. She found a road — followed it — running breathlessly. The rucksack

6

became a heavy weight, and her heart-beats hurt her.

Then she came to cross-roads and a signpost. It was darkish now, but the lightning lit up the words: '*To Rossdown 1 mile.*' Ah! that was a village. She would find shelter for the night there. She ran, lowering her head as the rain beat into her eyes. The thunder crashed on.

Her sense of humour prevailing, Terry thought:

'Mummy and Barbara would be so pleased if they could see this finale to my first day's hiking. 'Serve you right,' would be the slogan . . . '

Half a mile more. Terry became drenched, hot, trembling with fatigue. She felt she could not move an inch farther. Rossdown village seemed to be at the other side of the world.

Then she saw lights twinkling mistily ahead through the driving rain. Turning off the road, she began to run over the moor, taking a short cut toward those lights. She could see many lights now.

She was near the village.

Then an exasperating thing happened. She caught her foot in a rabbit-hole, stumbled and wrenched her ankle. It was fortunate she did not sprain it. It hurt enough, anyhow. Grimacing, she limped slowly, now, toward those beacon lights. She was nearing a human dwelling, and she did not care to whom it belonged — prince or pauper; she was going to ask for shelter and rest and get out of this horrible storm.

The pain in the ankle intensified. Terry's face whitened under the golden tan. Setting her teeth, she moved on, limping badly.

At last she came to the house — a biggish one with a walled-in garden. A vivid flash of lightning showed her a wrought-iron gateway; a brick pathway, flanked by shaped yews. She was utterly exhausted when she reached the door which was just inside the old porchway, and knocked upon it; too exhausted even to look for a bell.

Nobody answered her knocking. She knocked again. She knew somebody was at home. She had seen a light. Her head felt queer. Was she going to faint? Surely not. Terry had never done such a thing in her life. But of course she had walked a tremendous distance, for her, and not eaten very much.

Then a light gleamed through the hall window on the left of the door, which was opened cautiously.

'Who is it?' said a woman's sharp voice.

'Can you let me in — please?' gasped Terry.

The door opened wide. Half blinded by rain and lightning, Terry saw an elderly woman wearing a black dress and white apron. At the same time a terrific peal of thunder echoed and re-echoed over the moor. The woman shrank back, shielding her eyes with her hand.

'Ugh! that dreadful lightning. Come in, for goodness' sake.'

Terry stumbled in. The door was shut

after her. She managed to smile and say:

'Thanks — awfully — '

Then the hall began to spin round her. She felt an arm about her, and heard the woman say:

'Hold up — don't go and faint. Gracious me — you're only a child — what on earth are you doing out in a storm like this? Soaked through — mercy on us!'

Terry was too exhausted to answer. She did not faint, but she was a little vague as to what happened for a moment or two — just felt herself being helped along to some room and put in an armchair. She sat with eyes closed, panting, fighting off a feeling of sickness.

Then the faint sensation passed and her head cleared again.

'You'd better have a drop of brandy,' the woman said, and left her alone.

Terry looked round. Heavens, what a relief to be indoors — out of that awful storm! It was most comfortable and pleasant in here. A long-shaped room with low, casement windows, and green silky curtains shutting out the stormy summer's night. The atmosphere was close, for it had been a very hot day, and there was a rich scent of roses in here. Terry saw several vases and bowls of luscious scarlet and yellow blooms; some on the window-sill; some on a small table beside her chair; a big crystal bowl full on a big mahogany desk in front of her.

She began to take note of many significant things in this room. A screen, half shielding a wash-basin; a glass and enamel tray on wheels, and a tall cupboard with glass doors revealing rows of bottles, jars, bowls, instruments, a couch covered by a rug. One wall completely lined with books. Medical and surgical books.

'This is a doctor's house — this is a surgery' — the thought leapt to Terry's brain.

Then the woman came back with the brandy.

11

'Better drink this,' she said.

'I'd rather not,' said Terry. 'I'm all right now, thanks.'

'Where on earth have you come from?'

'The forest.'

'Are you a stranger here, then?'

'Very much so . . . ' Terry laughed a little shakily. 'I only left London this morning — on a walking-tour. I've never been to this part of Sussex before.'

'A walking-tour,' repeated the woman, and stared at the girl.

Terry took off her rucksack and her beret. Water dripped on to the thick green carpet. The woman hastily took them from her.

'Gracious — you'll make the place wet . . . '

'I'm so sorry. I'm afraid I am — drenched through. Is this a doctor's house?'

'Yes. This is Russet Place — Dr. Farlong's. He and Mrs. Farlong are away for the night. I'm Mrs. Clarke, the housekeeper.'

'I see,' said Terry.

'It's getting on for nine,' added Mrs. Clarke. 'Where on earth do you intend going?'

'To tell you the truth,' said Terry, 'I don't feel I could go a step farther. I'm played out.'

'You look done in,' admitted Mrs. Clarke. 'It's a nuisance. There's no car — the doctor's away in it — and the house-parlourmaid's gone home to the village for the night. There's no one here but me and my little boy, and I can't see how to get you into the village. You might get a room at the Crown — but you're not fit to walk a hundred yards with that ankle.'

'I know,' said Terry weakly.

'I'd 'phone up the man at the Crown to come and fetch you, but the storm's put our line out of order,' the housekeeper continued in a grumbling voice. 'I tried five minutes ago to get through to a friend to come and stay — I don't like to be alone in these storms — and the line seems dead.'

Terry gazed up at her. She did not think the housekeeper a very pleasant-looking woman. She had an angular, cross face with hard lips, and short-sighted eyes behind black-rimmed glasses. Yet she seemed quite kind. Terry looked round the doctor's room. It was charming — flooded with soft light from an alabaster bowl hanging from the ceiling. She heard the rain beating against the window-panes. The thunder rolled on sullenly. Her heart sank at the idea of going out into the storm again. She was shivering now, cold in spite of the sultry atmosphere, and every bone in her body ached.

Suddenly she said:

'Mrs. Clarke — couldn't you be an angel and let me stay here for the night? You say everybody is away. You could give me a shake-down, surely. I'll be off early — before a soul comes back. Honestly, I can't move again tonight. I'm not fit to. I feel so rottenly tired and chilled.'

'Gracious! I couldn't let a stranger

14

sleep here — ' began the housekeeper primly.

'I'm quite respectable, really,' broke in Terry with a faint smile. 'My name is Miss Manstone, and if you look in the London directory you'll see my mother's address — The Cedars, Poyning Avenue, Wimbledon.'

Mrs. Clarke looked down at the bedraggled young figure. Certainly she was a lady — Mrs. Clarke knew one when she saw her. A pretty thing, too. She looked very young, with her slight, boyish figure, sun-browned face and throat, bright hazel eyes, and wet brown hair tumbled over her head.

'Mrs. Farlong would give me the sack,' said Mrs. Clarke, after a pause. 'I can't risk it. I've got my little boy. He's a half-wit, poor laddie, and the doctor and Mrs. Farlong allow him to live here with me, which most folk wouldn't do. I wouldn't like to lose my place.'

'I'm sure you're right, but nobody will know,' said Terry wearily. 'Do let me stay . . . '

She fumbled in her coat-pocket for a small leather purse, and pulled out a pound note.

'Will this compensate the risk? It's awfully wrong of me to tempt you, but I am so done in, and the storm is still raging.'

Mrs. Clarke peered through her glasses at the pound note. Again Terry had the feeling that she was not a pleasant woman. She had a horrid expression. A half-wit son, too, poor creature! Terry added:

'Dr. and Mrs. Farlong won't be back till tomorrow, will they?'

'No. They went up to a dinner-party. They said they'd be down by car first thing tomorrow.'

'I'll be gone frightfully early,' said Terry.

The pound passed from her slender fingers to the woman's claw-like ones. Mrs. Clarke said:

'Well, I'll do it, and I daresay no harm will come.'

Terry sighed with relief.

16

'Oh, thank you. I am really grateful.'

'Better come upstairs and get off your wet clothes and have a hot bath,' said Mrs. Clarke, 'and I'll give you some liniment and a bandage for your ankle.'

'It sounds too good for words.'

'I'll cook you a scrambled egg and make some coffee.'

'How marvellous!'

Terry stood up and stretched her cramped limbs. The feeling of pleasure in her new freedom, in this adventure which had been intoxicating her ever since she left Wimbledon this morning, returned once more.

'Mummy and Barbara wouldn't be able to sneer at my 'hotel' for the night,' she thought, as she followed Mrs. Clarke out of the room. 'It's a delightful place.'

Passing the doctor's desk, she saw a leather-framed photograph of a pretty woman with a baby in her arms. 'Is that Mrs. Farlong?' she asked.

The housekeeper eyed the photograph grimly.

17

'That's her — taken five years ago with the little girl.'

'How pretty she is.'

'She is that!'

'Is the child away too?'

'No, she died, over four years back.'

'Oh, how dreadful! Poor Mrs. Farlong.'

'I don't know that she felt it like the doctor did. She's one for Bridge and dances and society. But he fairly worshipped that baby. Never got over it, I'm told.'

'Poor Dr. Farlong.'

'Quite a young pair they are.' Mrs. Clarke waxed confidential as she led Terry up a wide oak staircase on to the top landing. Terry, limping after her, noted the beautiful rugs on the polished floor; the charming coloured sporting prints on the cream-coloured walls. A nice house, Russet Place. Georgian, probably, and well furnished. The Farlongs seemed well off. 'They married seven years ago,' continued Mrs. Clarke. 'The doctor's only thirty-two

18

now, and missus is thirty. Only had that one baby. He wanted more, but she don't care for them.'

'I see,' said Terry, a trifle coldly, feeling that the woman was being a little too confidential about her employers.

'Now they do nothing but quarrel,' added Mrs. Clarke, and looked over the rim of her glasses at Terry with a rather malicious expression. 'The doctor's strong-willed and so's she. He likes gardening and music and animals; crazy about his delphiniums, he is; and she wants to be gadding about. I was engaged here when they first came to Rossdown three years ago. She wanted him to practise in London, and his health broke down. He had to come to a quiet place. Rossdown is quiet enough. The practice is very small, but she has a bit of private money, so they can keep up appearances.'

She rambled on while she showed Terry into a small bedroom and switched on the light. Terry was too tired to really take in all that the woman said, but she was given the impression that the Farlongs were not very happy together, and it seemed as though the doctor was the one to be pitied and that his wife was thoroughly self-centred and selfish.

'But I really don't care whether they are happy or not,' thought Terry, as she unhooked her sodden grey skirt and slipped the blouse over her head. 'All I want is bed and a good hot bath.'

The housekeeper went downstairs to make the coffee.

'You'd best get straight into bed,' she said. 'It's the doctor's dressing-room, and his bed was made up clean this morning. Best take that and I'll make it up fresh tomorrow. The spare room's being spring-cleaned, and I don't want to mess up the missus's room.'

Terry agreed to anything and everything. When she was out of her wet things and wrapped in a dressing-gown — a grey flannel one, lent by Mrs. Clarke, and hideous in the extreme —

she looked with some curiosity about her. This was a typical man's room. Rather spartan: one nice tallboy; a Georgian wardrobe; a bow-fronted chest of drawers and a divan bed. Chintz curtains, brown and yellow; two good rugs on the floor, and only one picture in the room: an enlarged snapshot of a laughing, curly-haired, two-year-old baby. The little girl who had died.

Terry looked at this and felt quite grieved for the unknown Dr. Farlong.

'Poor thing — to have lost a child he worshipped so!'

Mrs. Clarke came back with a bath-towel over her arm and a photograph in her hand.

'This is one of the doctor,' she said. 'I found it torn in half in Mrs. Farlong's waste-paper basket a few nights back and saved it — pasted it together. I expect she did it in one of her tempers.'

Terry's cheeks felt hot. She felt that she was being let into intimate details and secrets of this family which she had no right to know.

However, she would never meet the Farlongs; she was only stealing this one night in their charming home, so what matter what she knew about them?

She found herself examining the repaired photograph of Dr. Farlong. It was signed: 'Blaise.' She said the name aloud.

'Yes — that's him,' said Mrs. Clarke. 'Some think him very good-looking. He's clever at his work.'

'Dr. Blaise Farlong.'

Terry studied the face with some interest. Certainly Dr. Farlong was good-looking — in a way which appealed to her. A rugged way. Powerful lines of jaw and chin; attractive eyes — the keen, serious eyes of a deep thinker; hair which looked thick and dark, brushed back from an intellectual forehead. A rather big mouth. The lips and eyes portrayed humour and kindliness. Yet withal it was a curiously sad face. An appealing one.

'He's a popular doctor,' said Terry's

informant. 'Folks about Rossdown dote on him.'

Terry handed her back the torn photograph.

'He looks charming; it's surprising Mrs. Farlong doesn't get on with him.'

'If you ask me,' said Mrs. Clarke with a little leering smile, 'there's another gentleman she likes better.'

That was too much. Terry gave the woman a chilly stare and marched out of the room.

Lying languorously in the hot water, her slim white limbs relaxed and a delicious feeling of well-being pervading her, Terry dwelt on the thought of Dr. Farlong and his wife. What an attractive face he had. She always liked doctors. She was sure she would like him. But she would never meet him. She would be gone early in the morning — carry on with her solitary walking tour through this lovely Sussex country.

Turning her reflections to Mrs. Farlong, Terry felt quite indignant.

'Beastly of her — to quarrel with him

— make him unhappy — and not have any more children,' was her youthful opinion.

Half an hour later, having eaten a good supper, her strained ankle bandaged, Terry went to sleep tucked up in the bed of a complete stranger. Certainly, if she had wanted to get away from her humdrum, conventional life at home in London and find adventure, she had found it on this, the first night of her tour.

2

The storm did not abate for several hours after Terry fell asleep. The lightning continued to play over the countryside and the thunder growled and grumbled intermittently.

At half past one in the morning the rain ceased and the storm passed over, and suddenly the moon broke through the clouds. The little village of Rossdown and the moorland fringing it lay wet and glittering with an unearthly beauty in the white moonlight.

At a quarter to two the gates of Russet Place were pushed open and a man walked quietly into the garden and up the brick pathway with the assured air of one who knew his way. The rain dripped off the yews and the feathery mass of montana clematis which grew profusely over the porch. The man took off his hat and shook it. It was like everything else — soaked with rain.

He had just walked a considerable distance from Crowborough, the nearest big station from which he was able to reach Rossdown so late at night.

In the moonlight his face looked pale and fatigued. He was wearing a light Burberry over his evening dress. He took off the coat and shook that also.

'Quite crazy,' he said to himself. 'But, my God, I'm glad to be home. At least it's peaceful here, and Ruth can't nag at me any more. If I'd stayed with her in that hotel, I think I'd have done something violent . . . '

He found a latch-key, inserted it in the Yale lock, opened the front door, and walked into the house, yawning.

It was very quiet. Old Prince, the retriever, in his kennel at the back of the house did not bark. He knew his master's footsteps.

Blaise Farlong walked into his consulting-room, switched on the light in there, and stood by his desk for a moment while he lit a cigarette.

He glanced at the letters lying on his blotter — nothing of interest; then at a telephone message on the pad beside the 'phone:

'Mrs. Deemer would like to see you in the morning.'

Blaise smiled grimly. Mrs. Deemer was a most trying patient. A *malade imaginaire*. The type he hated to deal with. But she had money. He must make something — anything, these hard times. His practice at Rossdown was very small. He was considered more in the light of a consultant than a G.P. Dr. Beggland, the other practitioner in the village, did all the panel work.

That did not worry Farlong. His health had been groggy since the war. A year in Mesopotamia as a youngster had started the trouble which had never really left him. He could not work too hard. But work to some degree he must. He adored his job. It was an unceasing grief that he could not have a big practice. He had the ability. He knew that. The fact that Ruth, his wife, had money of her own made things difficult. It made them easy for her, of course, and easier for him in a way. It enabled them to live much more comfortably than they could have done otherwise. Blaise had only three hundred a year private means and what he earned. But he had grown to loathe depending upon his wife for any contribution toward the mutual maintenance.

It had been all right in the beginning — when she had cared for him and they had been happy together. Now that she had so utterly ceased to care, her money was a curse — something she could choke down his throat — a subject which never failed to make him writhe. Oh, God, those ghastly money discussions! When Ruth, coldly sarcastic, reminded him that *she* had paid for this, for that, for the other. She continually reproached him for not being in a better position than this one in Rossdown.

She wanted him to buy a practice with her money in London. He loathed town — the life up there. He only asked for a garden; a little time to grow his flowers; the country wherein to exercise his dog. He had tried for Ruth's sake to live in London, but he had felt unable to cope with the rush — the artificiality of London — since that bad breakdown in his health, after Priscilla had died.

Priscilla had been the one perfect gift that Ruth had given him — and she had even begrudged that — the temporary discomforts of producing a child. But Priscilla had been born, and Blaise, who had always loved children, expended all his starved affections on the delicate little thing — too delicate, alas, to survive a sudden attack of pneumonia when she was nearly three years old.

From that shock Blaise had never recovered. His hopes of parenthood had died with Priscilla. Ruth told him brutally, soon after the child's death,

29

that she would never go through the business again.

Today Blaise was better, stronger in health than he had ever been. If Ruth had been different, he might have sold Russet Place, sacrificed his love of the country for her sake and taken a new practice in London. But what was the use now? They were so utterly out of sympathy these days — poles apart. Going to London could not bring them together again. Ruth was still pretty and attractive. But her attractions were not for him. She had told him more than once that she loathed him to touch her. She was sick of him. Gradually his intense, whole-hearted devotion to her — a very real and passionate love it had been in the beginning — died of starvation. He concentrated entirely on his medical work and withdrew into a shell of reticence, of bitterness, foreign to his nature which was an open, simple, and affectionate one.

Ruth spent a great deal of her time in town these days and left him here alone. But yesterday they had both gone up to town, guests of a Harley Street surgeon — an old friend of Blaise's, who was giving a party at the Carlton. Ruth, insatiate for pleasure, wanted to go to this party, although as a rule she despised her husband's friends — called them 'dry medical sticks' and avoided them.

The evening started badly. Ruth was in a bad temper because a new frock, ordered from a Bond Street dressmaker, did not fit as she wanted it. She vented her temper on Blaise. Snapped at him while he was dressing — criticised the way his hair had been cut — sneered at the shabbiness of his 'tails'; nagged until, his own patience snapping, he had turned on her and said: 'Leave, me alone, for God's sake, Ruth. What the hell's the use of my ordering new 'tails'? I so rarely go out.'

She had answered:

'No, because you're so eaten up with this passion for the garden — you're becoming a weed yourself. I'm ashamed to go out with you.'

His nerves were raw — he had slept so badly lately — and Ruth in a nagging mood drove all the good humour and kindliness out of him. He snapped back at her again. They quarrelled all the way from their hotel to the Carlton. He had thought: 'How long is this sort of life going on? I can't stand much more . . . '

And he had looked at his wife's lovely figure — and the pretty face which had grown so terribly hard — and wondered what he had done to make her hate him. He had given her everything — body, heart, soul, brain. All that he had. Not much, he knew. He had failed in many ways. His health had failed — his career as a medical man was not a big success. He just carried on — steadily — but in a small way. Not enough for Ruth.

He realised that he ought never to have married her. He could not satisfy her greed for a good time and she could not share his interests, which were of a much more simple kind.

Once, in a blazing temper, she had demanded a divorce. She would not leave him herself. She had no wish to be a *divorcée*. She asked him to give her evidence. He — equally angry, but quieter — had refused, definitely, to do what she demanded.

'I have never been unfaithful to you, Ruth, and if our marriage is not a success, it is your fault as much as, if not more than, mine. You've never been decently kind to me since Priscilla died. I loved Priscilla. For the sake of her memory I refuse to be mixed up in a shoddy, sordid, *arranged* divorce. We made a compact six years ago. We must stick to it.'

At the Carlton tonight, in front of Herringford, his friend, Ruth had openly sneered at him — slighted him. Blaise, raw, furious with her for her lack of taste, if nothing else, waited until the party ended, then took the first train he could catch from Victoria to Crowborough.

'I won't stay up in town with you. You've gone too far, Ruth,' he had told her, white-lipped. 'You can come down in the car in the morning with the luggage.'

She, a little chastened, said:

'Don't be a fool. You can't walk home at midnight from Crowborough Station to Rossdown.'

He had said:

'That will be preferable to sleeping beside a woman who shows her contempt for me in front of my friends.'

She, red and sullen, had flung a coarse, parting remark at him as he left her:

'Perhaps you want to sleep beside some other woman . . . '

To that he had made no reply. It was too humiliating — and the whole thing was futile.

In great bitterness and loneliness he had trudged home through the tail end of the thunderstorm and wished himself in that little church graveyard at Rossdown beside his baby daughter.

Since Priscilla's death, these years had been hell to Blaise Farlong. Terrible, empty years, leaving him sick of soul — physically and mentally fatigued — sterile of all that he had dreamed and wanted when he had first loved Ruth, and made her his wife.

He saw no light on the horizon — no possible change. He could not alter his own nature, and Ruth certainly could not alter hers. She was selfish to the core — shallow — ungenerous. Yet even now he remembered with a pang the girl he had married. A sweet, yielding, passionate Ruth, who had loved him.

For a long while he stood lost in bitter reverie.

Then he glanced at his reflection in the mirror over the mantelpiece, pitched his cigarette-end into the grate, and turned away, grimacing.

'I'm an ugly fool of a man who has achieved nothing. Why should I expect anything?' he thought.

Herringford, his friend, who had been a student with him at Bart's, was now a successful consultant in the West End of London. Blaise remembered him as he had just seen him at the Carlton — a prosperous, handsome, smiling man. Ruth had sat at his right hand. Ruth, looking her best — she was still so pretty, with her youthful figure, her smooth dark hair, her narrow blue eyes which she could use so engagingly. Blaise had watched her smile and talk to Herringford with that particularly charming manner which she affected at will for men whom she wished to impress. He had thought with bitterness what a long while back it was since she had expended any of that charm upon him, and wondered if anybody could be more cruel than a woman to the husband she has ceased to love.

Blaise Farlong switched off the light in his consulting-room and walked slowly upstairs.

Opening the door of his dressing-room, he switched on the light in there. It came softly from the standard-lamp, shaded with orange parchment, which stood on a table beside his bed.

Then his heart gave a startled jump, and he stared in blank amazement.

'Good God!' he said.

A girl lay in that bed, asleep. A girl — or was it a child? — in an old-fashioned white nightgown, unbuttoned at the chin, showing a curve of sun-browned throat. She slept with one hand under a tanned cheek, upon which the long dark lashes were spread fan-wise charmingly. Her brown bobbed hair was tumbled; one thick strand tossed against the white pillow.

Dumbfounded, Blaise stood staring and thought:

'Who in the name of Hades is this? What's old dame Clarke up to — putting strange girls in my bedroom when Ruth and I are away?'

And then Terry, as though her subconsciousness warned her that somebody was there beside her bed, opened her eyes, saw the tall figure in 'tails,' and sat up with a little cry.

'Oh!' she gasped.

Blaise found himself looking into a pair of very bright hazel eyes which were a little hazy with sleep and considerably frightened. Now that she was sitting up, and he could see the faint curves of young round breasts, he knew that this was a young woman and not a little girl. He coughed, cleared his throat, and said:

'You must pardon me, but I am Dr. Farlong, and this happens to be my room. I had no idea that I would find anybody sleeping in here.'

Terry, wide awake now and crimson-cheeked, pushed the brown hair back from her eyes and clutched the bedclothes tightly about her. She looked what she felt — overcome with embarrassment — which amused Blaise somewhat.

'I'm *dreadfully* s-sorry!' she stammered. 'I — I had no idea you — you would be coming back.'

Blaise knit his brows.

'Are you a friend of my housekeeper's? No — surely not — ' He stopped.

He was a fool. The girl was a lady — her voice was well bred, her hands exquisite — she was obviously not a friend of Mrs. Clarke's.

'No — it's like this — l-let me explain — ' stammered Terry.

'And I must get up — go at once — of course.'

Blaise, more than ever amused, said:

'Go where?'

'A-away,' she faltered.

'What — at two a.m.? I'm not really so inhospitable that I would turn you into the wet and chilly dawn just because I don't know who you are.'

'Well, let me get up — explain, anyhow.'

'No need to turn out. Stay where you are, please. There are other beds in the house.'

Terry, her heart beating fast with shame and embarrassment, sat staring up at Dr. Farlong, unable to cope with her explanations for a minute or two. It was a most awkward situation for her — a distinct shock to find that the

master of Russet Place had come home
and discovered her in his bed. That
stupid old housekeeper had assured her
that he was not expected until tomorrow. At least, it was *today*. It was two
a.m., he had just said. She must have
been sound asleep for the last four
hours.

What an awful thing to have done!
And she had got the wretched Mrs.
Clarke into trouble too. Had Mrs.
Farlong also come home?

The doctor's next words dispelled
that fear.

'My wife is still in town,' he said. 'I
suddenly went crazy after a party and
rushed back home — I do these things
sometimes. I know Mrs. Clarke didn't
expect me.'

'It's all my fault,' broke out Terry.

'What's your fault?' Blaise smiled at
her.

She thought it the nicest smile she
had ever seen. It was so infinitely kind,
and softened the rather stern curve of
his big mouth. He was very like his

photograph, but thinner. He had rather a gaunt face, with grave and very grey eyes and a touch of grey in the darkness of the hair just over both ears.

What struck her most forcibly was the quality of sadness in his smile — in the whole of his face. Not the face of a happy man. Yet there was humour hidden away somewhere. Terry remembered, suddenly, the stories which the garrulous Mrs. Clarke had poured into her ears about the unhappy married life of Dr. and Mrs. Farlong, and her embarrassment seemed to increase. She began to stammer out her story.

'I'm on a walking-tour — got lost in Rossdown Forest — a frightful thunderstorm came on — I hurt my ankle — found this house — and nearly fainted. I begged Mrs. Clarke to let me stay — then meant to go off early tomorrow. She didn't want to. I'm afraid I behaved rottenly — bribed her. Do forgive me — and don't blame her . . .'

Blaise listened with the smile still

playing about his lips and his grave eyes fixed on her. He was thinking how extraordinarily attractive the child was — only a child, surely — still in her teens. He liked her funny little nose, tip-tilted, and her round, stubborn chin, and the eagerness in her eyes. She was blushing and stammering with such genuine discomfiture, and was so unaffected; he liked her at once. Blaise always knew immediately whether he was going to like people or not.

When Terry finished her tale, he said:

'I quite understand, and I assure you I don't mind in the least. I think Mrs. Clarke did the right thing. How could she have turned you out with a bad ankle in a storm like that? It was a pretty bad storm, I gather, from the state of the ground. I noticed our lawn is under water.'

'You won't be cross with Mrs. Clarke, will you?'

'No crosser than I am with her as a rule. To tell you the truth, I can't stand the old woman and her chattering tongue, but she suits my wife's requirements. It's so difficult to get servants to stay in these out-of-the-way country houses.'

'Y-yes — isn't it?' said Terry, trying to recover her equilibrium.

He added, with a slight touch of the professional:

'Is the ankle quite all right now?'

Terry moved her leg gingerly up and down underneath the bedclothes. 'M'm. More or less. It's a bit painful. Mrs. Clarke rubbed embrocation on it and bound it up.'

'You must let me have a look at it in the morning if it still hurts you. You say you're on a walking-tour. Is this the result of all the newspaper talk about 'hiking'?'

'No. Only a desire to get away from London.'

'Well, that's easy to understand. I loathe London.'

'I live in Wimbledon.' She was more at ease with Dr. Farlong now. He had an easy, friendly manner, and was being so nice to her, she thought. It was really awful cheek to have used his house as an hotel.

'Wimbledon?' He raised his brows. 'My wife used to live there. I know it well.'

'Do you know Poyning Avenue?'

'Poyning Avenue? Let me see. Not far from the Common?'

'No — it leads out of Chigwell Road.'

'Ah, I know. Chigwell Road was once quite pleasant, before they built over it so extensively.'

'It's awful now,' said Terry. 'Our house, the Cedars, is surrounded by other houses — and, even though we've got a bit of garden, I feel it's very much town.'

'Then you prefer the country?'

'I adore it,' she said fervently.

'So do I . . . ' Blaise forgot that it was two a.m. and that he was standing here in the bedroom, blithely chatting to a strange young woman who was sitting up in his bed. She was so entirely natural and it was pleasant to talk to a girl who preferred the country to London, after Ruth's incessant nagging at him to leave Russet Place. 'I feel hemmed in in London, and my great hobby is gardening. When I'm not visiting the sick, I'm in my garden.'

'You are lucky,' she said.

'Aren't you able to indulge in it, then?'

'Gracious, no. Our miserable plot is attended to by a gardener, who won't let anybody touch an inch of it, and my mother won't have him interfered with, so I have to sit and weep because he plans it all stiffly and formally like a park and I want an old-fashioned garden. I want a flagged path and an old well or a really old sundial, and lavender and rosemary and mignonette and lots of hollyhocks and lupins and delphiniums — oh, you know!' She stopped, flushed, breathless.

Blaise nodded.

'Yes, I know,' he said. 'In the morning you'll find most of what you like here. I've got an ancient well and all the old-fashioned herbaceous things, and a herb-garden.'

'Oh, how glorious!' she sighed.

Blaise seemed to hear Ruth's cold, sarcastic voice, saying: 'The garden's a mess, anyhow. Why can't you have proper, tidy beds, with tidy plants and some sort of design? . . . '

Terry said, with a touch of shyness:

'By the way, my name is Terry Manstone.'

'Terry's a boy's name, surely.'

'I was christened Teresa Mary . . . ' She grimaced at him. 'Can you imagine me being called Teresa?'

'No — it's a little inappropriate.'

'My father nicknamed me Terry.'

'I like it. You know my name — Farlong.'

'Yes. Mrs. Clarke told me. I say, Dr. Farlong, would Mrs. Farlong be horrified about this?'

Blaise hesitated to answer. He could well imagine that Ruth would be horrified. She would probably sack Mrs. Clarke and rant about the thing for hours. Of course, it *was* wrong of Mrs. Clarke. How was she to know who or what the girl was? She might have been admitting a thief, or a thief's decoy, into the house — might have found half the Georgian silver missing in the morning.

But, looking at Miss Teresa Manstone — nicknamed Terry — Blaise Farlong smiled and considered that for once Mrs. Clarke had shown discretion and taste. The girl was charming — quite a dear — and after his own heart. He did like simple and natural people. No shingle-caps and permanent waves and lip-stick or any kind of artificiality here. Just a sun-browned, very human young woman, with brown hair, straight as God intended it to be, except for that one delightful wave tumbling across her flushed cheek.

'I'm sure Mrs. Farlong would be appalled — and rightly,' Terry was saying.

'Oh, well I don't suppose my wife will voice any opinion in the matter,' he

47

said, with a faint laugh. 'She won't be down till midday. You won't see her.'

'I shall be gone long before then, but I feel very guilty and apologetic.'

'Please don't feel either. It's most exciting to come home, feeling rather depressed and solitary, and find a pleasant companion,' he said.

Terry's cheeks burned.

'It's awfully nice of you. Were you depressed?'

'Very. Do you ever get depressed? No, of course you don't. You're much too young.'

'But I do terribly at home, and I'm twenty-one — that's not young.'

'Are you twenty-one? You look about seventeen! Well, twenty-one is absurdly youthful when you consider my grey hairs.' Blaise touched his head and smiled. 'I'm rising thirty-two . . . '

'You oughtn't to have grey hairs at thirty-two.'

'Ah,' he said sadly. 'The worries of this wicked world . . . '

She remembered that he had a wife

who quarrelled with him and got into such tempers that she tore his photograph in half. How could she? What a difficult woman she must be. Dr. Farlong seemed so charming. Terry did not think she had ever met a man she liked better or had felt more friendly with at a first meeting. Then there was the little girl he had adored and who had died. Poor man!

'You have all your life before you,' he added. He was walking up and down the room, staring at the floor thoughtfully, hands in his pockets. 'Why should you ever feel depressed?'

'I don't fit in at home very well.'

'Don't you?'

'No. I'm a bit of a disappointment to my mother . . . ' Terry made a little *moue*. 'You see, she is very much a society woman, and adores Bridge teas and bazaars and committee meetings and dressmakers. I have a sister, Barbara, who is just like her, and has just done the correct thing and become engaged to an excellent young man in

Lloyds'. He's 'society', like mother and Barbara. I'm always in disgrace — I can't bear having clothes tried on and parading in the park on Sunday and going to these awful teas and luncheons. They're such a waste of time.'

'How right you are,' said Blaise. He paused at the foot of the bed, looking at the girl with sympathy and understanding. It was strange, but this child seemed to suffer in her home-life from the restrictions and persecutions with which Ruth constantly threatened and tormented him. Bridge teas . . . luncheons . . . dress-parades. Things that Ruth adored and from which he shrank.

'I adore animals, and mother won't have a dog in the place because of muddy paw-marks in the drawing-room. I oughtn't to grouse, really . . . ' Terry checked herself, half ashamed. 'I mean, Mummy and Barbara are dears, and I daresay I am a great disappointment — but everybody can't like the same things.'

'I understand,' said Blaise gently. He

smiled wryly. Hadn't Ruth groused and nagged because his little Cairn, Rip, had brought muddy paw-marks into her drawing-room — nagged until, exasperated, he had given Rip away and contented himself with old Prince, the retriever who was kennelled up in the garden?

'Mummy hopes some nice, proper young man like my sister's *fiancé* will come along and marry me and make me settle down,' Terry added, with another burst of confidence. 'But I'm sure I never shall. We are supposed to be taking the annual summer holiday next week in Eastbourne or Bournemouth — you know: a little discreet bathing; walks on the front; drives in the car. Kid gloves again. I can't bear it. I just packed up and rushed away on this walking-tour by myself. The family are furious. Mummy wouldn't even say good-bye. But I did adore my day — before the storm spoiled it. I bought a sausage roll and had my lunch in a field by a brook somewhere near

Tunbridge Wells, and took off my shoes and stockings and paddled. Lovely!'

She sighed, and clasped her hunched knees with her arms. Blaise Farlong smiled at her a little wistfully. He thought:

'What a dear thing — a jewel of a woman she'll be. And they want to tie her down to a society life and marry her to a City gentleman who'll put her in a flat in London and dress her up and stifle the soul out of her . . . '

He said:

'Look here, it's latish; you ought to go to sleep. I'll say good night.'

'Oh, but what about you?'

'I daresay my wife's bed is made up. I'll be all right.'

'You've been most awfully nice to me,' said Terry. 'I do apologise again for being here.'

'Don't,' he said. 'I'm glad we've met. We have many views in common. And tomorrow before you go you must see my garden. I've got a rockery I'm proud of. Do you like those tiny roses they call

Dresden China? You must see them.'

'I'd love to,' she said eagerly, and on an impulse held out her hand. 'Thanks awfully,' she repeated.

He took the hand in his. She looked down at his long fingers, as sun-tanned as hers — thin, strong, with darkish hairs at the wrist. Terry, who was very particular about hands, liked them. She could imagine them being very sensitive and gentle at his doctoring; good at budding a rose or potting a delicate plant.

She thought of Kipling's poem:

And some can pot begonias and
*   some can bud a rose,*
And some are hardly fit to trust
*   with anything that grows.*

To Blaise Farlong so much might be trusted.

'Good night,' he said. 'Sleep well.'

He left her, shutting the communicating door through which he passed into his wife's bedroom without a sound. Terry switched off the table-lamp and lay down, wide awake, staring into the darkness, thinking. And she thought how strange it was that she should be lying here in Dr. Farlong's bed and he just through that door — in the other room. Just as though they were an old married couple. How queer! What on earth Mummy and Barbara would think — thoughts failed Terry, and she knew words would fail them!

She mused on the subject of Blaise Farlong's wife. A peculiar woman if she could not be happy with such a man. Terry, if she had never before dwelt on the thought of her own marriage, considered it now. And she believed that she could have been very happy married to a man like this sensitive charming doctor who loved his garden and his dog and his country life.

'What a tangle it all is,' thought Terry. 'I'm sure I shouldn't like Mrs. Farlong, and she'd simply detest me — so there it is.'

She turned over on her pillow, punching it into some shape. She felt hot and restless. And she was sorry that she must walk away from this place in the morning and never see Dr. Farlong again.

3

Terry slept soundly, the healthy sleep necessary for her tired young body, and she did not awake until Mrs. Clarke knocked on her door and came into the room with a cup of tea and Terry's suit and blouse, which had been dried and pressed.

'You'd best be up and off, miss,' she said a trifle shortly. 'It's half past eight. I overlaid.'

Terry's heart missed a beat. She sat up, her bright hazel eyes looking at the woman guiltily. For a moment she did not know what to say. Mrs. Clarke laid the tea on the table beside her, drew aside the brown and yellow chintz curtains, and let a flood of sunlight into the bedroom. Through the open window came the ecstatic song of birds and all the sounds and scents of a glorious summer's morning.

56

'Better weather than last night,' the woman remarked, coming back toward Terry. 'Soon as I've served your breakfast I must walk down to the post-office and tell them about our phone. It won't do for the doctor to find his telephone out of order.'

Terry, with hot cheeks, glanced in the direction of the communicating door. Well, it had got to come out sooner or later, so best tell Mrs. Clarke at once and get it over.

'I'm terribly sorry,' she stammered. 'But the — the doctor came back — at two this morning.'

The housekeeper, who had been about to pass through the door, swung round, startled.

'What?'

Terry repeated the confession.

'But you needn't worry,' she finished. 'Dr. Farlong says he won't blame you. He knows it's my fault.'

Mrs. Clarke put her hands on her hips; her sour, leathery face was a study in astonishment and chagrin.

'The doctor's *home*?' she exclaimed. She nodded towards Mrs. Farlong's bedroom. 'In *there*?'

'Yes. I'm afraid so.'

The woman looked so dumbfounded, it made Terry smile a little. She slipped out of bed, sat on the edge, and sipped her tea.

'I must get up — quickly. Dr. Farlong will want his clothes. He was simply petrified when he walked in here and found me in his bed, as you can imagine.'

Mrs. Clarke made no answer. Her face had assumed a stony and forbidding expression. And, before Terry could attempt to soothe her, the communicating door opened and Blaise Farlong walked into the room. He looked younger and less haggard than he had seemed to Terry last night. His thick, dark hair was ruffled over his head like a boy's. He had an embroidered spread wrapped round his shoulders to hide his pyjamas.

'I'd like to get a suit of clothes, if you

don't mind,' he began. Then he saw his cook-housekeeper, coughed, and pulled his ear.

Terry, suddenly aware that she had nothing on but Mrs. Clarke's voluminous nightgown, pulled a blanket over her knees.

Blaise cleared his throat.

'Ahem! Morning, Mrs. Clarke. Rather a surprise — finding Miss Manstone here when I turned up. Sorry I didn't let you know I was coming.'

The woman looked at him with her thin lips pursed. She tossed her head.

'I'm sorry, too, doctor. I told the young lady I wasn't doing right and — '

'That's all right. I'm glad you took her in — nobody could have turned her out in that filthy storm,' broke in Farlong cheerfully. 'Now what about a spot of breakfast for both of us?'

'Yes, doctor,' said Mrs. Clarke in the same sour voice, and, with heightened colour, she marched out of the room.

Terry's lips quivered into laughter.

She caught Blaise's eye and became aware of the comic side to the whole situation. Blaise looked so funny with that embroidered cover so modestly wrapped about his big tall figure, and she knew she must present a queer spectacle in her Victorian nightgown.

They began to laugh together. Blaise said:

'Dame Clarke's furious about it. I can well see I'm in her bad books for coming back to my own house without letting her know.'

'It's all my fault,' said Terry. 'But I expect she'll get over it.'

'I really don't mind if she doesn't. Do please dress in peace and I'll go to my bath and shave meanwhile.'

'I'll be quick as lightning,' said Terry.

Blaise put his head out of the window.

'A topping morning. But that deluge has done in some of my roses.'

'I'm dying to see the garden,' said Terry eagerly.

'I want to show it to you,' he said. 'By

the way, how's the ankle?'

'A bit stiff, otherwise all right this morning, thank you,' she said.

They exchanged friendly smiles. They might have known each other for years. Terry felt that she had not a care in the world, and Blaise Farlong was suddenly glad to be alive. It was a pleasant thing to hear a sympathetic voice and see a young, eager, friendly face, instead of waking to the usual discord and irritation. But the light-hearted sensation departed as he went along to the bathroom and remembered Ruth. When Ruth came down there would be a hell of a row. He knew it. She would not easily forgive him for clearing out and leaving her to sulk alone last night.

Terry washed and dressed rapidly. Mrs. Clarke, however disagreeable, had pressed her grey flannel suit beautifully, she thought. She looked spruce and charming in the neat, well-cut skirt and freshly ironed silk blouse, open at the throat, and with a leather belt around her slender waist, when at length she strolled downstairs and out into the garden.

It seemed to her a wonderful and enchanting place with the old, high walls of grey weathered brick, half hidden by creepers — tall herbaceous plants — all the ones she loved.

Terry stood still a moment; listened to the rapturous song of a thrush; drank in all the sweet, fragrant beauty of Blaise Farlong's garden, and adored it. How could that woman who shared it with him, wish to leave it — for London?

From his dressing-room window, Blaise looked out and saw the girl's figure in the short grey skirt and white blouse standing by the well with her tanned face lifted to the sun and her hands thrust boyishly in her belt. He thought regretfully:

'She's loving it all. If only Ruth cared for my garden — like that child would do!'

From outside his door came Mrs. Clarke's voice.

'I've put breakfast on the table, doctor. Cold ham and boiled eggs and coffee. If you'll excuse me, I'm taking Willy down to the post-office to tell them to get our telephone put right.'

'Oh, is it out of order?' he sang out.

'Yes. Owing to the storm.'

'Right you are, Mrs. Clarke,' he said cheerfully.

The woman went downstairs, bridling.

'Coming home without telling me,' she muttered as she went into the kitchen. 'Sleeping there with that door unlocked between them — him and that young girl. Not proper, I don't call it. And I bet they had a nice talk before they said good night.'

She was an unpleasant woman with an unpleasant mind. The one good point about Ada Clarke was her passionate and absorbing love for her idiot-son. For him she would have made any sacrifice or committed any crime. He sat at the table, eating a slice of bread and butter. A big, loutish child with a vacant, grinning face — a little snout of a nose and small, pinkish eyes. A miserable, dreadful child with the mentality of a baby of two. But to the mother, her son — all she had, all she had ever had, for, although she had told the Farlongs that she was a widow, she had no right to the name of Mrs. Clarke. In her thirty-fifth year, a soured, plain spinster, she had been the victim of her inordinate passion for a farm-labourer, already married. And the miserable Willy had been the issue of that unlovely union, ten years ago, since when she had called herself Mrs. Clarke and supported the child as best she could.

It was only by luck she had got this comfortable job with the Farlongs, and she was furious with herself this morning for the risk she had taken when she had fallen for Miss Manstone's bribe and let her stay.

But who could have dreamed the doctor would steal back like that at dead of night? He might condone what had been done, but Mrs. Farlong wouldn't. Ada Clarke knew what *she* was like in a temper.

Half an hour later, holding the shuffling, grinning Willy by the hand, she walked down the sunlit road from Russet Place toward the post-office.

She had barely gone a few hundred yards before she heard the loud blare of a motor-horn. A car was coming round the corner. Mrs. Clarke stopped and pulled Willy to the side of the road. Surely she knew the sound of that horn?

Then a car with a black fabric coupe body came in view. Mrs. Clarke uttered an exclamation.

'Mercy on us. It *is* the doctor's car . . . and Mrs. driving it . . . '

The woman in the car saw the two familiar figures by the roadside, applied all her brakes, and skidded to a standstill beside them.

'Hello,' she said. 'What are you doing out so early?'

'Good morning, madam,' said Mrs.

Clarke primly. 'Willy and I was going to the post-office to tell them to mend our telephone. It's out of order.'

Ruth Farlong pulled a case from her bag and lit a cigarette. In the strong sunlight her face looked haggard and cross. But she was a pretty, *soignée* woman, who always looked *chic*. Her powder-blue cardigan suit came from Bond Street. The tweed coat with the fox collar, on the seat beside her, was perfectly cut. The small blue cap-hat with a diamond brooch in it, pulled over the sleek, dark head, was an expensive one and there were two good pearls in the lobes of her small ears. Ruth Farlong looked what she was — expensive; extravagant. Impossible to imagine her grubbing in the garden in old clothes and shoes.

She was in one of her worst moods this morning. When Blaise had lost his temper and left London last night she had vowed to make him pay for it. She hated sleeping alone in a London hotel. She hated being thwarted, too. She had swallowed pride and asked Blaise to stay and he had refused.

There was, at times, a quiet but immovable obstinacy about Blaise which drove her mad. She hated him for that very stubbornness which prevented her from always getting her own way. In fact, she had no love left for him and little respect. Hc was, in her opinion, a dull fool, a failure. She had been crazy to marry him. She was thirty now, and still young and beautiful enough to enjoy life in her own fashion, and she meant to do it.

The trouble was that she could not get a divorce. Blaise would never give her evidence, with his high-falutin ideas about marriage compacts and Priscilla's memory, and she, Ruth, was not going to leave him and bear the blame. Even in these free-and-easy days, a woman must have some sort of reputation.

Ruth valued public opinion. She was essentially conceited and arrogant. But she kept on telling herself that she could not stand her boring life with

Blaise much longer. Besides, there was another man on the horizon. A certain Naval officer with money, good looks, a position. He was crazy to marry her. If only she were free! But it would ruin him if the divorce were on Blaise's side.

She had got up long before her usual time this morning, because it was unbearably hot in town, and driven down to Rossdown with every intention of having a row with her husband before he started on his rounds.

The car was going badly. She had taken an hour and three-quarters to get there, and she was in a more evil mood than usual. She sat back in her seat, smoking her cigarette, frowning.

'The doctor's home, isn't he?'

'Yes, madam,' said Mrs. Clarke. Then, squirming, she added: 'By the way, madam ... there ... there's a young person at home, too — they're having breakfast together.'

Ruth Farlong looked up sharply.

'A young person? Who? What on earth do you mean?'

Mrs. Clarke glanced at her son, who was grinning vacantly at the car. She licked her thin lips. Now for the storm of abuse which she expected to break over her head.

'It's like this, madam. I'm terribly sorry. I did a wrong thing . . . '

'What?' asked Ruth impatiently. 'What on earth is it?'

Mrs. Clarke told her story. The woman in the car listened, scowling, smoking hard. Then gradually the scowl disappeared. A queer little sneering smile curved lips artificially red.

'Oh!' she said slowly. 'So this girl spent the night in the doctor's bedroom and he in mine, eh?'

'Yes, madam. I — the doctor said it was all right.'

'Oh, did he?' said Ruth. 'A nice thing — when I'm away.'

Mrs. Clarke's small eyes rested nervously on her mistress.

'Yes, madam. I reckon the young person should have woke me up when the doctor come in . . . '

Ruth Farlong did not hear that speech. Her mind was working furiously. She remembered what she had said to Blaise when he left her last night. She had said: '*Perhaps you want to sleep beside some other woman . . .* ' Only in temper — of course. She had known perfectly well that Blaise was physically faithful to her. She had told herself, in a passion of hatred, that she wished to God he would be unfaithful. Anything so that she could get her freedom. They would both be happier apart. She was quite sure she would not feel half so antagonistic towards Blaise if she were not forced to live with him — drag on with an existence at Russet Place which bored her to tears.

Then there was the Naval commander. Hugh Spalderson. Hadn't he told her many times that if only she could get rid of 'her doctor' he'd marry her — take her to Malta, where she would have a marvellous time?

This girl, Miss Manstone, was young

and pretty, Mrs. Clarke said. On a walking-tour, by herself. That didn't sound as though *she* were too careful of her reputation.

Blaise was flesh and blood — passionate enough when he was roused. Ruth was well aware of that. Supposing he *had* spent last night with that girl? Mrs. Clarke to prove it. Sufficient evidence, then, to get her divorce.

The most evil temptation of Ruth Farlong's life assailed her in this moment, and she gave way to it. She sat there brooding, her blue eyes glittering under their narrow, pencilled brows. Then she pitched her half-smoked cigarette into the hedge and leaned over the side of the car to her housekeeper.

'Mrs. Clarke,' she said. 'Do you realise that if I liked to make a fuss I could get a divorce . . . on this business of last night?'

The woman shot her mistress a quick look, then smiled downwards.

'Oh, the sly one,' she thought. 'So that's what she's after — a divorce . . . '

Aloud she said: 'Oh, madam, not *really* . . . '

Ruth Farlong's small, greedy fingers, with their highly polished nails, closed over the steering-wheel — opened again.

'Yes, quite easily,' she said. 'The doctor . . . and that girl . . . in communicating rooms . . . and you saw them together in their night attire . . . when you took this girl in her tea . . . '

Mrs. Clarke made no reply. Ruth Farlong gave a short, nervous laugh, but her pretty face was cruelly hard. She added:

'You've got to *prove* misconduct in a court of law today. You could prove it. You might, for instance, have seen quite a lot by just opening the bedroom door without them knowing — you were disturbed by noises early this morning — are you following me?'

Mrs. Clarke peered through spectacles at her mistress.

'I follow you, madam. But I can't say I did see anything like that, and the doctor's always been decent to me and — '

'And you have a child who ought to be put away in a mental home,' put in Ruth Farlong mercilessly. 'And no money to support him, and no means of getting another job if I sack you — eh?'

Mrs. Clarke shrank visibly and pulled the boy nearer her. 'I won't have my Willy in no mental home.'

'But you'd like a nice sum of money — something to put by and know he's safe and you're safe . . . later on . . . ?' said Ruth.

Mrs. Clarke swallowed hard.

'What do you want me to do?' she said uneasily.

Ruth Farlong hesitated. Her heart beat at an abnormal rate. Her face was pale. She knew that she was about to do a very wicked thing; a thing which would ruin Blaise as a doctor, and an unknown and possibly innocent girl into the bargain. But her own obsession to be free and her fast-growing passion for Hugh Spalderson submerged her better instincts.

'You won't have much to do, Mrs. Clarke,' she said. 'Just to swear in a court of law that — the doctor and that girl spent last night together.'

'It might land me in gaol.'

'Rubbish. How can it? They can't disprove it. I've got money, Mrs. Clarke. A few hundred pounds — for you and Willy — '

The housekeeper licked her lips. After all, Willy counted first, and she had never had many scruples or high principles. If Mrs. Farlong wanted a divorce from the doctor, let her get it.

'I don't mind swearing whatever you tell me,' she said.

Ruth Farlong drew a deep breath. She lit another cigarette. A little colour returned to her cheeks. She pressed the self-starter.

'Get in — don't mind about the phone,' she said briefly. 'You're coming back with me. I'm going to surprise those two, and you're going to back whatever I choose to say. Is that understood?'

'Yes,' said Mrs. Clarke meekly.

Blaise Farlong and Terry had finished breakfast and were walking through the garden, looking at the havoc wrought upon the flowers in the herbaceous border by the storm, when Ruth Farlong drove up to the gates of her home.

4

Blaise Farlong was tying up a drooping delphinium and Terry was watching him, thinking that the rain-washed blue of the tall flower in the sunlight was the most exquisite thing she had seen. It was she who first saw that car drive up and stop outside the gateway of Russet Place.

It did not strike her at once that the driver was Dr. Farlong's wife. She said casually:

'Hallo! You've got an early visitor, Dr. Farlong.'

Blaise cut the piece of raffia with his pocket-knife and looked up. There was no more astonished man than he when he saw the tall *soignée* figure of his wife. Ruth — home at this house! Why, she usually spent an hour or more bathing and dressing. He had to confess to himself that he was not pleased to see her. He knew she would not approve of the fact that Terry Manstone had spent the night at Russet Place.

He looked at Terry's happy, sun-browned face.

'It's my wife,' he said quietly.

'Oh, Lord!' exclaimed Terry, like an embarrassed boy. 'What will she say, Dr. Farlong?'

Blaise did not answer. Ruth was coming toward them with that quick, slightly imperious walk which he knew so well. And on her face was an expression which he also knew very well. A look which had so often in the past menaced his peace and heralded a row.

'Now for the peroration,' he thought.

Ruth Farlong, having made up her mind to do a very wicked thing, did it thoroughly. She was a good actress. She looked from her husband to the slim girl in the grey flannel skirt and white blouse. She said in a hard voice:

'So, Blaise, *this* is why you quarrelled with me and came home last night at such an unreasonable hour. Now I understand.'

Then she turned on her heel and walked toward the house.

Terry looked at Blaise. Her cheeks were hot. Her heart beat fast. Mrs. Farlong's manner and tone of voice had given her a shock. They were sinister, to say the least of it, although she did not quite understand what lay behind it all.

Blaise Farlong's cheeks were also hot. But his eyes were furious. What the devil did Ruth mean by that speech, and how dared she look at the girl in that insulting fashion?

'I was afraid,' said Terry, 'that Mrs. Farlong wouldn't like me being here.'

'Oh, rubbish!' said Blaise. 'There's some mistake. I'll go and speak to my wife.'

He pocketed his penknife and followed Ruth into the house. Terry walked slowly after him, frowning. Her ankle was hurting her again, but that did not matter. What worried her was the fact that she had made such a mistake in sleeping in this house last night. The situation was an awkward one — becoming more awkward now that Mrs. Farlong had come home unexpectedly and seemed so angry about things. Terry remembered what Mrs. Clarke had told her about the unhappy married life of the doctor and his wife. She felt very uneasy. What had Mrs. Farlong meant by saying that she *understood now* why Dr. Farlong had quarrelled with her and come home last night? Surely she could not think — Terry's thoughts carried her no further. She reached the hall and stood, hesitating outside the door of the consulting-room. The door was ajar, and she could hear Blaise and his wife talking. The woman's voice shrill, sarcastic, The man's quiet, indignant.

Terry, after one look at Ruth Farlong, had instinctively disliked her. Pretty, smart, yes. Typical of the hard society woman dear to her mother's heart. Terry had met plenty of them in London. Women who made a fetish of dressing well; who spent half their time and money beautifying themselves, and the rest playing Bridge or Poker. Terry had no use for them. And that was why she was not a success with mother or sister Barbara.

A few hours in Blaise Farlong's company had proved what manner of being he was. Utterly different from his wife. A man whose interests lay in his work and his garden. Terry could imagine how great the gulf must be between him and such a wife. When she had first met him in the early hours of the morning he had seemed melancholy — weary — saddened by life. Yet at breakfast later on he was a different person; full of enthusiasm about his flowers — ready to laugh with her. Yes, they shared a sense of humour. And she had felt more than once that she was sorry she must go away and never see him again.

It was obvious, however, that she was not destined to leave Russet Place in peace. A fresh and very real sense of shock descended upon Terry when she heard Ruth Farlong's high, accusing voice:

'I tell you, Blaise, I don't believe a word you say. You spent the night with the girl. You were very clever — picking a quarrel with me so as to justify your leaving me after the party. I asked you in fun if it was because you wanted some other woman, but it wasn't so much a jest as I thought.'

Then Blaise's voice — horrified:

'You must be crazy, Ruth! Absolutely crazy to make such an unspeakable suggestion. You know perfectly well that I don't know the girl — never set eyes on her until — '

'That's all rubbish,' broke in the woman. 'It's quite true that *I've* never seen the girl before, but that doesn't say that *you* don't know her.'

Then Blaise Farlong's voice — louder — angrier:

'Good God, Ruth, you must be off your head! I tell you, Miss Manstone got caught in the storm and Mrs.

Clarke put her up. She, herself, will tell you so. It's a most damnable thing to suggest that that girl — that child and I — could — '

His voice broke off. Outside the door Terry stood like one rooted to the spot. She was quite white under the tan. She felt a little sick. It was not difficult for her to realize what was happening between those two in there. Mrs. Farlong was accusing her husband of having come home especially because of *her*. And she was accusing them of having spent the night together. It was ludicrous. If it hadn't been so serious, Terry would have laughed. *She and Dr. Farlong* — indulging in a liaison — two complete strangers. Mrs. Farlong must, indeed, be off her head. Jealous to the pitch of madness to think such a thing.

It was not Terry's nature to shirk any issue of her own conduct. The whole thing was her fault, she told herself, and it was up to her to rectify the mistake. Bravely she walked straight into the consulting-room and faced the woman who was in the middle of more violent accusations.

She had known for some time, Ruth was saying, that Blaise was sick of her and wanted somebody else. He had pretended to be so virtuous, but *she* knew he was no saint about women, etc., etc.

Terry, shaking a little, hardly dared look at Blaise. One quick glance showed her that he was livid with rage. Then she looked at Mrs. Farlong. Ruth had taken off her hat and was leaning against her husband's desk. Her long fingers with their highly polished nails plucked nervously at the little cap which she was holding. Her red lips sneered. Her eyes were like blue stones — relentlessly hard.

Terry summoned all her courage. She said:

'Mrs. Farlong, forgive me for butting in like this, but you're making a terrible mistake. I couldn't help hearing what you said just now to Dr. Farlong. Of course it isn't true.'

'Of course not,' echoed Blaise. 'I must apologise to you, Miss Manstone. It's most outrageous that such things should have been said to you in my house. But I am quite sure my wife will beg your pardon — '

'I shall do nothing of the kind,' said Ruth Farlong. 'This girl' — she looked Terry up and down — 'ought to beg mine. It's a low-down thing to take another woman's husband away from her.'

'But, Mrs. Farlong — ' began Terry, crimson-cheeked.

'Don't bother to deny it,' said Blaise. 'It's too preposterous. Ruth!' He seized his wife's arm. 'Have you taken leave of your senses?'

She wrenched her arm away.

'Don't touch me, Blaise. You've behaved unspeakably to me, and it makes it all the worse — trying to brazen it out that you've never seen this girl before. I've stood too much from you lately. This ends it. I shall see my solicitors and file my petition at once.'

Blaise looked at her as though he could not believe his ears. Terry put a finger to her mouth and wished that she could stop shaking. This was growing worse and worse. *File a petition.* She meant *divorce.* But, really, the whole thing was insane.

Then Blaise broke out in a violent tone:

'You are going too far, Ruth. For the last time I tell you that you are making a ghastly mistake. Miss Manstone and I never set eyes upon each other until we met here in the early hours of the morning. There was no question of a liaison — of us being lovers — ' He stumbled over that word, and Terry gasped a little. 'If you really think such a thing, call in Mrs. Clarke. She'll explain the whole situation.'

'I've already spoken to Mrs. Clarke,' said Ruth Farlong. 'It was she who told me what has been going on behind my back.'

Blaise put a hand to his head. He was conscious more of bewilderment than anger now. The whole affair was assuming such outrageous proportions. He had expected Ruth to be annoyed because Mrs. Clarke allowed a stranger to sleep here. But that she should put such a sinister complexion upon the incident — accuse him of infidelity — talk about filing a petition — that stunned him.

'But, Mrs. Farlong' — Terry found speech again — 'you're absolutely mistaken — honestly! Your housekeeper will tell you that I got lost in the storm — hurt my ankle — and she let me sleep in Dr. Farlong's room.'

'I refuse to discuss anything with you,' said Ruth Farlong in an insulting voice.

Scarlet to the roots of her hair, Terry fell back and remained mute.

'Of all the damnable things — ' Blaise began, and then added: 'There must be an end to this. You're crazy, Ruth, but we'll have Mrs. Clarke in here and she'll explain exactly what did happen.'

Ruth Farlong took a matchbox from the desk and coolly lit a cigarette, but inwardly she seethed with excitement.

'Go ahead. Let Mrs. Clarke come in,' she said.

Blaise rang the bell. The three of them waited in silence for the house-keeper to come. Terry felt that these were the most ghastly few minutes of her life. She had never been more hideously embarrassed. She could not face the doctor. She heard the telephone bell ring. Blaise answered it. In a curt, professional voice:

'Hello . . . Oh, yes — the line is all right again. You've been working on it, have you? Right — I'll take the call. Hello . . . Yes, this is Dr. Farlong speaking . . . Yes, I shall be with you within the hour. I'm late starting on my rounds this morning. I am sorry the pain's so bad — yes, I'll do what I can to relieve it . . . No — no more morphia until I come.'

Silence again. Then the door opening and the entrance of Mrs. Clarke. Terry looked up at the woman. She felt strangely uneasy about Mrs. Clarke. There was a nasty, covert look in the short-sighted eyes behind those black-rimmed spectacles. What was she going to say? Terry did not trust her.

'You rang for me, madam,' said Mrs. Clarke.

'Look here, Mrs. Clarke,' said Blaise. 'I very much dislike having to drag you into this, but it's got to be done. Mrs. Farlong is labouring under the delusion that Miss Manstone and I — ' He swallowed and cleared his throat, loathing the whole situation. He had never liked Mrs. Clarke, and to have to include her in an intimate discussion of this sort grated on him horribly, but it had to be done since Ruth persisted with her unspeakable accusations. 'Mrs. Farlong thinks,' he began again, 'that I came home last night on purpose to — er — be with Miss Manstone. You know the real facts of the case. Kindly place them before Mrs. Farlong.'

'Yes, Mrs. Clarke,' put in Terry

eagerly. 'You know that I am a stranger here — that I asked you to let me stay — please explain everything to Mrs. Farlong.'

'And don't be long about it,' added Blaise. 'I have patients waiting.'

Ruth Farlong looked hard at her housekeeper. Mrs. Clarke looked back. They exchanged significant glances. Mrs. Clarke folded her hands primly in front of her and said:

'I am sorry, doctor, but I must do what's right. I've already told the mistress that you and this young person were together here last night.'

'What do you mean by *together*?' Blaise asked violently.

Mrs. Clarke raised her brows.

'She told me,' said Ruth, 'that she doesn't know where you met the girl or when, but that she *does* know that you shared the same room — that you were together when she brought in the morning tea — and that you bribed her not to tell me. But she has shown her loyalty by ignoring the bribe.'

Terry gasped. Her very ears tingled and felt hot. She would not have been more surprised if a bomb-shell had burst at her feet. It seemed incredible to her that such lies could pour from anybody's lips. She stared at Ruth Farlong, then turned to Blaise. He looked stricken — too stricken to speak.

Ruth turned to her housekeeper.

'Is that or isn't it true?' she said.

Mrs. Clarke hesitated for the fraction of a second. Somewhere deep down in her stirred shame — for, after all, Miss Manstone was a very young girl and the doctor a good man. She was aiding and abetting a very dirty thing by upholding Mrs. Farlong in this. On the other hand, there was Willy — her wretched, idiot son — and it would be nice to feel there was some money in the bank for the future.

'It's quite true, madam,' she said.

'It's a damnable lie!' broke from Blaise Farlong's lips. For a moment the usually self-possessed, easy-going man

90

was half crazy with anger. He seized the housekeeper by the wrist and shook her. 'How dare you tell such wicked preposterous stories to my wife? You know that it's a damned lie — that we did not share a bedroom. I'll have you in court for libel — '

'Oh, no, Blaise,' said Ruth Farlong, 'I'm going to have *you* in the divorce-court first of all. Let go of Mrs. Clarke. You're not going to bully her just because you've broken our marriage vows and ruined my life!'

The man's fury cooled down. He released Mrs. Clarke. She nursed her wrist sullenly. She felt uneasy about the whole business. But she must stick to her story now. And she'd see that Mrs. Farlong paid for it too.

'If the mistress divorces you, doctor, she'll be in her rights,' the woman said defiantly. 'She's got the evidence, and me to prove it.'

Terry, feeling that her heart would burst with its frantic beating, was the next to attack the housekeeper.

'What have I ever done to you,' she said, panting, 'that you should tell such dreadful lies? You know quite well that Dr. Farlong and I didn't — ' She broke off helplessly.

Ruth interrupted.

'That's all right, Mrs. Clarke, we shan't want you any more. I'll see you later.'

The housekeeper left the consulting-room.

Blaise Farlong looked at his wife.

'What devil's game is this?' he asked in a low voice. 'Is this a put-up job between you and Mrs. Clarke? It must be — she couldn't lie like that just for the sake of lying. You've wanted a divorce for a long time. Is this your way of getting it?'

Ruth's lashes drooped. She could not meet the clear blaze of her husband's eyes. She flicked the ash from her cigarette and shrugged her shoulders.

'It's perfectly true that I want a divorce from you,' she said. 'Our marriage has never been a success. But

I was prepared to stand anything from you but infidelity.'

'You know perfectly well, as God is my judge, that I have not been unfaithful to you, Ruth,' he said, shaking from head to foot. 'And it's a dastardly thing to drag a perfectly innocent girl like Miss Manstone into this business.'

Ruth glanced at Terry and curled her lips.

'Hardly innocent, since Mrs. Clarke found you — '

'But that's a lie!' broke in Terry.

'If you wish to defend the case, Blaise,' said Ruth gently, and with an unpleasant smile, 'you will be given a chance to do so in the divorce-court. But I shall file my petition tomorrow, and as Mrs. Clarke can prove misconduct I don't think you will stand a chance. Mrs. Clarke knows Miss — er — Manstone's address. Wimbledon, I think she said. If she has parents — I am sorry for them. But it's her own fault if she's got herself into this mess.

She should leave other women's husbands alone.'

'Oh!' said Terry, and dropped into a chair because her legs refused to support her. She sat there, her hands locked tightly together, staring from husband to wife. It was all too horrible — too amazing. It was impossible for her to collect her scattered wits and dwell on the thought that this woman meant to divorce Blaise Farlong and name her, Terry Manstone, co-respondent. She could not begin to think what her mother and Barbara would say.

Blaise said:

'Ruth, will you or will you not believe that Miss Manstone and I are strangers — and that there was no question of an affair between us last night? Either Mrs. Clarke is off her head — or you are.'

'I don't think we'll continue this discussion,' said Ruth. She pitched her cigarette-end out of the open window. Terry's gaze followed it mechanically.

Out there in the garden was sun-light, flowers, trees, and singing birds. Beauty, peace, nature. Impossible to believe that such an incredible argument was going on inside this room, and that she, Terry, was involved in it.

Ruth Farlong walked toward the door. Blaise sprang after her and caught her arm.

'Ruth, you can't mean to go through with this outrageous business? You can't! It's the most criminal thing. Miss Manstone is a girl of twenty-one — a lady; a thing like this will ruin her reputation. You can't divorce me — break up our home — ruin my practice. I keep telling you you're making a mistake, and that there is no possible cause for you to divorce me.'

Ruth drew her arm away from her husband's fingers. She looked up at him. All her petty annoyances and irritations of the past — her disappointment because she could not always get her own way — her boredom — her interest in another man — culminated into one tremendous desire to hurt this man.

'I have made no mistake,' she said, 'and I'm going to divorce you, Blaise, and cite Miss Manstone as co-respondent. That's final. I shall pack up and leave this house at once, and go to town to my brother.'

She walked out of the consulting-room and shut the door behind her.

Terry looked blindly at Blaise. He was still shaking, and there were two white, grim lines on either side of his mouth. He met her gaze. A horrible little feeling of shame smote her. Guiltless though she was, Ruth Farlong had made her feel ashamed. She covered her face with her hands.

'Oh!' she said under her breath.

Blaise Farlong pulled at his collar as though he felt choked. He stared at the girl's bent brown head. Then he said hoarsely:

'I don't know what to say to you. I never dreamt that such a thing would happen. It's damnable. But of course my wife won't do as she says. She can't.'

Terry uncovered her face. He saw tears glittering on her lashes and he was stricken with remorse. Poor little thing! Innocent as daylight — an honest, healthy-minded, charming child — to be dragged into such a sordid affair! Even now he could not believe that Ruth meant to behave in such a dastardly fashion.

'I am afraid, Dr. Farlong,' said Terry in a shaky voice, 'that my staying here last night was disastrous. I blame myself — but of course how could I know that *this* was going to happen?'

'How, indeed,' said Blaise.

'But why is that old housekeeper lying so terribly?' Terry asked in a piteous voice.

Blaise, hands clenched behind him, paced up and down the consulting-room.

'I've always loathed that woman — she's a treacherous old hag. She'd do anything for money. She's been bribed.'

He gave a mirthless laugh. 'My wife's at the bottom of it. I knew she was sick of me. But God knows I never thought she'd go to such lengths to get rid of me.'

'Do you think,' said Terry, 'that she really is going to pay that woman to swear in the divorce-court that you and I — '

'It seems like it,' said Blaise. 'But it can't be allowed to go as far as that. There's my practice to think of. But that's nothing compared to your reputation.'

'Heaven knows what my mother will say,' whispered Terry.

'She shan't know. I tell you it shan't be allowed to go any further,' said Blaise. He paused in front of her. 'Look here, child, I can never tell you how sorry I am — how ashamed — '

She looked up and met his gaze. Her lips quivered into a smile which he thought the nicest thing he had ever seen. She was so game.

'It isn't your fault,' she said, 'but I

think it's going to be difficult for you to stop your wife divorcing you if she really wants to.'

'You shan't be dragged into it, anyhow,' said Blaise.

'It looks as though I'm going to be,' said Terry dryly, 'especially if that horrid old woman is going to substantiate her story.'

'Unfortunately, my wife has the money, but in any case I'm not competing if it's a question of bribery,' said Blaise Farlong between his teeth. 'It's all going to be settled in quite another way. I shall speak to my wife and make her come to her senses.'

'And supposing she doesn't?' said Terry.

'She must.'

But Blaise Farlong — a man of simple and direct action, a man of honour, of integrity — was not so ignorant of the complexities of a woman's mind as to feel certain of winning the day. He knew Ruth — God, how well he knew her! Her meanness — unkindness — her lack of principle over trivial things. In this last year, particularly, she had stripped herself of glamour for him and revealed herself as she really was.

He had had to face the fact that she was sweet and charming only when it suited her book so to be. When she was in love she was soft and acquiescent. When she had grown tired of him she had become a nagging, complaining, selfish creature. But even then he had not thought her a bad woman — a woman who would stoop to such despicable conduct as this. With a queer sense of shock, of wounded pride, he realised how bitterly she must loathe him now — how anxious she must be to get rid of him.

'Wait here,' he said abruptly. 'I'll go and have this out with my wife.'

Terry stood up. She faced him nervously.

'Yes, I suppose I'd better wait until you've made sure what is going to happen. It's not much use me going on blithely with my walking-tour, is it?'

The blood rushed to the man's cheeks. There was something so unaffected and at the same time so courageous about this child.

'I am damned sorry,' he said under his breath, and walked quickly out of the room.

Terry stood where he had left her. Her gaze lit on the photograph of Ruth Farlong with her baby in her arms. She wondered how any woman who had lived with Blaise and borne his child could behave like this to him now. She thought:

'If the baby had lived, she couldn't have done it!'

Yet when she recalled the pretty, hard face of Dr. Farlong's wife it was easy to believe that Ruth could do anything. She was a woman without the quality of mercy.

What a position to find herself in! Terry thought of her conventional, rather prudish mother, and sister Barbara — the family paragon. She visualised the horror with which they would receive her account of this dramatic adventure. Mummy had said that she strongly disapproved of a young girl going on a walking-tour alone. Barbara had intimated that Terry would come to grief. Well, she certainly had — though not through any fault of her own.

Terry had always been different from Barbara, who was a replica of their mother. In their childhood Barbara had been an obedient little girl cut to pattern. The kind held up as an example by the mothers of more refractory offspring, who secretly labelled her 'a prig.'

But Terry from the start had not poured herself meekly into her mother's excellent mould. She had been a naughty, untidy, rebellious child. She had said and done comic things and made strangers laugh. But her mother had never laughed. And her father, who would have adored her, had died when she was a baby. He, like Terry, had existed with rebellion in his heart, unable to live up to his wife's standards.

He had bequeathed to Terry that sense of humour which saved her from being driven mad by a surfeit of discipline and organisation.

Barbara fitted so beautifully into the circle of her mother's friends. Terry liked unconventional, human people. But those whom she brought into the alien atmosphere of the Cedars were speedily driven away by Mrs. Manstone's frigid courtesy and disapproving eye.

Just before Terry came away on this walking-tour Mrs. Manstone had delivered one of her regular lectures. Couldn't Terry behave with more dignity, dress with more taste, curb that wayward tongue of hers? The things she said were not funny — only shocking. Now Barbara was engaged to nice Francis Colroyd, Terry ought to be careful and not jeopardise Barbara's chances.

It was soon after that that Terry had felt she must get away from the home circle. Her mother had said:

'I only hope you come to no harm, Terry.'

Terry had laughed and answered:

'What do you suppose can happen to me, Mummy? Do you think some ravening wolf disguised as a man will leap out from a hedge and make an attack on my virtue?'

Mrs. Manstone had flung up her hands in horror, and Barbara, with that prim look about her small mouth which Terry found so irritating, had said coldly:

'Don't be so coarse, Terry. I know mother is right — you ought not to go on this tour by yourself. Francis and Colonel and Mrs. Colroyd would be horrified.'

Those words echoed in Terry's brain as she stood in Blaise Farlong's consulting-room this morning. Certainly the excellent family of Barbara's *fiancé* would have cause to be horrified now. And if, indeed, she were to be publicly concerned in a divorce-case, her mother would never get over it.

Terry was bound to admit the prospect was not a pleasing one.

Through all the anxieties, however, Terry never swerved from her belief that Blaise Farlong was a much-to-be-pitied man and a very charming person.

'Poor dear,' she thought. 'I suppose at this very moment he's having a hideous argument with that woman upstairs.'

She began to walk up and down the consulting-room restlessly.

5

The row between Blaise and his wife was not a prolonged one. It was brief and fierce. When Blaise marched into Ruth's bedroom, she was sitting at her dressing-table sorting the contents of an untidy drawer, flinging things into a suitcase open on the ground beside her, only pausing now and then to puff at a cigarette. Through the mirror she saw the reflection of her husband's tall figure when he entered her room. With the cigarette in the corner of her mouth, she smiled, a maddening, sneering little smile.

Perhaps, through all the dark days to follow, that hateful smile haunted and irritated Blaise more than anything else in his life. He began to understand how a man could murder a woman he had once loved.

'Look here, Ruth,' he began, 'of

course you're not going to do this dastardly thing. You can't mean it. That child downstairs is an absolutely decent girl, and you know perfectly well that she and I are strangers. Either Mrs. Clarke is making mischief for the sake of making it, or it's a put-up job between you. Whichever it is, it's damnable. You can't divorce me.'

Ruth Farlong lifted her eyebrows in a supercilious fashion and threw a few handkerchiefs and some odd ribbons into her suitcase.

'I told you downstairs that I hadn't anything more to say to you,' was her answer.

'But you have. Damn it all — '

'It's no good swearing at me. Get out of my room.'

He came up to the dressing-table and looked down at her as though incredulous that she could behave in this fashion. She took the cigarette from her sneering lips with fingers that shook slightly. She was a woman without much conscience, but what she had was troubling her a little at the moment. She was anxious to be done with this business and get away from Blaise and Russet Place for good and all.

My God, but she was glad that she had taken the plunge in this fashion; that she was going. She was sick to death of Blaise — his medical work; his medical friends; his passion for gardening and animals. The very decency and kindliness which were intrinsic parts of his nature irritated her beyond belief. The quiet, rather sweet personality of the man, with his keen sense of humour, which had attracted her in the beginning, bored her utterly now.

She was the type of woman who liked a streak of viciousness in a man. Blaise lacked it. Perhaps that was why he bored her. Hugh Spalderson had a spice of the devil in him — an insolent, arrogant sort of way with him which fascinated her. Yes, she wanted Hugh. And she would get him once the divorce with Blaise was over.

'Don't stand there scowling at me,

Blaise. Get out, I tell you,' she snapped at him.

'You actually mean that you are going on with this damnable affair?' he asked her. 'Mean to divorce me and cite that innocent girl — '

'Oh, bah to the innocent stuff!'

He changed from red to white and white to red again. The muscles in his cheeks were working. He breathed quickly, like a man making some tremendous effort. He was trying to control himself — to prevent himself from taking Ruth's long white throat between his fingers and strangling her. The whole thing was so iniquitous — he felt half off his head.

'Ruth, have you lost all sense of decency?' he stammered. 'Can you sit there calmly and tell me that you believe that I slept with that girl last night?'

'Yes,' said Ruth, and went on coolly with her packing.

Blaise clenched his hands, unclenched them.

'You don't believe it — my God, you don't!'

'You'll soon see that I do, when I've filed my petition.'

'If that old hag downstairs is misleading you, I'll choke the truth out of her.'

'If you don't get out of my room and stop this violent stuff, I'll ring for the police,' said Ruth.

'For the love of God, be reasonable — if you've any affection left for me at all.'

'I haven't any.'

'Then for Priscilla's sake — '

'Priscilla is not alive.' Ruth Farlong flushed a little at the mention of her dead baby.

'It's just as well,' said Blaise in a choked voice, 'if this is how things are going to turn out for her mother and father.'

Ruth stood up and faced him in a fury.

'Will you *get out!*' She screamed the words. 'I won't be bullied by you. For the last time I tell you I'm going to divorce you, and Mrs. Clarke will prove misconduct. Defend the case if you like, but you won't get much change out of it.'

Blaise Farlong stared at his wife in silence, panting, beads of moisture on his forehead. That she, the woman whom he had loved passionately and married, to whom he had given everything, should turn round and strike this treacherous blow at him, was beyond his comprehension.

He became suddenly calm. In a quiet voice he said:

'I suppose you realise that not only will you ruin that girl's reputation but you'll do in my career as a doctor? Whether I defend the case or not, it'll get into the papers. Rossdown will hear of it soon enough. Not many people will go to a doctor who is supposed to have committed misconduct under his own roof with a young, unmarried girl. I love my work. Do you want to take that away from me as well as everything else?'

She hesitated for a moment. It was, perhaps, an unfortunate moment for Blaise. She happened to have taken from her drawer a small shagreen cigarette-case. Hugh Spalderson had given it to her for her birthday a fortnight ago. Her fingers caressed it. Hugh had said when he had given it to her:

'If only you were free to marry me, I'd give you so much more, lovely, clever Ruth!'

Yes, he appreciated her brains — he didn't call them 'Bridge-brains' and prefer that she should know all the long, tiresome names of flowers.

'I'm sorry if it's going to upset your career, Blaise,' she said tersely. 'But that's your look-out. I daresay you'll be hard up when I've gone. But hasn't your girlfriend any money?'

For an instant Blaise looked at the hard, unrelenting face with its red sneering mouth. He felt, suddenly, that if he went on looking at it, listening to her, he'd kill her.

He turned on his heel and swung out of the room. There was a blind, bewildered look in his eyes. On the staircase he collided with the angular figure of his housekeeper. She shrank back a little when she saw his white, distorted face.

'Are you going to substantiate that damnable story about last night, when you know what a foul lie it is?' he said between his teeth.

'I am on the mistress's side,' she muttered, and got away from him quickly before he could touch her.

He knew then that Ruth had bribed the woman. He saw through the whole treacherous, beastly affair. He was filled with a nausea which made him feel incapable of further fight.

He stumbled rather than walked into his consulting-room. The telephone bell was ringing. Vaguely he saw Terry Manstone's slim figure by his desk. Just for the fraction of a moment he wished to God he had never set eyes upon this girl — that she had never entered his house. She had raised a hornets' nest about his ears. Then that feeling passed. He was ashamed of it and sorry for her — infinitely sorry. She was the innocent victim of Ruth's unscrupulous desire for freedom.

Why hadn't he given Ruth her divorce long ago? He might have saved Terry Manstone's name and reputation from being sullied. But he had upheld the sacredness of his marriage vows because to him they were not lightly to be ignored, and because of the beloved little daughter who had been the sweet, tangible link between him and Ruth.

Last, but not least, there had been the question of his profession. It did not do for a doctor, a public man, to be divorced by his wife. Even in these free-and-easy days a medical man — especially one with a small country practice — must have no stain upon his character.

Terry, who had been walking miserably up and down the consulting-room wondering what was going to happen next, saw Dr. Farlong's face and her heart sank. The expression in his eyes told her that no good had come of his attempt to put things right with his wife.

The telephone bell went on ringing shrilly. It buzzed through Terry's head. Blaise said:

'Can you answer it? I can't.'

Terry, feeling as though she were in a bad dream, picked up the receiver and said:

'Hallo.'

A woman's voice said:

'Is that Dr. Farlong's house?'

'Yes.'

'Could I speak to him, please?'

'The doctor is engaged for a moment.' Terry said the first thing that came into her head.

'Will you ask him to come as soon as possible to Mr. Webster, Oakways. He seems a little worse, and Mrs. Webster is worried.'

Terry conveyed this message to Blaise.

'Say I'll be along in a moment,' he said.

Terry hung up the receiver. Biting her lip nervously, she leaned against the desk, facing Blaise.

'Well?'

'I ought to have been on my rounds an hour ago,' he said dully. 'I must go. I've got two rather bad cases.'

'W-what's g-going to happen?' Terry stammered the words.

'I don't know, but I can't make my wife understand — I don't think she wants to understand. And that fiend of a woman Mrs. Clarke means to bear out her lying story.'

Terry's heart-beats hurt her. Crimson-cheeked, she looked at the doctor. She was frightened — badly frightened. Yet even now her sympathies were for him. He looked ghastly, poor man.

'Do you mean,' she said, 'that Mrs. Farlong is going to divorce you, and cite me as — as co-respondent?'

'Yes,' said Blaise heavily.

'But — how absurd!' said Terry, with a queer little laugh, and put her hand to her forehead in a bewildered way.

'It's inconceivable. I've done everything I can — but I can't prevent it,' he said.

Terry's youthful spirit of brightness and optimism quailed suddenly at the thought of her mother — of Barbara — the accusing finger which would be pointed at her by the family and friends. She might explain things to her mother, but would she believe her? So few people would credit it if she told them that this was a put-up job between Mrs. Farlong and the house-keeper. One could not get away from the fact that she had stayed the night in this house while Mrs. Farlong was away, and that she and Dr. Farlong had slept in communicating bedrooms. He was a youngish man, not unattractive. She was very young and not unattractive herself. Easy enough for the world to put the worst construction on the affair. And since Mrs. Clarke was ready to swear that she found them 'together' when she brought in the early cup of tea — what use for them to deny it?

Never, never when she had started on this walking-tour and sheltered from the storm in this house last night, had Terry dreamed that such a preposterous thing could happen to her. There was a comic side to it, no doubt. But it was much too critical and serious for laughter now. Her name, her character, were about to be blackened for ever, and this poor doctor was in the same boat. She knew perfectly well that it meant ruin to him, professionally.

It was queer and terrifying to find herself up against things like this with a man whom she scarcely knew. It would have been a difficult enough situation to face had Blaise Farlong really been her lover. Terry believed that she could have faced much without flinching for the sake of a man who meant everything to her. But it wasn't quite so easy to accept disgrace with a man whom one did not love and to be condemned for a sin which one had not committed.

Terry was no more ignorant about life than most girls of her age, but perhaps she was a little more unawakened to sex than most. She had grown up with a boyish love of sport — outdoor things — golf, tennis, motoring, swimming. Dressing up, posing to attract the other sex — which Barbara did — had never appealed to Terry. She was essentially natural; free of guile. Whenever she had turned her thoughts to matrimony, she had visioned herself falling in love with a man not at all like Barbara's *fiancé*. Francis Colroyd was, undoubtedly, a most excellent young man, a social success; danced well, played good Bridge, and worshipped at the shrine of Barbara's and mother's gods. Good Form. Good Taste. Good Breeding.

The man of Terry's choice would be a far more natural and primitive being; a companion who would do as she had done — sling a rucksack over his back and walk beside her through the countryside with a dog at their heels. She could not imagine Francis Colroyd or any of the young men in mother's set in town doing that.

Dr. Farlong was more of her temperament. She had known it as soon as she met him and liked him. But she had not expected to find herself landed with him in this grave and extremely awkward situation.

'We shall have to talk it out and see what can be done,' she heard Blaise say in a weary voice. 'It seems all wrong of me to leave you at this particular moment — everything's in such a ghastly muddle — but I must go on my rounds. My patients, you understand — '

'Yes, of course,' said Terry. 'Please do go.'

'You can't stay here,' he said, looking at her in a worried way. 'My wife is packing — she means to leave the house at once — but you won't want to be here — '

'No. I ought never to have come. I feel horribly to blame.'

'You're not,' he said. 'Don't reproach yourself. My wife — God forgive her — is answerable for it all.'

'I'll get my things and go to the local hotel, shall I?'

'Yes. The Crown. It's the one and only pub — on the corner of the cross-roads in the middle of the village. You'll see it. As soon as my round's over I'll come along there. No, perhaps I'll come back here first of all and talk to Ruth again. But I'm afraid it's no use.'

In the hall, Terry found her Burberry, her rucksack, and her beret. She followed Dr. Farlong into the garden. There was a horrid sinking feeling in her heart. And there was great bitterness in the soul of Blaise Farlong as he passed down the flagged path and caught a glimpse of his beloved delphiniums and the gay herbaceous border which he had planted when he had first come here with Ruth.

What an end to their life at Russet Place! What an end to his practice in Rossdown! He couldn't believe it.

Yet when he reached his car, turned and saw the small figure of Terry with her red beret on her brown bobbed head and her rucksack over her back, looking more like a forlorn, scared child than anything, he forgot himself and thought only of her.

'Jump in,' he said. 'I'll drive you to the Crown. I'm going that way.'

Terry bit her lip.

'Ought we to be seen together?'

'Wise child,' he said with a wry smile. 'But what's the use of worrying about *that*? Nobody will notice us, and why should you tramp a mile and a half? Your ankle isn't too good, is it?'

'Only a bit stiff.'

He opened the door of the car for her. Terry climbed in, sat down, and found, suddenly, that she wanted to cry. The shock of this thing that had happened to her had been so acute, it had at first left her dazed. Now came reaction. There was a dry feeling in her throat and a hot, pricking sensation behind her eyelids. As Blaise Farlong drove away from his home, she stared ahead of her at the dusty, sunlit roadway. For once she was blind to the beauty of lush green meadow-land; of the growing corn, rippling with exquisite shadows in the breeze; of hedges blue-starred with birds'-eye and the dark, picturesque silhouette of an old black windmill against a clear blue sky.

Blaise Farlong, slowing down behind a farm-cart as they rounded a corner, glanced at the girl and noticed the droop of her lips and the scared look in her eyes — a look that caused him a pang because it reminded him how young she was.

'Poor child,' he said. 'This is damned hard on you. God knows I'm sorry you sheltered under my roof and that we landed you in this disgraceful affair.'

'It isn't your fault,' she said.

'That's kind of you.'

'Well, it isn't.'

'I'm bitterly ashamed, nevertheless.'

'I'd certainly like to know how it's going to end.'

'Unless I can make my wife see reason, it can only end in a public scandal. I'd give my life to prevent it — for your sake; but I don't know that I can if Ruth and Mrs. Clarke persist with their lies.'

'It's pretty bad for you — your reputation as a doctor.'

The man, weary, bitterly ashamed of the thing Ruth was doing to this girl, crushed by his own sense of impending disaster, was moved by Terry's thought for him. It was like a tiny beacon of light in the pitch blackness that surrounded his mind.

'It's unexpectedly sweet of you to think of me,' he said. 'But what do I matter? Things seem to have gone wrong for me from the start ... my life's half over, anyhow. Yours is only just beginning. It's ghastly that even a breath of suspicion should touch you.'

'Oh, well, that can't be helped,' said

Terry; then added with a touch of her old humour: 'My mother and sister have told me ever since I was a kid that I'd disgrace the family one day.'

'Heaven knows why.'

'Well, I can't say I've ever had affairs with men or anything of that sort.'

'Good God, no — I'm perfectly sure you haven't.'

'But I've been a disappointment to the family in various ways, and this will give them real cause for complaint, won't it, Dr. Farlong?'

She was plucky and amazingly sweet to him, but he winced as he listened to her. He loathed the whole business. He wondered why he had not strangled Ruth up in her bedroom a few minutes ago.

'Don't look too far ahead, child,' he said. 'We may yet be able to prevent this thing. I won't give up hope till I've seen my wife again. If it's a divorce she wants, perhaps she'll consent to let you drop out of it. I'll find some woman who won't mind —

these things can be arranged — '

He stopped, sick at heart. Terry's cheeks burned. She said in a low voice:

'Of course, I'd like to be kept out of it — if possible.'

'You shall be, if I can move heaven or earth to manage it.'

'If not — well — there we are,' she said in a small voice.

They had reached the local 'pub' of Rossdown — a charming old grey stone house, possibly seventeenth century, with an archway which led into a paved courtyard. Terry looked at it, and in the midst of her troubles admired it.

'What a nice place,' she said.

'It's quite a good little pub, but the food isn't much. I'll drop you here, if I may. I must get on to my patients. I'm late enough as it is.'

'I understand,' said Terry, and jumped out.

'Go through the arch. You'll find the hotel door on the left. Not the other — that's the bar.'

'Seems to me that's where I shall

end,' said Terry, grimacing. 'Swallowing quarts of beer to drown my sorrows, having been branded as the bad woman of Rossdown.'

Blaise looked at her dumbly. He would like to have hugged her, as he would have hugged a kindly child.

He leaned over the side of the car.

'I want to tell you how — how grateful I am,' he said with difficulty.

'Grateful? But why?' She dropped her lashes nervously.

'To you — for being so very decent over this . . . '

'I don't see how else I could behave.'

'I do.' Blaise bit hard at his lip. 'Good-bye. I'll see you later. I'll come back — if you'll wait here for me.'

'Yes,' she said, and smiled as he drove away. When his car had vanished, she stayed a moment outside the Crown, staring at the cross-roads.

She was haunted by a picture of the doctor's face when he had leaned out of the car just now and told her that he was grateful. He had looked so terribly strained and haggard — and ashamed. Poor Dr. Farlong! There was something so attractive about his thin, strong-featured face with the very grey eyes, and the streak of grey in the thick dark hair. Especially did she like his wide, sweet-tempered mouth. Meant for humour, that mouth. The whole personality of the man was naturally a sunny, kindly one. And that woman, Ruth, had tried to crush all the gaiety out of him; embitter him. Well, she had succeeded this time. He had looked crushed — defeated — by this, her last and most serious cruelty.

'How could she!' thought Terry. '*How could she?*'

It was not as though Blaise Farlong was the type of man who would dream of entering the bedroom of a girl who was a guest under his own roof. Every time Terry thought of Ruth Farlong's accusations, and Mrs. Clarke's insinuating evidence, her whole body felt hot.

It seemed queer that a girl could go through life doing her best to keep herself clean and decent, in body and mind, for the one right man whom she would eventually care for and marry, and have this sort of thing happen to her. Terry, sitting in the stuffy little hotel lounge, depressing with its horse-hair sofa, and plush armchairs of faded green, and Nottingham curtains, brooded over the whole business for the rest of the morning.

6

It was half past one before Dr. Farlong's car drove up to the Crown again. Terry was sitting forlornly by the window in the lounge, watching for him. It had seemed the longest, blackest morning of her life. When one is alone, worrying, things always seem doubly bad and the outlook blacker than it need be.

Terry felt that she had little humour left by the time Blaise Farlong rejoined her. She liked him — liked him better, perhaps, than any man she had ever met — but after all he was a stranger to her. What did she really know about his character? Who knew but that now he found himself involved in this scandal with her he would desert her — leave her to get out of it the best way she could? All manner of dark and depressing thoughts were weighing down

Terry's mind when the black fabric coupe came down the road and turned slowly under the archway into the courtyard of the hotel.

Terry was quite relieved to see it. She walked out into the sunlight and met Blaise at the door. He looked more than ever weary and haggard. There was a queer sort of grimace on his face when he returned her gaze. He took off the soft hat he was wearing and ran his fingers nervously through his hair.

'I'm afraid you've been waiting a long time,' he said, 'but I had a longish list of people to see and then I went back to Russet Place. I hoped to talk things over with my wife and find her more reasonable. But she had gone.'

Terry's heart missed a beat.

'Gone!' she echoed.

'Yes,' said Blaise grimly. 'Packed and taken her luggage with her. Mrs. Clarke has gone, too, with that unhappy child of hers. Nobody about but the little daily maid and the gardener who comes three times a week to mow the grass.'

He gave a short laugh and took Terry's arm. 'We'd better go in, child, and have a spot of food. I feel rather as though we're in a nightmare, but we must eat and keep ourselves going, I suppose.'

To Terry it was certainly as though she moved in a nightmare. She felt the doctor's long, sensitive fingers trembling against her arm. She could see that he was labouring under a tremendous strain. It could not have been easy for him — seeing his patients, adopting the bedside manner, trying to cure bodily ailments, and his own mind in a torment of doubt and worry.

She allowed him to lead her into the dining-room — a more attractive room than the lounge, with its oak beams, original old stone fireplace, with shining rows of copper utensils hanging above it. Save for an elderly couple and a commercial traveller, there was nobody here. Blaise and Terry sat down at a window table.

'We'll have the lunch,' Blaise said to the waitress. 'And a whisky and soda for one. Would you like something to drink?' he added to Terry.

'No, thank you,' she said, and felt a hysterical desire to laugh. It was such a ludicrous situation. Yesterday, carefree, happy, she had sat in a field by a brook munching a sausage-roll. Now, twenty-four hours later, she was having lunch in a country 'pub' with a man with whom she was supposed to have committed adultery.

'I don't usually drink whisky at this time of the day,' said Blaise in an apologetic voice. 'But I really do need one at this particular moment.'

'I should think you'll need more than one,' said Terry trying to laugh.

He bit his lip, and brought one clenched fist down on the other.

'God! What are we going to do about this damned business?' broke from him in a low, hoarse voice. 'Ruth must be off her head. She's doing the thing thoroughly, anyhow. She left the con-ventional note for me — and one or two pieces of jewellery which had belonged to my mother. I wonder she didn't take them with her; it would have been less shameful than what she's doing to you — to me. I'm convinced that she knows the truth — that it's a put-up job between her and Mrs. Clarke. But we've no redress since she chooses to carry on with the story and Mrs. Clarke intends corroborating it. In her note she merely said that she was going to her brother's house in Lancaster Gate. He's married — a lawyer — and she's going to file her petition through his firm.'

Terry's eyes dilated slightly. The sunlight came warmly through the window-pane upon her, but she shivered with nervous excitement. She had dropped her rucksack and Burberry on the floor beside her. She took off her beret and smoothed back the rebellious wave of brown hair which would insist on falling across her cheek.

'So it really means,' she said, 'that she's going to divorce you and bring me into it?'

'Yes,' said Blaise Farlong. 'Let's face

it. That's what it means. Of course, I shall try and see my wife in town. But I know her. She's obstinate, and when she gets an idea into her head nothing will move it. She obviously wants to get rid of me at any cost — and she doesn't care who she hurts so long as she gets her way. That's Ruth.'

The waitress put two plates of mulligatawny soup in front of them. They both toyed with it — talked and talked and let it grow cold. The usual English country hotel fare followed. Roast mutton, boiled potatoes, cabbage. Apple tart and rice pudding. Cheese and biscuits. The waitress must have thought them queer, for neither of them seemed to eat more than a mouthful.

Drinking her coffee at the end of the meal and nibbling at a biscuit, Terry looked at the man opposite her, feeling bewildered and at a loss for further speech. He, too, was dumb. He had asked her permission to smoke a pipe, and puffed at it steadily, looking out of the window with eyes which saw nothing.

Terry smoked a cigarette, gloomily. It seemed futile to go on discussing the affair. They had looked at it from every angle — the thing went round in a vicious circle. They came back to where they started. They were guiltless. They knew it. Victims of a dastardly plot. Both implicated in a thing which would inevitably become a frightful scandal. But they had no defence. They could protest innocence. But the world is not a kindly judge, and why should anybody believe that they had slept with that communicating door closed between them, if a servant swore that they were sharing the same bed when she took in their early tea?

Blaise Farlong was conscious of defeat. The whole thing was so baffling, and, whatever terms he had been on with Ruth, he had not expected her to strike at him in the back like this. He knew in his own heart that it would be a waste of time to go up to town and see her. Probably she would refuse to interview him. In any case, she would not be so certain of getting her divorce if he *arranged* it with another woman. Terry Manstone having slept last night at Russet Place gave Ruth such a golden opportunity of securing her freedom. The housekeeper would back her up. She would not be likely to throw her chance away.

Her brother, Victor Keyland, would of course also back up whatever story she told him. Unfortunately for Blaise, his brother-in-law was no friend of his. Keyland was ten years older than Ruth, and had been her guardian since the death of their parents. A prig and a snob of the first water, he had never thought Blaise, with his small country practice, good enough for Ruth. Victor himself had done well as a solicitor, and married money into the bargain. He was prosperous and arrogant, and he led the type of life in London that Blaise loathed. They had nothing in common.

Blaise had little hope of sympathy or help from Ruth's relations. Victor's wife, Marjorie, whom Blaise had once attended professionally when he was in town, had always been nice to him. Ruth had once told him that Marjorie maintained she would rather Blaise doctored her than any physician she knew. But Marjorie would have no say in this matter. She was always well under the thumb of her overbearing husband.

In the midst of these bitter reflections Blaise allowed his thoughts to wander to the memory of the baby girl whom he had adored for the brief while that she had lived.

Ruth had been a good mother in her fashion, but the child's death had never meant to her the irreparable loss that it was to Blaise. He wondered whether she would have done this incredible thing to him had Priscilla been alive. Perhaps not. But futile to indulge in thoughts of the might-have-been. There was this crisis of the present to tackle.

Sighing heavily, he put his pipe in his pocket and let his gaze rest upon the girl who sat opposite him. This was her tragedy as well as his. They stood together, helpless targets for Ruth's marksmanship — her callous wish to get rid of him at any cost.

'For the hundredth time,' he said, 'I'm dreadfully sorry this has happened.'

'Well — and what's going to happen next?' asked Terry.

'I shall go up to town directly after lunch,' said Blaise. 'I'll try and see my wife. It may be futile, but I've got to make every effort.'

'I think I'd better go back to town,' said Terry in a low voice.

'Will you give me your address and telephone number?' said Blaise, taking out his notebook.

Terry bit hard at her lips.

'How queer that you don't know the address or phone number of your partner-in-sin.'

He knew that she was being flippant

because she was trying desperately not to give way to tears. She was gallant, and he liked her for it tremendously. It made him feel more than ever ashamed that she should be implicated in this sordid affair.

'I suppose,' added Terry, 'that even if I could prove I have never left home before, and never had a chance of meeting you and that sort of thing, it wouldn't help?'

'I'm afraid not,' said Blaise, 'if Mrs. Clarke lies about last night. What I mean is, even though we are strangers, if we acted as we are supposed to have done, it's enough in the eyes of the law.'

'Oh, well,' said Terry, knitting her eyebrows fiercely. 'Give me your little book and I'll put down my address and telephone number.'

'I'll phone you as soon as I've anything to tell you,' he said.

He watched her write. She had pretty hands, he thought vaguely. Small, narrow, sun-browned. Sensible little hands. She was built altogether on *petite* lines which, with her straight bobbed hair and complete lack of make-up, gave her such a youthful appearance. He thought, guiltily, that it was like dragging an innocent child into the mud. How unutterable of Ruth! And how impossible to even imagine himself being Terry's lover. The red blood ran up under his skin. He said tersely:

'Are you going to tell your people about this?'

'Not if I can help it,' said Terry. 'You don't know my mother — she's about the most conventional person in the world, and she'd never forgive me.'

'Surely she'll believe you!' exclaimed Blaise. 'She must know what you're like.'

'I'm afraid neither my mother nor my sister will be very sympathetic. They didn't want me to come on this tour by myself. And they've always said I was a crazy sort of person who would get into a fix one day. Simply because I hate conforming to society life in London.'

'It makes things more difficult if your

family won't believe you,' said Blaise.

'Even if they do, there's the scandal to face.'

'I know! It's the very devil! But there's still a chance that I may be able to keep you out of it.'

'I don't know much about married people,' said Terry, 'but I can't understand how a woman could behave like this to the man she's cared for and married.'

Blaise smiled bitterly.

'No, it is queer. But you see, my child, how transient the human affections can be! Two people who have been madly in love — and my wife and I were, I think, six years ago — end up like this! Quite frankly there hasn't been any love between us for some time. But I did try to carry on as best I could. I always hoped Ruth would do the same.'

'I don't mean to be catty,' said Terry, faintly apologetic, 'but do you think Mrs. Farlong has somebody else in view?'

Blaise stared, then laughed.

'It never entered my head, but you may be right. Ruth's pretty, and most attractive when she wants to be. There may be somebody else in the offing. But, knowing Ruth, I'm quite sure she'll never do anything to bring justice down upon her own head.'

'She seems rather mean,' said Terry.

'I think that describes it — yes, *mean*. It's the word — it's what she is! It goes against the grain,' he added, 'to talk against my wife — you understand — but I've got to talk to you because, after all, we seem so mixed up in this confounded affair.'

'I do understand,' said Terry, 'and I like you to tell me things. I'm perfectly certain you don't talk against your wife as a rule. Personally I think you've been awfully nice about her.'

'You've been awfully nice to me,' he said, and for a moment the suspicion of a smile lit up his gloomy features. 'Well, it's no use threshing out the affair any further. I must get hold of my gardener's wife — she'll be caretaker at the house for the moment, I'm sure — and I'll ask Beggland, the other doctor here, to do my work for the next twenty-four hours. If I tell him I've got to go away on very vital business, he won't mind. He's a decent fellow.'

Terry picked up her beret and pulled it over her head.

'What an end to my walking-tour!' she said, grimacing.

'Poor child!' he said.

'I'm not so young — quite old enough in the eyes of the law to be condemned for a crime. But you know, Dr. Farlong, it never once entered my head when you came home last night that it would be dangerous for me to sleep in that house just because your wife was away.'

'Under normal circumstances there would have been no danger in it,' said Blaise. 'I'm afraid you struck a bad patch in my life with Ruth. Believe me, I wouldn't have let you sleep there if I thought she was so anxious for evidence for divorce.'

They walked together out of the dining-room.

'I feel too worried,' said Terry, 'to carry on with my holiday. I don't want to go home — I dread it — but I must.'

'Well, say nothing to anyone until you hear from me,' said Blaise.

They stood a moment in the courtyard by his car. Blaise regarded Terry with worried eyes. Twenty-four hours ago he had not known of her existence. Today he felt strangely responsible for her. He said:

'Look here, I've got to go back home and settle things up and have a look at one of my patients who's seriously ill. Then I'm going straight up to town. There's a train to Victoria in twenty minutes' time — a fast one. If I drop you at the station now, you can catch that.'

'Very well,' she said.

In the car, driving to the station, her philosophic spirits drooped a little. She was filled with depression. In a funny sort of way she wished she did not have to part from Blaise Farlong. His presence gave her a sense of protection — of support. It was going to be pretty ghastly, she thought, facing mother and Barbara — concocting some story to account for this abrupt finale to her walking-tour. And heaven alone knew what was going to happen after that.

Neither she nor Blaise spoke until they reached the station. Then, as Blaise stopped the car, Terry looked at him and said:

'Supposing your wife won't listen to reason and she *does* file this petition?'

His cheeks burnt. He returned her gaze grimly.

'In that case we're finished. We'll have to face it. Of course, we can and will defend — but the harm will have been done both to your reputation as a girl and mine as a physician.'

Her heart began to beat at an uncomfortable rate.

'Oh!' Her voice was suddenly panic-stricken. 'It's — *awful.*'

Impulse moved him to take both her small hands in his. They were shaking. He held them tightly.

'My dear, what can I say to you? I've told you so many times how sorry and ashamed I am, and none of that is any good — apologies can't help you. But you've been so plucky; don't give way now. I swear I'll do my uttermost to make my wife keep you out of it.'

She was on the brink of tears. She hung on to his fingers and tried to smile.

'Well, I suppose it will be all right. Please try and forgive me for staying in your house last night. I did such a wrong thing bribing that old woman to let me stay — I started it all.'

'No, you musn't blame yourself. Come along.' He gave her fingers a little squeeze and dropped them. 'Let's get your ticket and pack you back to town.'

Terry pulled herself together, jumped out of the car, and slammed the door.

'No. You stay where you are. I'm all right now. I can look after myself. You've got plenty to do — you get back. You're a busy doctor, and this must be terribly worrying and trying for you from every point of view.'

His heart warmed to her. He thought how much he would have liked the friendship of this girl under happier circumstances.

'I'll ring you in town,' he said. 'Thank you again, and good-bye.'

She felt thoroughly unhappy after she had bought her ticket to Victoria and stood on the platform waiting for the train to come in. It was a close summer's day. Her head was aching. Her nerves were on edge from over-excitement and not enough food. She took the rucksack off her back. It felt heavy. She did not want to go back to London. Under the circumstances, it was going to be frightfully hard for her to return to the family circle and behave as though nothing untoward had happened.

'I feel almost as though I *had* — spent the night with Dr. Farlong,' she thought gloomily, and tried to laugh at herself. There was nothing much to laugh at now.

It was all a frightful mess. She could see nothing ahead but chaos — if Mrs. Farlong turned a deaf ear to her husband's pleading.

The atmosphere of a railway station is never, at its best, a stimulating one. Today it seemed to Terry the most depressing place in the world. The sky overhead looked grey with heat. Across the ugly coalyards one or two trees displayed their green leaves bravely — but even the green appeared grey with dust and soot. The platform was sun-baked — hot under Terry's feet. The lines glittered cruelly in the sunlight, and the boards between looked incredibly dirty and unattractive.

The train steamed in and Terry got into an empty smoker. She felt in need of a cigarette. The carriage was stifling.

Both windows were closed, and there was an odour of stale tobacco which made her wrinkle her nose in disgust. She let down the windows, sat in a corner, lit her cigarette and stared out of the window. Her gaze was suddenly attracted by a poster on the platform.

Rossdown Cottage Hospital.
Annual Garden Fête.
Tickets can be obtained from
the Hospital and from Mrs. Blaise
Farlong, Russet Place, Rossdown.

Rather ironic! Mrs. Blaise Farlong was not likely to attend that fete. Blaise Farlong was on the medical staff, of course. How closely she, Terry Manstone, was connected with these people now, and in what a way!

The train steamed out. Suddenly Terry pitched her cigarette out of the window, put her face in her hands, and burst into tears.

7

Mrs. Manstone and her daughter Barbara were preparing for a Bridge-party. Until half past three a sacred silence had presided over the Cedars. Mrs. Manstone, as usual, rested in her bedroom. Barbara, bored but patient, sat in a deck-chair in the garden reading a library book.

The garden was as Terry had described it to Blaise Farlong, a neatly planned and perfect product of an unimaginative gardener. All the plants in rows — not an inch out between them; borders clipped; lawn mowed and rolled; hedges immaculately trimmed. The Manstones' garden was like a park and not a place wherein one could dream and feel the real glory of a garden.

In keeping with her surroundings was Miss Barbara Manstone. A tall slim girl, a little like Terry in feature, but with much fairer colouring, and such different expression as made her altogether unlike her young sister.

She was as perfectly produced as the garden — prim from the top of her well-waved blonde head to the soles of her well-shod feet. Her small mouth was self-satisfied, the tilt of her chin a little supercilious. Her eyes were a cool, clear blue. There was scarcely a crease in her yellow skirt of pleated *crêpe-de-Chine*, or in the silky blouse which was of her own making. People thought it so clever, the way Barbara made and embroidered her own things. It was one of Mrs. Manstone's grievances that Terry could not sew. Lack of patience, of course. But then, in her mother's estimation, Terry lacked so many things.

Barbara held a sunshade over her head, because she believed in preserving her fair complexion. Francis, to whom she had recently become engaged, always told her how much he admired her unblemished and beautiful skin. He thought that Terry, who did not mind exposing her complexion to sun and wind and rain, looked most unattractive in an evening dress, with her tanned arms and shoulders.

At a quarter to four Barbara folded her sunshade, took her book, and walked into the drawing-room. Her mother had just come down and was arranging cards and Bridge-blocks on two tables.

It was dim and cool in here. The French windows opened on to the lawn, but blinds were drawn to keep out the sun because of the carpet. Blinds were always drawn all over the house during the summer months, which fact irritated Terry who revelled in sunlight.

'They'll be here soon, dear,' said Mrs. Manstone as Barbara entered the room. 'I've told Davis to set tea under the cedar, and to serve ices afterwards. It's such a warm day.'

Barbara concealed a yawn.

'Your new dress looks nice, mother.'

Mrs. Manstone glanced at herself in the mirror over the mantelpiece. The reflection showed her a stately, rather full figure in dark blue georgette with long tight sleeves. A face like Barbara's — that same smug, prim expression and tight, hard little mouth. Her hair, which had gone grey, and had been permanently waved, was beautifully 'set.' She had never conformed to fashion and cut it; it was pinned in the old-fashioned way, with large tortoiseshell combs on top of her head. Her eyes, which had been fine and large in her youth, were still handsome, but she wore pince-nez, which gave her an added touch of severity.

She was the sort of woman who delighted in heavy gold bracelets, and was never without long necklaces of beads wound several times around her neck. People thought her distinguished. She had a stately way with her. A little condescending, but always charming to her friends, she was quite a popular hostess in Wimbledon.

Whatever Mrs. Manstone did, she did properly. Her parties were noted for their taste and discretion. She had been a Miss Fylson-Wise — *the* Fylson-Wises of Leicestershire; an old hunting family. Mrs. Manstone never forgot it. She had little or nothing to say about the family of the man she had married in her youth, when romance had meant more than money or social position. The late Robert Manstone had been on the Stock Exchange — seen years of prosperity and died leaving his wife and two daughters quite well provided for. But he had had the artistic temperament, and most of his relations, of whom Mrs. Manstone had disapproved, had been what she called Bohemians. The word Bohemian conveyed to Mrs. Manstone all that was distasteful — an ill-bred, ignorant crowd. She had tried to forget that her husband came of such stock.

Continually, however, she spoke of her own family — proud of their

breeding and aristocracy. Dear Barbara
was a typical Fylson-Wise. So elegant,
so reliable. But Terry — alas! Terry
seemed to have little of that precious
Fylson-Wise strain in her. She was all
Manstone. There were times when she
reminded her mother, painfully, of her
father. Poor Robert had been just such
an impulsive, erratic person. Mrs.
Manstone had always secretly feared
that one day he would kick over the
traces. Most of their quarrels had been
because he would not worship with her
at the shrine of Society.

It was a great pleasure to Mrs.
Manstone when Barbara became
engaged to Francis Colroyd. Colonel
Colroyd was Indian Army — one of
the old school; Mrs. Colroyd a very
valued friend; and Francis — just what
she had wanted for her daughter.
Eton, Oxford, and the rest of it.

If only Terry would emulate Barbara's example, Mrs. Manstone felt that
she would be a happy woman. But
unfortunately Terry was a law unto

herself and a constant source of anxiety to her mother.

Waiting for their friends to come, carefully arranging in a silver vase a bunch of carnations (from their own greenhouse), Mrs. Manstone spoke of her youngest daughter.

'We haven't heard a word from Terry, Barbara.'

Barbara shrugged her shoulders.

'Goodness knows where she is, mother. I really do think she should have respected your wishes and not gone off on this ridiculous walking-tour.'

'Terry never has respected my wishes. While she was at school I had some control over her, but now she is twenty-one — ' Mrs. Manstone spread out her hands with a gesture of despair.

'Francis was only saying last night that he thought it rather dreadful for a girl so young to be tramping the country alone,' said Barbara.

'What Margaret Colroyd and the Colonel must think, I don't know.

Please don't mention it to Lady Carisdon or Mrs. Furnaby or any of them when they come this afternoon,' said Mrs. Manstone. 'I'd rather people did not know that my daughter has gone on one of these vulgar hiking affairs.'

'I can't think what fun she'll get out of it alone like that,' said Barbara. And Barbara meant it. She hated being alone. It was incomprehensible to her that anybody should find birds, flowers, trees, all the living moving things of nature, satisfying companions. But then she did not understand her sister, and never had done so. 'I'm sure something will happen to Terry,' she added.

Mrs. Manstone glanced quickly over the rim of her pince-nez at her eldest daughter.

'Barbara — what?'

'Well, you never know, a young girl — a madcap like Terry — '

'Barbara!' broke in Mrs. Manstone. 'Don't upset me just before people come. I shan't be able to concentrate on the cards. Your father would turn in his grave if anything happened to Terry — he adored that child. But my patience is at an end. She hasn't done anything that I've wanted her to for months. She's just gone her own way. It will come to this — one of these days I shall refuse to be worried any longer, and I shall tell Terry she can find another home.'

A latent sense of loyalty and affection to Terry stirred in the elder sister.

'I think it's only Terry's way, mother. She doesn't mean any harm. She's frightfully young for her age.'

'I'm sure you were much more responsible when you were twenty-one,' said Mrs. Manstone.

Barbara looked self-consciously at her finger-nails.

'I think I'm more like you, mother.'

'Well, I am very hurt about this walking-tour, and I do think she might have sent us some message before this,' said Mrs. Manstone.

It was at that precise moment that

Davis, the well-trained parlourmaid who had been with the family for eight years, opened the drawing-room door and said:

'Please, madam, Miss Terry has come home.'

Mrs. Manstone and Barbara exchanged glances.

'She's back!' exclaimed Barbara.

'But she only went away yesterday,' said Mrs. Manstone. 'She told us she would be away for at least a week.'

'Perhaps something's happened,' said Barbara.

'Where is Miss Terry, Davis?' Mrs. Manstone asked the maid.

'She's gone straight up to her room, madam.'

Mrs. Manstone sniffed.

'So like her.' She waited until Davis had retired, and then added: 'She might have had the good manners to come in and see me.'

'I'll go up to her,' said Barbara.

Mrs. Manstone called after her:

'Don't be long, Barbara. I shall want

you for Bridge as soon as they come. Terry won't play — but she might be a help at tea.'

Barbara walked upstairs to her sister's bedroom.

The house, which had been built about 1900, was well planned, on three floors, the maids occupying the top rooms.

Mrs. Manstone had her own bathroom, and there was a second bathroom at the end of the corridor which the two girls shared — Barbara's room leading into it and Terry's just opposite. Not since they were little girls had they slept in the same room.

Temperamentally so different and so unsuited, it could almost be said that they had led separate lives since their mother allotted them their own rooms. Now and then they shared a confidence, but never a very important one. Terry was always in disgrace and Barbara backed her mother up over most of the disagreements.

Since Barbara's engagement the breach between the sisters had widened. Barbara, engrossed in her *fiancé* and the purchase of a trousseau — she hoped to be married in the autumn — had no time for Terry these days. Terry, on her part, could not become wildly enthusiastic about clothes, neither could she share Barbara's ecstasies over Francis. Barbara had her own girlfriends in Wimbledon, and was with them far more than with Terry.

It was with a certain amount of curiosity, however, that Barbara now entered her sister's room. She wondered what Terry had been up to; why she should have come back like this so suddenly.

Terry had just taken off her blouse and skirt. She sat on the edge of her bed, slim and straight in her cami-knickers, unpacking the contents of her rucksack.

'Why on earth have you come back so soon, Terry?'

Hearing the cool, slightly disdainful

voice of her sister, Terry looked up.

'Oh, hallo, Barbara.'

'What's happened?' asked Barbara.

Terry returned to her rucksack.

What had happened? Heavens! Nothing that Barbara would care to hear. And for the moment Terry had nothing to tell. She was on the edge of a precipice — waiting for Blaise Farlong to telephone to her.

Long before the train had reached Victoria she had dried her tears and got her emotions well under control. To a more friendly, sympathetic sister she might have confided everything, and it would have done her good. She felt the strain badly. But nothing would have induced her to tell Barbara anything. The very sight of her cool, precise, and well-regulated sister irritated Terry more than usual.

'Well, what has happened?' repeated Barbara.

'Nothing,' said Terry.

'Then why have you come home?'

'I got fed up with my walking-tour,'

said Terry with a certain degree of sincerity.

'Oh!' said Barbara, in a tone of relief. 'Mother and I were afraid something awful had happened to you, rushing back like this.'

Terry said nothing. She began to whistle, stood up, and, ignoring Barbara's presence, took a linen dress out of her wardrobe and removed it from its hanger.

'We thought you'd get fed up with your tour,' said Barbara. 'It was too absurd. Mother's been awfully upset about it. It's rather mean of you to worry her like you do.'

Terry stopped whistling. A mutinous look came into her bright hazel eyes.

'Home with a vengeance! Lectures start again.'

'You needn't be nasty,' said Barbara.

'Neither need you,' said Terry.

'And you can't wear old things,' added Barbara, glancing at the blue linen dress. 'Mother's got a Bridge-party on. Lady Carisdon, Mrs. Furnaby and Rita, and some others are coming. Mother says you must appear at tea.'

Terry shut her eyes a moment. Yes, she was indeed home again! She had come back straight into the bosom of the family; the centre of the life which she found so trying. Mother's Bridge-parties — how insufferably boring they were! And those old snobs! Lady Carisdon with her patronising manner and passion for cards. Mrs. Furnaby with her continual chatter about her wonderful son who was going into Parliament. Rita Furnaby, Barbara's age, with nothing to talk about except clothes and what was going on in the South of France.

How could she tolerate it, today when her mind was in chaos and her world tottering under her feet? At any moment Dr. Farlong might ring her up to tell her that his wife refused to see him. Then for the *débâcle*. Confession — scenes — reproaches — disgrace. Terry felt as though nothing were real today — as though even this familiar bedroom was strange to her, and Barbara a person whom she had not met before. It was as though she had been away for years instead of twenty-four hours. What a lot can happen in a day and a night!

'Terry,' said Barbara's high, clear voice, 'didn't you hear what I said about your dress?'

'Oh, very well,' said Terry.

What was the use of making a fuss? Better to do what was required of her and have peace. She might not have peace for much longer.

She put on a flowered *crêpe-de-Chine* dress which had a little cape to it and a long skirt flaring from the hips, reaching her ankles. It altered her completely. It made her look older, more graceful, and not at all like the child in the short skirt with the beret on her head who had sheltered in Blaise Farlong's house last night.

Changing her shoes and stockings, Terry paused to rub her ankle, grimacing as she did so.

166

'What's the matter with your foot?' asked Barbara.

'I caught it in a rabbit-hole on the moor,' said Terry.

'What moor?'

'Oh, down in Sussex,' said Terry vaguely.

'What on earth were you doing on a moor?'

'Hiking,' said Terry, and brushed her hair vigorously. Barbara, who slept in a shingle-cap and combed her own sleek waves gingerly, shuddered with horror at this sight.

'Where did you sleep last night?' The cross-examination continued.

The one unruly lock of brown hair fell across Terry's face. She allowed it to stay there, thankful because it hid the fact that her cheeks suddenly burned.

'Oh, I got a room somewhere.'

'You're very vague about this tour,' said Barbara, staring at her sister. 'I'm beginning to wonder what object you had at the back of your mind — going off like that by yourself.'

'I never have objects at the back of my mind,' said Terry sweetly. 'I leave that to you, darling. You do love to be suspicious, don't you?'

Barbara tossed her head.

'What you do or don't do doesn't interest me much, my dear Terry, only I think you might consider mother a bit more.'

'God gave you all the virtues and me none of them,' said Terry.

'How rude you are!'

Terry, her nerves on edge, was not in the best of humours.

'Well, don't start nagging at me as soon as I get back. I'll be down in a minute. What time are the old cats coming?'

'If you mean mother's friends, they'll be here any minute.'

'That means tea at five. I can take a book in the garden and have some peace until then,' said Terry.

Barbara walked out of the room. And then Terry's face changed. Her forehead wrinkled; her lips twisted in a worried way. She had not realized quite how difficult things were going to be. Her mind kept reverting to the thought of Blaise Farlong and his wife, and of the terrible position in which she found herself. What was happening? Would Mrs. Farlong see her husband? Would she keep Terry's name out of it?

Terry sighed, fixed a slide in her hair, picked a book from her shelf — *Tarka the Otter*. She had read it a dozen times, and could never read it too often. She adored Henry Williamson's wonderful pen-pictures of Devonshire and animal life. Going through the hall into the garden, she caught a glimpse of her mother, in the drawing-room, shaking hands with a large lady in black lace with a huge black hat on her auburn head.

'*Dear* Lady Carisdon! How *are* you?'

'The queen of the cats has arrived,' thought Terry, and hastily escaped into the garden. She flung her book on to the deck-chair which Barbara had recently occupied.

169

Davis was spreading a spotless cloth over the table under the cedar. Restless, troubled in her mind, Terry could not settle down even to her beloved book. She wandered through the garden. The roses were sweet, but everything else was much too stereotyped to please her. Inevitably her thoughts wandered to Blaise Farlong's garden — that paradise of his own making. The gorgeous riot of flowers in his herbaceous border — the flaunting pink and scarlet of sweet williams, the matchless blue of delphiniums and anchusas, the tall sweet hollyhocks, the pink and purple stocks; the lavender walk and the flowered creepers twisting around the old disused well. She had not seen enough of it. She would like to have stayed there, intoxicated with its wild loveliness — wild yet designed by an artist's clever hand.

No wonder Blaise Farlong loved his garden. It struck Terry not for the first time how awful it would be if he had to leave it because of his wife!

She felt suddenly very tired. Emotional stress and worry are always tiring, and she had had a disturbed night into the bargain. Her heart gave a queer little jump at the memory of Dr. Farlong beside her bed — smiling at her in that grave and kindly fashion when she woke up, covered in confusion.

The nicest man she had ever met — and she stood side by side with him in the worst predicament of her life. How would it all end? He must dislike her for having caused all this trouble, and yet he had been so charming to her at the Crown when they had lunch together. He had thanked her when they said good-bye, for being decent to him.

If only she knew what was happening! If only he would telephone quickly and she could know the worst!

The afternoon seemed interminable. She could not settle down to her book. She paced restlessly round the garden. Then at five o'clock the Bridge-players poured out of the drawing-room into the garden, chattering, Terry thought, like a lot of crows. There was no longer time or solitude for thought. Eight people descended upon Terry. She was swept into a circle of people whom she did not like and whom she felt sure did not like her; forced to talk a lot of nonsense; to hand round tea and sandwiches and cakes and make herself generally agreeable.

Terry did what was required of her, but all the time she knew that her ears were straining for the sound of the telephone-bell. Would she hear it out here in the garden? If Davis answered and came out with the message that 'a Dr. Farlong wished to speak to Miss Terry,' an avalanche of questions from mother and Barbara would fall upon her. After all, she did not want them to know that such a person existed unless it were necessary. And that necessity might arise only too soon.

The afternoon passed. Tea was over. Ices were eaten, amidst murmurs of:

'How delicious!' — the Bridge-party returned to warfare, further armed for the fray.

Mrs. Manstone seized a moment alone with her youngest daughter whilst her guests wandered back to the drawing-room.

'Well, my dear, the famous walking-tour wasn't such a success, eh?'

Terry hunched her shoulders.

'I told you it was an absurd idea,' added her mother. 'What brought you to your senses?'

'Nothing much.'

Mrs. Manstone's keen eyes, through the pince-nez, scrutinized Terry's face. She did not notice the pallor under the sunburn. But she was quick to see something that perplexed her. The girl looked harassed — tired.

'Is everything all right, dear?'

The condescending kindness did nothing to comfort Terry. Long ago she had learned that she and her mother were, temperamentally, poles apart. As a child she had never been able to open her heart to the one woman who should have been her confidante. She answered now as she always answered — in non-committal fashion:

'I'm a bit tired, that's all, Mummy.'

'Ah well,' said Mrs. Manstone, 'I must say I'm thankful to see you back safe and sound. But you annoyed me very much — going off in that silly fashion.'

Mrs. Manstone returned to the Bridge. Terry was alone again. Up and down the garden path outside the house she wandered, waiting for the telephone-bell to ring. The suspense began to try her nerves badly. She felt quite sick.

It was six o'clock before that expected call came through. Thankful that her mother and sister were still safely tied to the Bridge-table, Terry fled from the garden into the hall. Davis was on the point of lifting the receiver.

'All right, Davis,' said Terry breathlessly. 'It's for me.'

The parlourmaid, looking grieved,

retired. She did not consider it Miss Terry's place to answer that bell.

In rather a shaky little voice Terry said:

'Hallo.'

'Hallo. May I speak to Miss Manstone?' said a man's deep voice.

Terry, almost certain that this was Dr. Farlong, although his voice was not very familiar to her, said:

'It's Terry Manstone speaking.'

'Ah! This is Dr. Farlong.'

'Thank goodness. I've been longing for you to ring.'

'I'm afraid my news isn't very good.'

Terry swallowed hard.

'You mean,' she said in a very low voice, 'that — that she won't — '

'We can't talk about it on the phone. Can I see you somehow?'

Terry, her heart beating at twice its normal rate, looked round the hall as though seeking assistance, and shook her head helplessly.

'I don't see how — it's terribly difficult — '

'But I must see you.'

'Yes, I want to see you. I'll have to manage it somehow. When? Where?'

'I'm at my club at the moment. I daresay it will be easier for you if I get on the Underground and come along to Wimbledon.'

'It would — of course.'

'Say about quarter to seven at the Underground Station entrance.'

'All right. I can say I've gone out for a stroll.'

'I'm terribly sorry,' said Blaise Farlong, his voice sounding tired and worried. 'Six forty-five. Till then, good-bye.'

Terry hung up the receiver. Her heart still beat fast. Her eyes were large and scared.

She could hear a bustle and hum of voices in the drawing-room. Lady Carisdon's high-pitched laugh. Her mother saying:

'Very naughty of you, getting me down two hundred. Now I shall have my revenge and go three no trumps.'

Terry secretly thanked her stars that the game was still in progress. She would get out now, quickly — tell Davis to let them know she had gone for a walk. She often did escape from the house and walk over the Common. Nobody would be surprised.

She would be late for dinner, that was a certainty. But it seemed such a trivial thing, now.

Ruth Farlong had, apparently, refused to listen to reason. That meant she would file her petition. Terry would be the co-respondent in the divorce-case. Incredible — frightening.

A lucky thing for her, she thought, that she had a nice person like Dr. Farlong to deal with. Things were going to be pretty nasty. At the moment the horizon was black as ink. But she never doubted that Blaise Farlong would make things as easy as he could.

If only there were some friend whom she could trust, with whom she could talk this thing over — someone who could help and advise her! Surely there was a way out of it? But she would see Blaise first of all. Perhaps he would have some suggestion to make. She knew that he was as anxious as she was to avoid a public scandal.

The only friend in whom Terry could possibly have confided was Gage Thornton — a queer name, Gage, pronounced Gaje. She was four or five years older than Terry, but had been at the finishing-school in Paris with her as a pupil teacher. Gage was charming and clever, with just that touch of unconventionality and Bohemianism which attracted Terry but had made Mrs. Manstone disapprove of her.

Gage's parents — both artists — were poor as church mice. Mrs. Manstone had never encouraged the friendship. But Terry, in spite of her, had managed to see Gage sometimes. In the early spring Gage had suddenly met and married Anthony Thornton, a young portrait-painter whose work had been in the Academy last year and who was rapidly making a name for himself.

Gage had written ecstatically from Italy where she had spent her honeymoon, and, although Terry was glad that her friend had found such happiness, she felt that she had lost her.

If only Gage were in England, what a help she might have been! She who understood life — had worked, suffered, loved — would be the best person in the world to give wise counsel now.

But, so far as Terry knew, Gage and her husband — whom Terry had met once and liked enormously — were in Paris for the Exhibition, and not due back in England until next week. Terry had to face this crisis alone.

She walked for half an hour across the Common. It seemed to her hot, dreary, unlovely. How she hated Wimbledon! Everything about it. Everybody in it. At a quarter to seven she was at the entrance to the Underground, and stood there scanning the crowds, waiting for Blaise to come.

Even now, in the midst of all her worry, her sense of humour asserted itself. She thought:

'Lord! Anybody would think I really was having an affair with a married man and waiting for him to turn up! What on earth will be the end of it all?'

8

Blaise Farlong emerged from the dimness of the Underground into a hot blaze of sunshine. The heat seemed to spring up from the hot pavements and smite one like a blast. It had been like this all day in London. Close, unbearable. He was deadly tired, and sick at heart.

Terry saw him before he saw her. For a moment he did not recognise the fashionably attired young woman in her flowered silk dress and big straw hat. Probably he had been expecting to find the familiar, youthful figure in the hiking kit, with the ruck-sack over her back and the beret on her head.

Then, when Terry moved up to him and he looked down and recognised the pretty, tanned face with the bright, hazel eyes, he pulled himself together and said:

181

'Ah! Here you are!'

Rattling along in the Underground from Oxford Circus, he had dreaded this meeting with her. He was so ashamed — so baffled by the whole situation. Now he felt an even greater embarrassment because in her smart clothes, her long skirts, she seemed so much a woman — a woman involved with him in a frightful *débâcle* from which he saw no escape.

'Where can we go and talk?' he said.

Terry avoided his gaze nervously.

'There are the Willow Tea-rooms just along here,' she said. 'They stay open until eight in the summer. We can go in there and have some lemonade or something.'

'Come along, then,' he said.

They walked down the street. Blaise seemed to her just the same as he had been at Rossdown. He was wearing the same dark grey suit and soft grey hat, only he carried a pair of yellow chamois gloves — the touch of 'London.' She had noticed when he first came towards her how tired he looked, and his sun-brown did not deceive her. He was livid in spite of it.

There had always been a kindly, almost maternal streak in Terry. A strain that made her want to succour stray dogs and cats and small, defenceless children. In spite of her personal anxieties, she was infinitely sorry for this man. It was the mother instinct which now conquered the scared-girl feeling and made her say:

'You don't look as though you've had any food or rest today.'

They entered the tea-shop — one of those mushroom places, furnished in pseudo-Elizabethan style, with spindle chairs, gate-legged tables, willow-pattern curtains, willow-pattern china.

'I'm all right,' said Blaise. Then, as they sat down at a small table in the corner, he added more gently:

'Nice of you to think about it. I wonder you're not cursing me.'

'Why should I? The beastly thing wasn't your fault.'

'We'd better have something,' said Blaise as a waitress walked up to them and cleared away two empty plates.

'Lemonade for me,' said Terry.

'I suppose there's no chance of anything stronger,' he said with a faint smile, 'so I'll have the same.'

'I'm sure,' said Terry, as the waitress moved away, 'it would do us both good to have three or four double brandies. Then we might stagger out on to the Common and shoot ourselves.'

For the first time since he had come up to London, Blaise felt his own spirits lifting out of the darkness. Heaven alone knew they had been crushed by the bitterness of his failure with Ruth.

'You're very game, child,' he said. 'As a matter of fact, I was thinking, myself, a few strong drinks and suicide would put an end to one's miseries. But I don't know that it would help you if I quit.'

'I should quit with you,' said Terry, with forced brightness.

'Seriously,' he said, 'we're in a

devilish hole. We've got to face it now. I've failed to do any good today. I went to my brother-in-law's house. My wife was out, but my sister-in-law saw me. She was very kind — I like Marjorie; she's much too good for Victor. But she couldn't do anything. She had, of course, been told that I'd given Ruth cause for a divorce, and that Victor was going to see things through for Ruth. I told Marjorie the truth about the affair, and she seemed a little incredulous.'

'There you are,' broke in Terry. 'Even people who like you are doubtful about it. Naturally. Oh!' she added passionately, 'it's simply *wicked* of Mrs. Farlong and that old woman!'

'In the middle of my conversation with Marjorie,' continued Blaise, 'my brother-in-law came home with Ruth. She went straight to her room. Victor — thoroughly insulting — told me to get out of his house and never enter it again. I asked to see Ruth. He said Ruth would not see me. I tried to explain things to him, and he laughed in my face and said that he wasn't a damn fool and wasn't going to waste his time listening to a trumped-up story from me.'

'But everybody will listen to Mrs. Farlong's trumped-up story,' said Terry bitterly.

Blaise drew a hand wearily across his eyes.

'That's the devil of it. I don't know why, but people are always so much more ready to believe the worst. God! It's — it's — '

'Pretty bloody,' Terry finished for him. 'I'm sure that's what you want to say. I've wanted to say it for a long time, but, being nicely brought up, I've tried not to.'

'Look here,' said Blaise, looking at her with strange, unhappy eyes, 'you're treating the thing very courageously, but the position is frightfully serious — you've got to face that. As I told you at Rossdown, I'd have cut off my right hand rather than that this should happen to a girl like you —

186

and I've done everything in my power to stop it. But Ruth won't see me. She must know she's doing a most damnable thing; and she doesn't want to face me. I see it was useless arguing with my brother-in-law — the fellow's a swine, and he's always hated me because I wouldn't soft-soap him. I was afraid I'd knock him down when he started abusing you, so I left the house. I spent the next hour telephoning — sending messages to my wife — begging her to see me. She only sent back word that she did not intend to see me again, and that I could deal with her through her solicitors.'

Terry, staring at him, bit fiercely at her lip. She left her lemonade untasted, although her throat felt hot and dry.

'You needn't think I don't realise how serious it is,' she said in a low voice. 'But if I don't make a joke about it I shall go off the deep end and burst into tears. That wouldn't help.'

'Poor child,' he said. He passed a

hand across his eyes again and drew a bitter sigh.

'What the hell can we do?'

'What *can* we do?' she asked.

'Nothing much. She means to file the petition. She means to cite you!'

'I suppose we can't get hold of Mrs. Clarke and either force her to tell the truth or bribe her to?'

'I haven't any money — frankly, I'm pretty hard up. I haven't been able to build up a very big practice, owing to my rotten health in the past. I'm pretty fit now — living in my garden between times has done a lot for me — but I haven't started to save much money. When I bought my practice I had to borrow the money. I have been paying it back gradually. It's quite certain my wife has bribed that old woman heavily.'

'Well, I haven't any money,' said Terry helplessly.

'I'm trying to think what's best to do,' he said, staring over her head. 'Mrs. Clarke is our only hope. I'll see her as soon as I get back to Rossdown, but I think for her own sake she'll be too afraid to swing round again and retract her story.'

'If my mother were different,' said Terry, 'I'd let her into the secret and ask her to help — she has a little money.'

Blaise Farlong's cheeks reddened.

'I'd be ashamed to ask help from your mother. God knows my wife has done you enough harm. My brother-in-law has got your name and address and the whole damn thing at his fingertips. Only too anxious to put the divorce through for Ruth.'

'Mother might help us bribe Mrs. Clarke just in order to save the scandal.'

'No. It's too late. Too late to save a scandal, anyhow. Ruth would go on with the divorce, and she and Victor between them might even suggest in court that we had bribed Mrs. Clarke to hide the truth. It could easily be discovered that we on our side had paid her money.'

'Oh, what a mess!' said Terry.

'I'm afraid we're in for it. But I'll get at Mrs. Clarke tonight and let you know.'

Her lips drooped a little.

'More ghastly suspense. Will you telephone again?'

'Yes. I'm so terribly sorry, Terry — I suppose I can call you Terry?'

'Please do,' she said, on the verge of tears. But she tried to laugh. 'You can't very well address the co-respondent as Miss Manstone.'

'I wish I had your pluck — but I can't laugh tonight.'

'I'm not laughing much,' she said miserably.

'No, I know — that's where the pluck lies. Through no fault of your own you're dragged into this hideous affair, and you're perfectly charming about it.'

'It's so terrible for you — your reputation as a doctor.'

'Oh, that's done for! Things will start to buzz at Rossdown tomorrow when the rumour gets round that my wife has left me.'

'And meanwhile this Mr. Keyland — the lawyer — is going to get on with the good work of filing the petition?'

'Yes.'

A pause. Then Terry said:

'Did you drive up?'

'No. I came by train.'

'And you're going back now?'

'Yes, there's a train at 8.40.'

'Have something to eat first, do, please, Dr. Farlong. You look so rotten.'

'Kind little thing,' he said, and a faint smile lit up his haggard face. 'I daresay I'll have a snack at Victoria.'

'I wish I could ask you home — but the fat would be in the fire if I did.'

'It's out of the question. You know, when I was showing you my flowers at home early this morning, I thought how glad I was I had met you — I was wishing Ruth and I might count you as a friend of ours. And now — '

'Now,' said Terry with a grimace, 'Mrs. Farlong scarcely regards me as a *friend*. Although I don't know what I have ever done to her that she should want to do for my reputation like this.'

'I didn't think her capable of it. She must have found life unbearable with me to use such measures to get away.'

'I don't know you very well,' said Terry, 'but I can't imagine you making life unbearable for a woman. It was just because she was bored — boredom sometimes drives people crazy.'

'You're right. But it's astonishing a child like you should look at it that way.'

'It was the country life — the garden — not you who bored her. Nobody could call you boring.'

There was something so young and disarming about that, Blaise Farlong's spirits lifted again. He looked at her with gratitude.

'You're doing more than your realize to help me through.'

'To tell you the truth,' she said shyly, 'I wished — just like you did early this morning — that we could be friends. And why shouldn't we be?'

'It's unexpectedly nice of you — '

'Well, we *must* be friends. If this thing goes through I shall be cast out upon a wicked world, and nobody will know me except you and, perhaps, my great friend, Mrs. Thornton. And you'll lose most of your friends too, I suppose.'

He stared at her. A sense of disaster had weighed him down all day. After his final failure to get at Ruth on the telephone he had felt at the end of his tether. His world was crashing around him. He was struggling in a morass of lies, deceit, intrigue, all springing from Ruth's bitter dislike of him. He was up against something against which he was powerless. He had been unable to be philosophic. His one thought had been:

'I've lost my wife, my home, my career, the old associations — everything but Priscilla's memory. What is there left?'

Terry Manstone had had no place in those thoughts. But now, facing her, listening to her, she was bringing it home to him that she would be hand in hand with him; that they would be flung on the rocks — ship-wrecked — branded with the same stigma of disgrace.

He and this girl, this pretty, charming child with her youth, her inexperience, her innocence, were partners in a disaster which must inevitably bring them close together in the most intimate way. While he sat there, brooding, watching her, he saw, suddenly, the glitter of tears in her eyes, saw her surreptitiously lift a finger and wipe away one tear which had rolled down her cheek. He was walking in shadows and confusion — tormented with doubts — full of despair. But the sight of that tear — the knowledge that this defenceless girl must be as terrified, as bewildered, as troubled as he — stirred him to infinite compassion, and bred in him a new regard for her. She was no longer a stranger outside his thoughts; he was responsible for her. He was a physician, a married man, years older than she was, experienced.

He must protect and help her to the best of his ability.

He reached out and took her hand.

'You've been marvellous; you musn't give way now,' he said.

She fought back the tears, but she felt an acute sense of trouble.

'I'm all right — it's getting on my nerves rather.'

'I don't wonder. Go home, child, take some aspirin, go to bed and try and sleep.'

She let her hand rest in his. His fingers were warm and strong, and the contact steadied her.

'Are those the doctor's orders?' she asked in a shaky voice.

'Yes,' he said with a faint smile. 'I only wish I could prescribe something better — cure your mind. But there I'm helpless. Only, believe me, if my friendship's worth anything to you, it's yours. I shall never forget how charming you have been all through this ghastly business.'

Terry stood up, and again he was

struck by the grace and budding maturity of her in her long silk dress and big hat. He paid the bill and they walked out of the shop together.

When they said good-bye at the corner of the street, Terry suddenly blurted out:

'I *am* glad that you and I are friends, and I *do* think your friendship's worth quite a lot. I don't care what anybody else says.'

'That goes a long way toward cheering me up,' he said with his tired smile. 'Now do as I suggest and try not to worry. I'll phone you tomorrow before I start on my rounds.'

She walked home like one in a strange, bewildering dream. Another night of suspense — another horrible wait for the phone-bell to ring and, so far as she could see, little hope now of Blaise preventing the disaster.

She spent a miserable evening. In order to escape too much criticism from the family, she pleaded a bad headache and retired to bed directly after dinner. When she was in bed she swallowed two crushed aspirin with some milk — remembering Blaise Farlong's orders. She could imagine him down in his lonely house, tormenting himself with the same sort of thoughts that troubled her tonight. She wondered why these things were allowed to happen. So little of importance had ever happened in her life, and now chaos — this disaster which was not her fault in any way except that she had, perhaps, been foolish to make Russet Place her shelter on that stormy night.

Mrs. Manstone came up to see her and fussed over her.

'Have you had aspirin? That's right. My dear child, your one day's walking-tour seems to have done you a lot of harm. Barbara and I both thought how pinched and tired you looked at dinner. You'd better see Dr. Collier in the morning if you are not better.'

Terry, lying with eyes shut and arms behind her head, moved her lips wryly.

She did not want the family physician. One doctor was enough. She was very much in Blaise Farlong's hands, if only Mummy knew it.

Mrs. Manstone, large and important in her black dinner-gown, eyed her daughter over the rim of her pince-nez and said:

'I can't quite gather from Barbara what you did last night or where you stayed. Aren't you going to tell me more about it?'

Terry, her nerves frayed, moved restively and said, without opening her eyes:

'There's nothing to tell — I want to go to sleep, Mummy. My head aches.'

She knew without looking that her mother's expression was now injured. Mrs. Manstone raised her brows and moved toward the door.

'I wish I understood you a little better, Terry. You're really very difficult.'

'I'm sorry, Mummy.'

The door closed behind her mother. Terry turned her face to the pillow and did not know whether to laugh or to cry. But she did know that there was something about her mother — about Barbara — that made it impossible for her to confide in either of them. She must face her difficulties alone. But a very strong feeling pervaded her tonight that she would have been happier in the company of Blaise Farlong than here. Somehow it was more comforting to be with a person with whom one was so involved. She did not feel that they had only met such a brief while, that they were comparative strangers. She felt that she had known Dr. Farlong a long time. They were friends. He had said so. It was funny, for they might have hated each other under the circumstances.

It was a long time before her head stopped aching and her mind stopped working and she drifted into sleep.

9

Blaise Farlong telephoned to Terry at a quarter to ten the next morning. Mrs. Manstone was not up. She generally had grapefruit and toast and coffee in bed. Barbara had gone out early for a fitting. Terry was able to speak to Blaise undisturbed.

She was nervy and wretched after a broken night's sleep. But somehow she was quite prepared for the bad news when it came. Blaise told her that there was no hope of a capitulation with Mrs. Clarke. Ruth had done her work thoroughly. The evil old house-keeper and her idiot son had already left Rossdown, and nobody in the village seemed to know where they had gone.

'I have no doubt that my wife knows,' Blaise told Terry, 'and that Mrs. Clarke will in due course receive a subpœna and turn up at the courts with the evidence.'

Terry's heart jerked uncomfortably. She was not quite sure what a subpœna meant, but she knew well enough what Blaise implied. She felt confused and frightened.

'Then — it really means we're in for it?'

'I'm terribly afraid so.' His voice sounded deadly tired. 'I must get through my work somehow and then see my solicitors this afternoon — no, not in town; my lawyer is in Brighton — an old pal who was at Cambridge with me. I shall take advice from him, but I'm pretty certain nothing can be done now except we defend the case at the time. There'll be a scandal anyhow.'

'So it seems,' said Terry in a small voice.

'I also had a letter from my wife,' he added, 'sent through that insufferable fellow her brother asking me not to pester her with telephone calls or demands for interviews, as she is quite through with me. I don't see a ray of hope now, Terry.'

Terry gripped the receiver tightly, her cheeks hot, her eyes wide.

'What shall I do?'

'There's nothing to do — that's the devil of it. I really feel I don't much care about myself, but I'm worried about you. It's so wickedly unfair.'

'Well, there we are,' said Terry, with a hysterical desire to laugh. 'We've got to face it, haven't we?'

'Yes,' came his low reply.

'I can't tell anybody at home — I simply can't — ' broke from her. 'Not yet. But I suppose I'll have to some time soon. Shall I get a subpœna or whatever you call it as well?'

'No — not unless we choose to defend. You'll just be named in court.'

'But what defence have we,' she asked frantically, 'if Mrs. Clarke bears out her story?'

'Is it safe for you to be speaking like this?'

'Yes. My mother's just gone into the

bathroom. The maids are in the kitchen.'

'I'd better see you again and have another talk,' he said.

'It's so difficult for me to get away. The family are suspicious as it is about my peculiar walking-tour.'

'We'll meet in town again,' he said.

'Will you let me know?' she asked feverishly.

'Yes, as soon as I've seen Heslop, my lawyer, and discussed the thing with him. I'll phone you.'

Terry shut her eyes. Her headache was coming back. More suspense. More waiting for the telephone. And this time nothing to hope for. The divorce was going through. The only question left to answer was whether they stood any chance if they defended the case. But her reputation would suffer, anyhow, and so would his.

'You know how terribly sorry I am,' he said.

'I am, for you as well as myself,' she answered.

And that ended the call. The nasal voice of the operator said:

'Six minutes — will you have another three minutes?'

Terry wandered into the garden. It was not such a sunny day. The sky was heavy with grey clouds, and the atmosphere was sultry. A thunderstorm had been forecast on the radio last night. Terry felt that a very big storm was crashing about her head. Even now she could not believe that she was to be brought into a divorce case as a co-respondent. It was so incredible.

She asked herself if she would have minded had she loved Blaise Farlong, and his wife had had just cause for the divorce! The mere thought of that made her cheeks burn. Yet, strangely enough, she did not find it difficult to imagine herself in love with Blaise.

All her life Terry had formed very few attachments. The people she really liked were few and far between. But she generally made up her mind quickly and definitely whether she did or did not like a person. From the beginning she had been attracted by Blaise Farlong. He was much older than she — but she preferred older men. Boys of her own age did not interest her.

This doctor with his tired smile and his unhappy marriage had in some peculiar way intrigued her from the start. She knew that she would have been furiously indignant — positively enraged — If such a thing had happened in connection with a man whom she disliked. She was indignant enough as it was — but the indignation was all against Mrs. Farlong. Her regard and her sympathy for Blaise were thriving in this sea of trouble.

Of course, it did seem outrageous that she should be named as the woman in the case when she had never done more than shake hands with Blaise Farlong. But her desire at the moment was not to run away from him — rather to run to him. And, with that realisation upon her, she felt suddenly shy of him — ashamed of herself. Altogether her thoughts were chaotic during the rest of the day.

Fortunately for her, her mother and sister were out until the evening. She was left in peace. But the moment they came back to dinner her ordeal began afresh.

'I want you to come with me tomorrow morning, my dear, to see Aunt Bertha,' said Mrs. Manstone during the meal. 'It means an early start — you know she has just built that house at Hampton Court, and she wishes us to spend the day with her.'

This speech caused Terry some distress. She did not want to spend the day at Hampton Court. Blaise Farlong might phone. The only excuse she could make was one of health.

'I really don't feel well enough to face Aunt Bertha for a whole day, Mummy. Do take Barbara instead.'

Barbara answered quickly:

'I can't go. I'm playing tennis with the Kestaways. Francis is joining me when he gets back from the City.'

'What is the matter with you, Terry?' asked her mother. 'You certainly don't look well. I insist on your seeing Dr. Collier.'

An argument ensued. Terry did not want to see the doctor. Her mother harried her until finally, in her nervy condition, her control gave way and she burst into tears.

Mrs. Manstone was astonished. Terry never cried. She was convinced that the girl was ill, and told Barbara to ask Dr. Collier to call in the morning.

Terry went to bed, subdued, and feeling that the whole thing was so futile. A few little rows like this at home were paltry in comparison with the *débâcle* which was descending. Her mother was troubled because she thought she was ill. But she would be more than troubled when she knew what was about to happen. She would be horrified — furious. Scandal was the one thing she could not tolerate, and Terry knew quite well she would neither be believed nor forgiven.

She felt half inclined to pack her things and tear down to Rossdown that night. But, quite aware that that wouldn't help the situation, she stayed where she was and brooded wretchedly over the affair.

The first disaster, in a small way, happened that very night. Blaise phoned from Rossdown about half past nine. Barbara answered the call. The next thing that happened was that Mrs. Manstone sailed into her youngest daughter's bedroom and said:

'Terry, may I ask who is ringing you up on a trunk-call at this hour of night?'

Terry's heart missed a beat. She sat up, crimson-cheeked.

'W-why?' she stammered.

Mrs. Manstone eyed her coldly and distrustfully.

'Something is going on that I don't know about. Davis tells me you are constantly on the phone. Barbara said that a man has just enquired for you on a long-distance call, and when she said that it was Miss Barbara Manstone speaking, and that you were in bed, he rang off.'

Terry knew at once whence that call had come. She felt bitterly disappointed that she had missed it. So much depended on any news from *him*. Now what was she going to say to her mother?

'I really don't know who it was,' she murmured.

'That's absurd. You must know. Terry, surely you are not having any sort of affair with some man that I don't know!' said Mrs. Manstone in a tone of virtuous indignation.

This might have been the time when Terry could have told her mother everything. But the cold superiority and disapproval of the elder woman checked the girl's instinct to confide in her. The story would leak out soon enough. But Terry was putting off the evil day. She refused to answer any questions. Her evasiveness annoyed Mrs. Manstone exceedingly, and that good lady marched out of the room quite convinced that something wrong was going on behind her back, and that this accounted for Terry's queer behaviour since she had come home.

Mrs. Manstone and her elder daughter discussed things at length together down in the drawing-room.

'I can't believe that Terry's having an affair. She's not like that — she's such a child,' was Barbara's comment.

'Well, I'd very much like to know who telephoned to her, and why he rang off so abruptly. I don't like it. I'm very worried,' Mrs. Manstone declared. 'Terry's such a stubborn little thing — so like her father; if he didn't want to tell me anything he used to shut up like a clam. It's most irritating.'

Barbara, on her own, made an effort to gain her sister's confidence. But Terry was just as non-committal with Barbara as she had been with her mother.

'Anybody'd think this was a convent — with the nuns flying into a stew because some man appears on the horizon,' she muttered when Barbara persisted with questions. 'I'm of age — I'm not going to account to you and Mummy for all my actions.'

'You're a little fool,' said Barbara coldly. 'But I'm not going to upset myself about you. Do what you like.'

As she walked to the door she turned and looked at Terry, who was sitting up in bed looking pale and harassed.

'By the way, tomorrow night you've got to come out with mother and me, and no nonsense about it. Colonel and Mrs. Colroyd and Francis are having a family gathering at their house. Francis has some cousins he wants me to meet and he's asked all of us to dine. I suppose you'll have the grace to turn up for my sake and make yourself pleasant.'

'If I'm wanted,' said Terry.

'Well, you're my sister,' said Barbara, in a resigned voice. 'so I suppose you'd better be present.'

'It's marvellous to be so popular,' said Terry with a strained laugh.

Long after Barbara had departed, the thought of Blaise haunted Terry. She wondered why he had phoned and what he had had to tell her. Perhaps he had seen his lawyer. Perhaps there was a way out of the tangle after all.

She rose early that next morning, before her mother and sister were awake. She did not want to risk being overheard on the telephone at home, so she put on a hat and walked to the post-office. She got on to the enquiry, found Dr. Farlong's number, and put a call through to him.

In the box, she spoke to him for a few minutes. It was queer how glad she was to hear his voice. In an impulsive moment she told him so.

'I haven't had a very easy time with the family — somehow things are better when I can talk to you.'

He heard the worried, unhappy note in her voice.

'Poor little Terry,' he said. 'It's a confounded shame. I've nothing very good to tell you. I rang up last night

212

because I'd seen Heslop and put the case before him. He thinks it's a pretty dirty business. He's a pal of mine, and he says he believes me, but I don't honestly know whether he does or he doesn't. The thing looks so incriminating. Anyhow, he says we can do nothing but use every defence we've got, and he sees no way of preventing the scandal. I wrote to my wife yesterday and the letter was returned unopened. So that doesn't look too hopeful. I must see you and talk to you about the defence.'

'But it isn't any good!' said Terry wildly.

'There is just one important thing I'd like to talk to you about,' he added.

'Oh, dear! My mother has got it into her head since last night that I'm having an affair with someone. It's more than ever difficult for me to get away. I feel like telling her the whole thing and getting it over.'

'How do you think she'll take it?'

'Badly. But I couldn't stand it if she

refused to believe me and started abusing me. I shall run away.'

'Oh, Terry!' came his voice. 'I'm beginning to realise with a vengeance the harm that has been done to you. But for God's sake don't run away or do anything until I've seen you.'

Tears were pricking Terry's eyelids.

'I'd rather be with you than anybody at the moment, because you're the only one who understands what I'm going through.'

'Poor child,' he said again. 'But I'm not fit for human company. I'm in a wretched mood. The village is buzzing with rumours. Everybody seems to know that Ruth has left me, and that old devil, Mrs. Clarke, took care to hint at our supposed 'affair' before she went. I had one or two rather chilly looks on my rounds this morning.'

Terry shook her head helplessly.

'It's all so preposterous.'

'I shall have to sell my practice and get another,' he said. 'I shall try and do that at once, whatever happens.'

'Oh! And your garden — your lovely garden!'

'Sweet of you to think of it. I must say it'll break me up to leave the garden. I've worked in it so many years now. It's been like a sort of child that I've nursed. My delphiniums have been so marvellous this year — '

He broke off. She thought gloomily how wrong everything was — the whole scheme of life. Why should a man who cherished his garden and shrank from the thought of leaving his delphiniums be treated in so shameful a fashion by the woman he had made his wife — by fate?

In a queer way, the mention of the flowers in the garden brought them closer together. A paltry yet significant thing in the midst of the trouble.

'But my garden,' came his voice, 'is nothing. It's you I'm most worried about.'

'It's all so hopeless,' said Terry. 'I'm a coward about telling the family until the last moment. But what is the procedure now?'

'My wife will sign a petition for divorce and send a formal refusal to my request that she should come back to me, then I shall be asked to put my signature to the petition or state whether I wish to defend the case or not. Then it will follow the usual dreary course and come up at the next assizes. It's a wretched business.'

'I wish, for my sister's sake more than anything, that I could have kept quiet about it for a bit. She's being married in the autumn. Her *fiancé*'s family are fearfully stuffy. I'm afraid this will be shattering for her.'

'Well, say nothing until you have to,' he said. 'Meanwhile, when can I see you?'

Terry racked her brains.

'Today's out of the question. I'm terribly involved with the family. We've got a party on with Barbara's *fiancé* tonight, but tomorrow — come to town in the afternoon if you can and I'll say I want to go into the West End and shop.

I'll meet you — say half past four — outside the Piccadilly tube.'

'I'll be there,' he said, and added with a faint laugh: 'It's pretty hectic — getting through my work and this business at the same time.'

'You must be worn out,' she said with a short sigh. 'I know I am, and I haven't got any work to do.'

That ended the call. Terry went back to the house, not very comforted. But her mood swung from one pitch to another. She trod ruthlessly on her worries and assumed a gay and cheerful aspect. She convinced her mother and sister that she was much better in health and more amenable. The day, therefore, passed without much friction.

They set off at half past seven, in a taxi, for the Colroyds' house. Barbara was looking pretty and flushed with excitement. It was rather an important dinner for her. She was to meet some future relations whom she had not hitherto seen. She was to be *the* person of the evening, and that always pleased her. Mrs. Manstone — the future mother-in-law — was equally important and in the best of humours. She looked resplendent in a new black dress with sequins, a Spanish comb in her hair, and a handsome Spanish shawl, embroidered with roses, over her shoulders.

Terry, to please her mother, had put on a frock which she hated and which had been bought for her. Mrs. Manstone considered it 'nice and girlish.' It was pale pink, with a lot of frills and flounces; modestly high at the neck. Mrs. Manstone did not approve of young girls wearing such low backs as were in the fashion.

With a little black velvet coatee over the delicate pink dress, Terry looked charming, but her small sun-browned face wore a harassed look, and, if she laughed and chatted a good deal, it was to hide the fact that she was extremely miserable and not at all in the mood for a party.

The Colroyds' house was in Pont

Street. Terry had been there before and found it as formal and awe-inspiring as the Colroyds themselves. Colonel Colroyd was not so bad. The old man had a human side to him. But it was rather crushed by a domineering wife who was almost as big a stickler for the conventions as Mrs. Manstone herself.

Francis definitely bored Terry. He had a drawling voice and a superior manner, and treated her as though she were a refractory child, which annoyed her.

She did her best, however, to be affable in the Colroyds' drawing-room. A butler brought sherry. The Colroyds boasted that they never mixed cocktails in *their* house. If Francis wanted one, he could get it outside. Francis, at the moment as much in love as a lukewarm nature would allow him to be, was content to sit beside his future wife and drink his sherry delicately.

Mrs. Colroyd — a tall, blonde, angular woman with sharp features — talked down everybody in the room, which was her habit. Her husband had long since ceased trying to get a word in when she was there. But he had a kind smile for Terry, whom he secretly thought a most attractive little thing, and reminded him sentimentally of a brown-haired, hazel-eyed maiden whom he had loved in his youth before he fell into the trap his wife had laid for him.

Terry always remembered that evening — one which marked the turning-point in her career. The first shock descended on her when Francis Colroyd dutifully crossed the room and spoke a few words to her:

'So glad you were able to come. Baa thought you'd still be away on this — er — holiday of yours.'

Terry looked up at him. His face bore the typical pallor of the City man, and he had a fair moustache, trained rather in the Guardee style. He was not bad-looking, but of rather an effeminate type. With a flash of humour she found herself thanking her stars that she had not been thrown into any kind of disaster with a man like Francis; and thinking how very much nicer Blaise Farlong was, as an individual.

Then came Francis's drawling voice:

'Baa hasn't met these cousins of mine yet. I think you'll like Eileen — she's a daughter of father's brother, Sir Alfred Colroyd. And then there's Ruth — whose mother was my mother's sister. Poor Ruth, so I hear, is going through rather a bad time just now. She married a doctor. Her brother, Victor, who is also coming tonight, with his wife, tells me the fellow is a howling cad. They're being divorced.'

Terry sat like a figure turned to stone. Every ounce of colour drained from her cheeks. She had no time to analyse what Francis had just said. No time to escape — to plead sudden illness and get away from this house before Ruth Farlong entered it. For of course it was Blaise's wife who was coming here tonight. Heavens! What a catastrophe! What a freakish coincidence — that Ruth and her brother, Victor Keyland, should be in any way related to Barbara's *fiancé*. It was a platitude to say, 'What a small place the world can be,' but it was certainly the truth, she reflected.

Never in her life had Terry been so petrified — so incapable of speech or action — as when the drawing-room door opened and the butler entered and announced:

'Miss Eileen Colroyd. Mr. and Mrs. Victor Keyland. *Mrs. Farlong.*'

Terry never had the slightest idea what Eileen Colroyd looked like. Her fascinated gaze swept at once to the figure of Blaise Farlong's wife. Only once had she seen the clear-cut, slightly aquiline features, the narrow blue eyes, the black shingled head. But they seemed painfully familiar.

Beautifully dressed in a long blue chiffon gown and little silver coat with a sable collar, Ruth came forward with that charming smile which she affected when she wanted to make herself popular.

'How are you, Aunt Margaret?' she murmured, tendering a cool cheek to Mrs. Colroyd, who pecked at it; and added gracefully, to Francis: 'Nice to see you again, Francis.'

'Yes, we haven't met for some time.' He took Barbara's hand and led her proudly forward. 'I want you to meet my *fiancée*. Baa dear, this is my cousin, Ruth.'

While greeting and congratulations were exchanged, Terry continued to sit in her chair like a frozen thing, her wide eyes never leaving Ruth Farlong's face. And now she heard Ruth's clear, metallic voice, saying:

'Did you say your *fiancée*'s name was Manstone, Francis?'

'Yes. Why? Have you met before?'

'No,' said Ruth Farlong slowly. 'But the name is rather a familiar one. As a matter of fact, Victor and I were saying at lunch that we knew that you'd become engaged but had no idea who to — neither of us having seen the announcement.'

'Well, here she is, and not too bad,' said Francis facetiously. 'Now let me introduce you to her little sister.'

It was then that Ruth's cold blue eyes roved round the room and fastened upon Terry. An instant of shock — then an expression of incredulity and something almost secretive and malicious — altered Ruth Farlong's whole face. Terry, feeling much like a rabbit fascinated by a snake, could neither move nor speak. She felt suffocated, and her heart beat so furiously she wondered if she were going to die.

It took Ruth Farlong only a few seconds to realise that this girl, sister to her cousin's *fiancée*, was one and the same as the Terry Manstone whom she was citing as co-respondent in her divorce case. She understood now why the name had been familiar.

Everybody in the room was talking. The butler was handing round sherry. There was an atmosphere of geniality, and the room seemed full of Mrs. Colroyd's shrill voice, still drowning everybody else's.

But Terry Manstone and Ruth Farlong faced each other like opponents in the ring before the gong sounds for the first round.

Somehow or other Terry managed to gain her feet. She was still too dumbfounded to speak, but a mute appeal came into her eyes. The elder woman saw it, but did not respond. If she allowed conscience to prick her now, her case would be lost. She would never break free from Blaise. And in the brocade bag she carried this very minute was a note from Hugh Spalderson — full of surprise and delight because she had written to tell him Blaise had given her evidence for divorce.

Whatever happened, she must set her teeth and carry the thing through. And, after all, she tried to salve her conscience, how did she know that her husband and this girl had been such saints that night? The younger Miss Manstone was decidedly pretty.

There was something peculiarly ruthless in the nature of Blaise Farlong's wife. That streak conquered her first impulse to show some mercy.

'Ruth, let me introduce Teresa,' said Francis, 'generally known as Terry — '

Then Ruth Farlong swung round and faced her cousin, with heightened colour and an expression of indignation.

'I must apologise, Francis,' she said in a high, clear voice, 'but if Miss Teresa Manstone is to be included in tonight's party, I must beg to be excused.'

Terry's heart galloped on. She went deadly white and then scarlet — a flush that spread to her very throat. So this wicked creature meant to carry on with her iniquitous accusation, and intended to shame her now in front of the whole family! Of all the dreadful coincidences, this was the very limit!

Ruth's voice penetrated through the general chatter. Everybody stopped talking. Terry's mother, who was sitting quite close to her, opened her mouth wide and let the pince-nez fall from her nose. Francis, who flushed easily, like most fair men, coughed, cleared his throat, and turned blinking to Barbara. Then Mrs. Colroyd came forward.

'Ruth, my dear, *what* did I hear?'

'I'm sorry, Aunt Margaret, but I must repeat that if this — girl' — she indicated Terry with a scornful gesture — 'is to be your guest this evening, I must beg to be excused from the party.'

The silence in the big drawing-room was now so intense that one could have heard a pin drop. All eyes were focused upon Mrs. Farlong. Mrs. Colroyd stared at her niece.

'My *dear* Ruth — but why on earth — '

'Really, Ruth,' put in Francis, in his most superior manner, 'I don't quite understand. Terry is my future sister-in-law.'

'That is to be regretted,' said Ruth. 'I

am afraid I can't explain — I feel much too upset!'

Mrs. Manstone stared at her youngest daughter.

'What on earth does she mean, Terry?'

Still no speech from Terry. She felt incapable of it, like one paralysed. Victor Keyland came forward and took his sister's arm.

'What is it, old girl?'

Ruth, shaking a little, inclined her head in Terry's direction.

'Forgive me, Victor, if I go home — nobody else need concern themselves, but it's impossible for me to stay here. That girl is Teresa Manstone — I know her only too well. And *you* know who I mean, too.'

With her head held high, she disengaged her arm from her brother's fingers and swept out of the room.

Another sickening silence. Eileen Colroyd, young and rather stupid, gave a nervous laugh, and said:

'This is all very dramatic.'

Then Victor Keyland, whose smug face made Terry understand why Blaise detested him, eyed her covertly for a second, coughed, and turned to his hostess.

'Perhaps I had better explain, Aunt Margaret. I think it is better that we should all know where we are. I dislike spoiling what should have been a delightful family gathering, but, as you all know, Ruth is divorcing her husband. Miss Teresa Manstone is the reason for the divorce.'

A long-drawn 'Oh!' from Mrs. Colroyd, followed by a spluttering noise from Mrs. Manstone. And now the attention was focused upon Terry. Shivering from head to foot, she faced the party. All colour had left her face.

Mrs. Manstone sprang to her feet.

'Mr. Keyland, do you realise what you have said? You're insinuating that my daughter — '

'I regret,' he broke in, 'it is not a question of insinuation. Facts speak for themselves. As a solicitor I am handling this case for my sister. Miss Teresa Manstone is cited as co-respondent. Most painful for you, as no doubt you know nothing about it. You have my deepest sympathy, but, on the face of it, my sister could not possibly stay here. The last time she saw your daughter was when she discovered her down in her own house with Dr. Farlong, during my sister's absence.'

Mrs. Manstone turned a crimson, horrified face to Terry. Barbara had clutched Francis's hand. They both looked aghast. 'Terry,' exclaimed her mother, 'are you going to stand there and allow Mr. Keyland to make such accusations? It isn't true — it can't be — '

Then Terry spoke. Her voice sounded like a whisper.

'It's quite true, Mummy, that Mrs. Farlong is citing me in her divorce case. I did stay at Dr. Farlong's house while she was away — but it isn't true that he and I — that we — '

She broke off and put her hand to

her trembling lips.

'Good heavens!' said Mrs. Manstone.

'Dear me, dear me,' came from Colonel Colroyd.

'What a terrible thing to have happened in my house!' said Mrs. Colroyd, and sat down under the burden of shame.

Victor Keyland spoke again.

'This is neither the time nor the place for a denial, Miss Manstone. If Dr. Farlong defends the case, you will be given ample opportunity to say what you wish in court. But I'm afraid you do not stand much chance. My sister's housekeeper is a witness to the — er — facts of the case.'

Terry looked about her helplessly. Mrs. Manstone spoke in a low, terrible voice to her daughter.

'So now I know — the reason for everything! This man who phoned you — your walking-tour — and that night you stayed away — it was in *his* house. Dear God! *My own child*!'

Like a trapped thing, Terry turned

her head from side to side. She felt that it was utterly impossible for her to say any more. Then with a little choked cry she fled from the room and shut the door behind her. She rushed out into the night and stood on the pavement, her teeth chattering, her small face livid. The intolerable shame of that scene bit like acid into her very soul — a proud young soul — for Terry had always held her head high, conscious that, whatever her faults, she did at least know the meaning of honour. Now she stood dishonoured for no just cause — but she knew that nobody would believe her. Not even her own mother. The evidence was too strong. Well, after all, this chaos had been bound to come sooner or later. Ruth Farlong's appearance at the Colroyd's party tonight had only precipitated it. The question now was, what could she do? What was there left for her to do?

Terry looked wildly down the road. A taxi came scraping along with its flag up. She hailed it desperately and gave her home address.

She sobbed to herself as the taxi drove her away from Pont Street in the direction of Wimbledon. She had not got enough money in her bag to pay for the fare. She would have to borrow from the servants when she reached home. She had no idea what she meant to do, but she went back to the Cedars in this crisis because it was the most natural thing for her to do.

If only Dr. Farlong had been there to help her — deny the beastly thing for her — with her. She could not face or fight those cruel, suspicious people alone.

She felt incapable of sane thought when finally she found herself in the deserted hall at home. Davis, staring inquisitively, paid the taxi for her.

But almost immediately another taxi drove up to the Cedars. Mrs. Manstone had come home in hot pursuit, firmly intending to get to the bottom of this terrible thing here and now. The good lady was crimson and panting when she marched into her house. In all her life she had never been so insulted — so ashamed. And in front of the Colroyds, too — a most terrible thing — poor little Barbara! Francis was being so kind, too; had refused to let her come back, and assured her that it made no difference to him. But Mrs. Manstone was quite sure it was going to make a difference to his mother, if not to the Colonel.

She was stunned by the realisation that her youngest daughter was mixed up in a divorce case — she had, apparently, been indulging in a secret liaison with a married man. Mrs. Manstone had always feared that one day Terry would do something crazy. But this — this public scandal — the Fylson-Wise blood congealed in Mrs. Manstone's veins.

She pursued her daughter up to her bedroom — stood on the threshold, panting, the chain of her pince-nez quivering, and hurled questions at her.

Terry, like a pale ghost of herself with

large strained eyes, sat on the edge of her bed and tried to answer quietly. But it seemed so futile, up against a stone wall of suspicion; so wretched to feel that her mother, who should have been ready to defend her, was one of the first to condemn.

'The disgrace — in the Colroyds' drawing-room — I shall never get over it!' came from Mrs. Manstone in a gasp. 'And this is what you've come to, Terry. You've had an affair with a married man unknown to me — to Barbara — and you are going to be cited as a co-respondent in a divorce case! My God! if your father had lived this would have broken his heart.'

'I tell you I'm not guilty and neither is Dr. Farlong!' Terry said again and again.

'How can you say you are not guilty. You went off on that walking-tour against my wishes — pretending that you wanted to be alone. You lied to me — to Barbara — about staying at some inn — and all the time you slept in this doctor's house. Mr. Keyland saw me to the door at the Colroyds, and sympathised — nobody knows how ashamed I was — *sympathised* with me for having such a daughter! He has all the facts, legally. The Farlongs' housekeeper found you with the doctor in the morning. *Oh!*'

Mrs. Manstone burst into tears and went on hurling questions and accusations in the same sobbing breath.

'How could you do such a thing? Haven't I done my best to bring you up in the right way — to teach you to be a decent Christian woman? There are girls today who play fast and loose — but that *my* daughter should so far forget her name, her up-bringing, her family, as to lay herself open to this scandal! I shall never forgive you — never, so long as I live. You've broken my heart. You've done irreparable harm to your poor sister! She'll never get over it either. Hadn't you more control — *more modesty?*'

Terry, who had hardly spoken at all,

sat staring at her mother, her heart sinking lower and lower while she listened to the stream of abuse. When at length the elder woman paused to breathe and applied her handkerchief to her eyes and nose, Terry said, with the quietness of despair:

'Aren't you going to believe me when I tell you that I did *not* sleep with Dr. Farlong?'

Mrs. Manstone shuddered.

'The shame of it!' she kept muttering.

'But I *didn't* sleep with him!' reiterated Terry wearily. 'It's all a most ghastly mistake. Mrs. Farlong knows it is — her housekeeper lied — it's a put-up job — '

'You can't expect me to believe such an absurd story as that,' said Mrs. Manstone.

'Very well,' said Terry, 'then you must believe the other thing.'

'My daughter — co-respondent in a divorce case!' whispered Mrs. Manstone.

Then something flamed in Terry — revolt against this easy way in which her own mother put the worst construction on the case.

'I should have thought that *you*, my mother, would have defended me!' she said passionately. 'I think it's beastly of you to believe what the others say. But you've never liked me — Barbara's always been your favourite. I don't care! I shan't ask for your help again. I know *my* conscience is clear. I've never done more than shake hands with Dr. Farlong — the whole thing's a wicked plot. But let them bring me into the divorce — I don't care — I'm going to get out of *here*, where I'm not believed, and go to the one person who does believe me!'

Mrs. Manstone had nothing more to say. Her own flow of language had stopped. Sniffing into her handkerchief, she stood there regarding her daughter as she would have done an unwelcome stranger. Terry gave a hysterical laugh and added:

'I'm quite sure you won't want me here any more.'

With trembling fingers she took off her evening dress, found a cardigan suit — the first thing she saw — and put it on. Mrs. Manstone stared at her in horror.

'You wicked girl — what are you going to do now?'

'I'm going away — I won't stay here and disgrace you any further.'

If Mrs. Manstone had said one kind or merciful word then, Terry would probably have flung herself into her arms and wept with her. But she said the one thing that finished Terry as far as her mother was concerned.

'So you're going to your *lover* — to live openly with him now!'

Scarlet to the roots of her hair, Terry turned on the elder woman. Then she checked the words that rose to her lips and gave a strange, hard little laugh.

'I'm sure it will give you a lot of satisfaction to believe that,' she said.

Somehow or other she managed to fling a few necessities into a suitcase, picked up the red beret which she had worn on that fatal walking-tour and pulled it down over her head, put on a tweed coat, and then rummaged in her drawer for a little leather case wherein she kept what was left of her month's allowance. She found a pound note. That would not last her for long, but it would take her to Rossdown. To Rossdown and Blaise she was going, whatever the consequences. She had nobody else to whom she could turn.

Without saying good-bye to her mother, who sat crying noisily, she walked down the stairs and out of the house which had been her home and would be a home no longer.

She had had no dinner. She wanted none. She reached Victoria, and by some lucky chance caught a train to Crowborough within five minutes of its departure.

How Blaise would receive her she had no idea. She went to him blindly and impulsively, because he alone could help her and share with her this trouble in which they were both involved.

10

At half past ten that night Blaise
Farlong sat alone in his study, writing.
His desk was littered with correspon-
dence. About half a dozen envelopes,
already addressed and stamped, lay
beside him. He had been struggling
with arrears since he had eaten his
supper — cooked and served by the
gardener's wife. He had paid off the
little house-parlourmaid in the village
and told her not to come any more. So
now he was alone, which was what he
wanted. He was wrestling with the most
bitter moments of his life, and he was
the type to seek solitude under such
circumstances.

There were so many letters to write.
Accounts to be settled — bills to be
paid and to be sent out. And he was so
deadly tired that his head throbbed, his
eyes ached, and the fingers holding his

fountain-pen were not very steady.

Blaise Farlong was facing disaster. If it had been of his own making he might have been more philosophic, and accepted ruin as the natural consequence of his folly. But he was defeated by the knowledge that he had done his best, and that this calamity was the machination of a woman whom he had once loved and married.

The photograph of Ruth with the baby in her arms still stood on the desk in front of him, just as it had stood there for years. But suddenly he looked up from a letter which he was writing to George Heslop, and as his gaze lit upon the portrait of Ruth and Priscilla a terrible look came into his eyes. He felt almost as though he would have liked to have torn the pictured child out of the woman's arms. She was not fit to be the mother of a child.

Because Priscilla was part of that photograph he could not bring himself to destroy it, but he took it and laid it face downwards in the drawer of his desk, then, with a bitter smile, went on writing.

He had thought a lot about Terry Manstone during these last twenty-four hours. He could not let his mind turn to her without a feeling of intense shame — helpless indignation — that such a girl should be dragged into the mire with him.

Already his own reputation was in tatters. This morning, on his rounds, he had tasted the first cup of humiliation. Ruth's departure and the invidious remarks dropped by Mrs. Clarke before she left Rossdown had done their work.

Everybody who was anybody in the village knew that Dr. Farlong's wife had righteously swept out of her home, because her husband had spent the night with some girl during her absence.

A fine morsel for the scandalmongers to nibble at. A grand piece of scandal to relieve the boredom of Rossdown life. Passing through the High Street in his car, Blaise had taken off his hat to one woman, a patient of his; a Miss Everdean, who spent half her life playing Bridge and the other making libellous remarks about her neighbours. Miss Everdean had given him a stony stare and passed him by. Rebuff number one.

Then Mrs. Deemer, at whose house he had called, had sent word by her maid that she was not at home and would not be needing the doctor any more. An unheard-of thing from a woman who telephoned to him frantically for every trifling ailment.

One or two more incidents of the sort had shown Blaise which way the wind was blowing. His reputation as a doctor was gone. It was the beginning of the end to his practice here, at any rate.

He was a man who loved his work; had been proud of his position; and God alone knew what bitterness lay in his heart when he returned home from that uncomfortable morning's round.

During the afternoon, without further ado, he put Russet Place and the practice up for sale.

At the end of that dark day his nerves were raw, and there was scarcely any room in his thoughts even for the girl who was also a victim of Ruth's wicked conspiracy. There was so much to tackle in the way of business before he could do what his feelings prompted. His main desire now was to pack up and get away from Rossdown — end it all.

Yet this evening he had taken a stroll around his beloved garden, and felt sick at the thought of leaving it. These lovely flowers were the fruits of many years' hard work. He felt sore at heart when he considered the hours and hours that he had spent out here, digging, hoeing, planting, weeding. Just before the light failed he had paused in front of a bed of delphiniums — a particularly fine show this year. The tall spikes, deepest blue, palest azure, lavender tinted, darkest purple — exquisite things — reared their heads proudly against the deep green of a hedge. They were delicately lovely in the twilight. All these he must leave, and his roses too — the result of years of budding, of vigilance, of care.

It was queer, but the idea of leaving all this behind him hurt him almost as badly as the loss of his reputation. But he told himself not to be a fool and sentimentalise about the garden. He must needs be practical when he was up against far more materialistic difficulties. Theoretically, he had only £300 a year private income. Things were none too good on the Stock Exchange, and dividends were being passed. In fact, he had a little less than £250 at the moment. And a man must live. Ruth, with £500 a year of her own, was not likely to demand a third of his income — he was grimly amused at the mere idea that she should do that and further deplete his means.

If his accounts were settled, he might rake in about £120 in cash. The practice was worth between £1,000 and £1,200. And whoever succeeded him would take over the house and its appointments. That meant, with luck, he might have just enough money to buy a practice elsewhere and start life again.

But did he want to start it? He was not old — thirty-two is no age — but he felt so much older than that, and the bitterness of his experience had robbed him of his zest for life. Priscilla's death had seemed the greatest calamity that could befall him. And now on top of it came the loss of his wife, his home, his career as a medical man.

He did not regret losing Ruth. There had been little love between them recently, and the final treachery on her part had crushed the last shred of feeling for her out of him.

But tonight he felt a lonely and embittered man — a failure. He wondered if it was worth while going on.

There was Terry — this girl whose name was linked with his own. What was to become of her? How was he to deal with that problem?

The pain in his head grew worse. He

ceased writing, stood up and walked restlessly round his consulting-room. Pausing in front of the white enamel cupboard with the glass doors revealing rows of tiny bottles, he thought:

'There's a way out — *in there* — many ways out — nice easy ones.'

With a brooding look in his eyes he opened a drawer in the cabinet and picked up one of a dozen small slender phials. A painless way out of all the difficulties — an end to heart-break and disappointment. At the moment, stunned by disaster, he felt unequal to bearing the load, to fighting down a disgrace which he did not deserve.

In a fascinated way he lifted the little glass phial and held it in the palm of his hand. Morphia. The blessed anodyne for physical suffering. Why not for mental pain as well?

Then he started violently. The silence of the deserted house was broken by a sharp sound of the front door bell. Blaise put down the morphia and wiped his forehead. It felt damp. He went to the door and opened it.

A girl's slim figure stood under the light which was flooding the porch. A young, pretty girl, with a beret on her head and a suitcase in her hand, looking as though her legs could scarcely support her.

He recognized her at once, and in a moment of shocked surprise uttered her name:

'Terry!'

'I had to come,' she said. Her voice held a note of exhaustion. 'I'm sorry — do you mind? But I've nowhere else to go.'

'Good God!' said Blaise, and took the suitcase from her quickly. He stared at her incredulously. 'What do you mean? Where have you come from?'

'I've just walked from the Crown. I came down from Victoria about an hour ago. I managed to get a lift from Crowborough Station to the Crown on a lorry. Then I walked here. I feel terribly tired.'

'Tired!' he echoed. 'You must be

exhausted, you poor child. Why on earth didn't you phone for me to come and fetch you?'

'I don't know,' she said dully, and swayed a little on her feet.

The professional eye of the doctor saw that she was on the point of collapse. He put her suitcase down in the hall, shut the front door, took her arm, and led her to his consulting-room. His own sensations of despair — that almost suicidal fit of a few moments ago — had passed from him completely. His brain was alert again, and that limitless compassion which was an intrinsic part of his nature for young defenceless things swamped all other feelings, as he felt the girl's slight body trembling against him.

He put her into his big armchair, pulled off her beret, took her pulse between his fingers, which were firm and cool again. Keeping an eye on her, he went to his cupboard, poured out a dose, and brought it back to her.

'Drink this down, my child.'

She obeyed him and smiled faintly. The table-lamp burning on his desk showed him the pallor of the small sun-browned face and the black shadows of exhaustion under her eyes.

'This is the second time I've arrived at your house in a state of collapse,' she said with a note of apology in her voice. 'I really am sorry, Dr. Farlong. The first time was fatal, wasn't it? I did an awful lot of damage.'

'Never mind, Terry. You can't do any more.'

She shut her eyes and sighed.

'*Oh*, how tired I am. It's good to be here.'

'But why *are* you here?' he asked, standing over her, hands in his pockets.

She looked at him for a moment without answering. He wore an old pair of grey flannel bags and a tweed coat — gardening clothes, no doubt. His hair was untidy. She had never seen him like this, but somehow she preferred it to the spick-and-span doctor. It was more friendly. She had rushed down to him in a hysterical mood, but now that she was with him she felt quite calm and amazingly glad to be in his company.

'The most awful thing happened tonight,' she said slowly. 'The truth all came out in the most unexpected manner.'

He knit his brows.

'You mean your family know?'

'Yes. We went to dinner at the Colroyds' house — my sister's engaged to Francis Colroyd.'

'Good Lord,' said Blaise. 'Colroyd. You don't mean the Colroyds from India who are related to my wife?'

'Yes,' said Terry. 'And your wife came to dinner too.'

Blaise stared at her, then sat down heavily in the revolving chair beside his desk.

'Good God!'

Terry blurted out the whole story.

'You can imagine what I felt — when Mrs. Farlong refused to be one of a party which included me, and walked out of the room. And then that horrible Mr. Keyland — telling everybody that I was the co-respondent — the family were appalled — staggered.'

Blaise put a hand to his head.

'My God!' he repeated. 'What a frightful thing! You poor little girl! It was damned hard lines that it should all come out that way — we certainly don't seem to have any luck.'

Terry grimaced at the memory of the subsequent scene with her mother.

'It was pretty awful. I felt so ghastly. I couldn't cope with it. I wish you'd been there.'

Impulsively he reached out, took her hand, and held it fast.

'I wish I had — I'd have knocked that fellow Victor Keyland to a jelly. God, what a swine he is!'

She leaned back in her chair, revived by the strong stimulant he had given her and amazingly content to let her hand rest in his reassuring clasp. Here was the one person in the world who knew and understood everything, and who would not argue with her, accuse her, drive her crazy.

'I just rushed out of the house,' she continued. 'I couldn't very well stay and argue with them, although I did try to deny it. Nobody believed me — I told you they wouldn't.'

He knit his brows fiercely.

'That's the most damnable part of it — nobody *will* believe us.'

She then described her scene with her mother.

'You see, I just had to come down to you — there was nobody else I could go to,' she finished simply. 'I couldn't face being looked at and doubted by even my nicest relations and friends. I *had* to come to you. Do you mind?'

He stared at her, feeling a little bewildered. But he said gently:

'Of course I don't mind. You have every right to come to me. I am more or less responsible for you now. But I don't know what I'm going to do with you.'

'I'm so miserable, and so ashamed,' she whispered.

Tears glittered on her lashes. He saw them, and his heart ached for her. She was bringing home to him the fact that she, too, was facing disaster and disgrace — sharing this calamity with him. He had been selfish to think so much about himself tonight.

'Have things been difficult for you, too?' she asked forlornly.

'Not too good,' he said. 'I've been cut by several of the old cats in the village. My reputation is gone. Just before you came I was asking myself if it was worth while going on!'

He still held her hand in his, but with the other he picked up the little glass phial of morphia tablets which he had dropped on the blotter when the front door bell rang.

Terry looked at it too, and her heart gave a horrid jerk.

'Oh, you weren't meaning to — you weren't going to — ' She could not finish the sentence, but her eyes grew wide and dark with horror.

He put down the phial and turned to

her, smiling sadly.

'No, I don't know that I was seriously contemplating putting an end to my life,' he said. 'But in a crazy moment I toyed with the idea.'

'But if you did that, what good would it do? How could it make things any better? The harm has been done; we're in this thing now, aren't we? And if you die — I'd be alone. I don't want to be alone — I'm frightened!'

She suddenly broke into wild weeping, tore her fingers away from his, covered her face, and sat there crying in a broken-hearted fashion. Blaise looked at her, shocked and startled by her outburst. He could not bear to see a woman cry, and it wrenched his heart-strings to listen to the desperate sobbing of this girl who was so young, so harmless, so inexperienced, brought to this pitch through no folly of her own.

Her passionate words reiterated in his brain.

'We're in this thing now . . . I don't

*want to be alone ... I'm fright-
ened ... '*

'Terry, don't cry like that, for God's
sake,' he said hoarsely. 'I can't bear you
to — I feel such an unutterable cur
when I think that you've been dragged
into this by my wife. It's unspeakable of
your mother not to believe you — to try
and protect you. You're such a kid.'

'No,' she stammered wildly. 'I'm not
— I'm quite old enough for the world
to look upon as a bad woman, anyhow.'

'A bad woman — you!' He laughed
grimly. 'It's outrageous.'

She went on crying as though her
heart would break. He knew so well
what she was going through. In a way
he envied her. It might have eased him
to break down like this — but he
couldn't. Men must not give way to
tears. But he could gauge the extent of
her mental suffering, for it was parallel
with his own. Today both of them had
been humiliated and condemned.

They were no longer strangers. Their
names were coupled — their lives also

must inevitably be linked. He felt that they were partners, intimately concerned with each other. He could not sit there any longer, detached from her, and listen to her crying.

He drew her out of the chair, sat in it himself, and pulled her down on to his knees. He held her as he would have held a child who had come to him for help, for comfort. She was slender and light, he was astonished at the fragile weight of her against him. Quite naturally she turned to him and hid her face against his shoulder and went on weeping. Gently he stroked her hair, smoothing the soft brown strands with his long, sensitive fingers.

'Hush, my dear. You'll only make yourself feel ill. Don't cry like this.'

Her sobbing gradually quietened down. She was immensely consoled by the warm curve of his arm and with her face pressed against the tweed coat that smelt so homey, earthy, of the garden.

And while he held her and caressed her hair, a strange new peace descended upon Blaise Farlong. He knew that he could not complain, after this, that he walked alone in the shadows.

When Terry lifted her head, he took out a big silk handkerchief and wiped her eyes. He gave her one of his wide, charming smiles.

'Better?'

'Much.'

'It's a damned rotten business, Terry, enough to make anybody weep.'

She pressed the handkerchief to her lips.

'Now I look a sight — my eyes are all bunged up. I can feel it.'

That human and feminine touch in the middle of calamity appealed to his sense of humour. He began to feel very much better himself.

'Powder your nose if you want to — but I don't object to it as it is.'

She gave a long sigh, then, suddenly acutely conscious that she was sitting on his knees, blushed crimson.

'Aren't I — rather heavy for you?'

'You're light as a feather, my dear.'

'You've been awfully nice to me.'

'It's you who've been so nice to me all the way along,' he said gently. 'But I suppose you realise, you poor child, that you've put the lid on it, as they say, by coming to me tonight. There isn't a soul now who'll believe we're a couple of angels.'

'Oh!' she said. 'No, I suppose that is so. It was rather silly of me.'

'Well, I daresay it won't make much difference. It's Mrs. Clarke's damning evidence that counts.'

'I had to come,' she whispered.

He picked up one of her hands and looked at it.

'I'm rather glad you did. Perhaps you've saved me from God knows what tonight.'

'But you would never have killed yourself!' she said in a horror-stricken voice.

'Who knows what one will do when one is alone and feeling there's nothing to carry on for? But now that you've come I see there *is* something to carry on for. I must stand by you — protect you as best I can.'

'You did want to see me, didn't you?' she asked. 'You said so.'

'Yes, I'll tell you about that in a minute,' he replied. 'But look here — what did your mother say when you left the house?'

Terry caught her breath.

'She said — that she supposed I was — going to live openly with my — my lover.'

He flushed to the roots of his hair. He had taken her in his arms as he would have done a child, but he was forced suddenly to the realisation that she was very much a woman, and an attractive one, charming, sympathetic, and she had come to him because there was nowhere else for her to go. His brain, in a single flash, revealed the possibilities of this thing and threw a new light upon the whole situation. He gave a queer, embarrassed laugh.

'Yes, no doubt that's what she thinks, and what others will be thinking.'

'Perhaps I'd better go away again,' said Terry in a forlorn voice.

'For your own sake and reputation, perhaps you had.'

'But where can I go and what's the use of worrying about my reputation now?' she asked piteously.

He suddenly dropped her hand, pushed her gently on to her feet, and stood up beside her.

'I must just get a cigarette. We'll try and work this thing out, Terry.'

Her heart beat fast. In a confused way she watched him while he lit his cigarette. And she knew definitely that she did not want to be sent away, and that she would rather face disaster with him than without him. A strangely exhilarating yet frightening feeling, that.

Blaise began to walk up and down the consulting-room, smoking hard, his face gaunt and tired in the lamplight. She sat motionless and silent, watching him, and waiting for him to tell her what lay in his mind.

11

A small clock on the mantelpiece in the consulting-room showed Terry that it was nearly eleven o'clock. She felt deadly tired. Her eyes began to close and her brown head drooped back against the cushion in the chair.

Blaise turned and saw the sleepy young figure, and an immense feeling of pity, even of affection, for this young thing who was supposed to be his 'partner in crime' softened his whole face. He stubbed his cigarette-end in an ash-tray, came over to her, and touched her shoulder.

'Poor child, you're almost asleep. But can you just give me your attention for a few moments?'

She started, looked up at him, and gave a faint laugh.

'Of course. Forgive me, but it's been a hectic day — *and* night. In fact, these last few days have been frightfully trying altogether.'

'Yes, you're right! But look here, Terry — there's something I must just explain to you. You know I've seen my solicitor and we've talked things over — I told him the whole circumstances. He said, of course, we can put in what defence we like and you can prove that you — ' He stopped, his brows knit, and bit at his lips. He was embarrassed and ashamed, and he did not really know how to put this thing to her. Her large candid eyes were fixed upon him so unswervingly. The very purity of her made him sick with disgust at the thing Ruth had done. 'Try and see what I mean — it can be proved that you and I, to use plain language, did *not* commit adultery,' he added bluntly.

Terry was no fool and she did understand, but now her lashes drooped, and her face and throat were scorched by hot colour.

'Oh!' she whispered. 'You mean I would have to submit to — a lot of strange doctors. *No!* Never! I shall never do that! I couldn't bear it. There'd be all the scandal, anyhow, and details about my virtue in the papers. It's absolutely *unthinkable*!'

Blaise spread out his hands with a gesture of despair.

'My poor child, I agree with you that, even if your innocence were proved by a dozen medical men, the scandal would remain. Ruth might not actually get a divorce, but there would not be much hope for either you or me after the damned Press had finished with us.'

'Then for heaven's sake let's leave it as it is.'

He gave her a quick, intense look.

'You realise that if we make no defence at all the divorce will just go through without further ado.'

'Yes. But is that worse than the other thing? It isn't as though we could both leave the courts without a stain upon our characters.' She gave a trembling little laugh, and with quickened breathing added: 'Think of the old cats talking about what we did or didn't do that night!'

He echoed her laugh, but his eyes were strained and his nerves on edge.

'It's the devil of a mess, Terry. What are we to do? Where are you to go? You're always so amazingly sensible, but I don't want to ruin your life.'

'It's already ruined.'

'I hate to hear you say it,' came from him in a low voice.

She looked up at him. His care-worn face, his sad, troubled eyes, gave her a pang. In her impulsive, generous fashion, she felt the need to help him — the inexplicable desire to drive away that wretched, broken look.

'Don't turn me out,' she whispered. 'Let me stay with you now. I haven't anybody else — neither have you, have you?'

He looked down at her a little incredulously, and answered with a queer intake of his breath:

'I certainly haven't anybody who cares much about me, Terry.'

'But I do — I like you, awfully. I did when I first met you — and this business isn't your fault and hasn't altered my feelings.'

'Oh, my dear, but that's sweet of you — God knows it's undeserved. As I've told you before, there was a lot about you that appealed to me — I felt we shared so many tastes and views in common — and I wanted to see more of you. But that it should all turn out like this is so disastrous.'

'Well, I may be a coward, but I can't face the disgrace alone,' she said. 'And my family will certainly cut me off after this.'

'Do you really mean that you want to see it through with me?'

'Don't you see,' she stammered, 'it might be easier for us both in the end. I can't bear to think that you wanted to kill yourself tonight — I'd like to help you feel differently.'

She was utterly transformed for him now. The defenceless child was becoming a woman anxious for his safety. He was speechless — immeasurably touched. He was beginning to know her well, and her sweet friendliness and understanding had never failed him from the beginning.

He put out his hands, took hers, and squeezed them hard.

'You're a dear, kind little thing, Terry. Much too kind. I can't think why you don't rave and rant at me.'

'I don't want to. You've never done me any harm.'

'But the world won't think that.'

'No — the world will say you're a cad, and that I'm one too — to come like a thief in the night and take Mrs. Farlong's husband away from her. We're both implicated, aren't we?'

He looked down at the brave young face, and felt a lump in his throat.

'You're a grand little thing, Terry.'

'I'm petrified, really.'

'I'd give anything to save you.'

'Seems to me *I*'ve got to save *you* — it would be just the last word for me if you took one of those horrid bottles full of poison.' She laughed nervously, and her eyes were bright with unshed tears. 'Don't think me a bore, but I *would* rather stay with you under the circumstances.'

He looked down at the small, trembling hands in his own. His breath quickened. The whole complexion of the affair was altering for him. It had never entered his head that this girl liked him or had any real regard for his happiness and safety. It made it impossible for him now to feel complete and utter bitterness. The simple, almost boyish way in which she said: *'Don't think me a bore — but I would rather stay . . . '* did more to stir him than if she had been the fully sexed type of woman setting herself out to attract him.

There had not been a woman in his life since his marriage with Ruth. Passion — even affection — had died between them so long ago that he had almost forgotten what it was to love or be loved. For the first time for years the swift thrill that is half an ache and half a rapture caught at his heart. But he felt that in such emotion lay madness. Whatever happened, he must keep his perspective and not allow sex to blind his vision. Terry was a sweet and charming child, and he a doctor, many years her senior. He had led a repressed and even solitary existence within himself for so long that it would not do for him to unleash the passionate impulses of which he knew he was perfectly capable.

He wrung her hands and dropped them.

'Terry, my dear, you frighten me a little — I'm frightened of myself. I can't let you stay.'

Her heart beat violently. She knew in that moment that she was utterly in love with this man. For the first time in her young life that age-old madness was upon her. Right from the start Blaise had appealed to her, and now that they were flung together on the rocks of disaster she was mortally afraid that she might be separated from him. Flushing to the roots of her hair, she stood there, her fingers interlacing nervously. She said in a small voice:

'You're fed up with me.'

Then he turned to her and gave her a long, deep look.

'Oh, you child! I'm not fed up with you — how could I be? Your coming down here tonight and saying these sort of things to me have made the hell of a difference — isn't it obvious? But you don't know what you're doing — what you're going to let yourself in for if you're too nice to me. I was faithful to my wife all the years we lived together, Terry, but I'm no saint, God knows. In a way you're an absolute baby — but in another way you're very much a woman, my dear, and a very sweet one. I've been feeling unutterably depressed — almost suicidal, as you know — and you come and make me want to pick you up in my arms and hold you there and forget the whole cursed business.'

She was suddenly exalted. A woman

in love. With all a woman's generous instincts to give rather than to receive, she said in a queer, hushed voice:

'Then, please, won't you forget it?'

He was shaking now. He shook his head at her.

'Child, for the love of God, go away. This won't do!'

Then, to his dismay, two great tears glittered on her lashes and rolled slowly down her cheeks.

'I don't want to go away,' she said forlornly. 'Don't make me go — please!'

'Terry,' he said hoarsely, 'you mustn't be silly — I'm all alone here, and I tell you I'm not to be trusted tonight. The thing's got me badly — I'm all to pieces. Oh, for Lord's sake don't cry — that will finish me!'

She hid her face in her hands.

'*You're* finishing *me*. You don't want me to stay. All right. I'll go away.'

'Be reasonable,' he said, more violently than he meant to. 'If you do stay with me it will confirm everything, and we shall have no defence left.'

'But you've told me that in spite of the beastly defence our reputations will be ruined.'

He put a hand to his head. It was swimming, and he was ashamed because he had scarcely the strength of will left to turn this girl away. Looking at her, listening to her, he knew that he had infinite need of her company in this deserted and dishonoured house, and that only she who understood could drive the devil of despair out of his soul.

'Yes,' he admitted. 'Our reputations are gone and our names are linked, whatever happens. But it isn't fair on you.'

She uncovered her face and looked at him blindly through her tears.

'It's unfair for both of us — but if I did stay and the divorce did go through, wouldn't it help you a little?'

'Heaven, yes — but do you *want* that to happen?' he asked incredulously.

She shivered a little. The pupils of her eyes were dark and big with excitement.

'I'm so tired and perplexed, I don't know which way to turn,' she said piteously. 'But I do know I'd rather stay with you than anything else, if you want me.'

He was powerless then to do anything but take her in his arms. She pressed her face against his shoulder, and he felt her slight body quivering from head to foot. The despair, the ugliness of the whole thing, which had been eating at him like an acid these last few days, seemed to vanish like magic in the strange sweetness of that embrace. It was amazing and satisfying to him to know that she wanted to stay and to face disaster with him openly and unashamed. But this was not the time to analyse his feelings, and on her part she was blind to all but the one great emotion — the hitherto unknown ecstasy of close mental and physical contact with a lover.

Blaise tightened his hold of her and put his lips against her hair.

'My dear, you bewilder me with so

much sweetness. You're a wonderful child. You've made me feel a different being. I didn't know I had it in me to feel like this about anybody again. It's like an intoxication — but I'd be a howling cad if I didn't conquer it.'

She put an arm about his shoulder and said, with her face still hidden:

'I do believe I've fallen in love with you, Dr. Blaise. Funny, isn't it?'

His heart jerked wildly.

'You — in love with me? Terry, you sweet little idiot, you don't know what you're saying.'

She raised a flushed and defiant face.

'I may be an idiot, but I do know what I'm saying, and I've never felt like this about anybody before. Oh, no, it's no good you saying it's just reaction or the madness of the moment because we're involved. I really do care about you — there, now you see how brazen I am! The bad woman of Rossdown living up to her reputation.'

Blaise felt the blood racing through his body. She was so different from anybody he had ever known — and so utterly different from the woman who had been his wife. Even in the days when she had loved him Ruth had always yielded her favours with a touch of condescension. She had liked to feel herself a queen granting her favours. He had been made to feel himself the supplicant and never the desired. But there was something so utterly generous and frank in the way Terry Manstone offered her affections that she touched a chord in him which had been asleep; supplied a long-felt need which even his beloved garden and his medical work had not wholly assuaged. But he was so afraid of taking advantage of her youth and her inexperience. His first wild instincts were to drown himself in the sweetness of her surrender. But he kept his head. He took her face between his hands, bent, and kissed her eyelids.

'Dear, lovely child, I can see that your chief fault is over-generosity, but I'm not going to let you sweep me right off my feet — I'd be a swine if I did.

276

The whole of this thing has happened so quickly — it's a bit dazing. I thought I was a broken reed, with nothing left to live for, and now I find there's a very great deal.'

Her heart had hammered at the touch of his lips against her eyes. She looked up at him with shining eyes and whispered:

'Then you like me a little?'

'Too much.'

'I'm glad.'

The simplicity of that went straight to his heart. They moved toward each other by mutual impulse, and she was in his arms again, this time more passionately. She put up a hand, shyly, and touched his thick hair just where it was greying at the temples.

'Poor Dr. Blaise!'

'I've no more pity left for myself. You've driven that away. Dr. Blaise is just a man, likely to fall badly in love at any moment.'

'Oh!' she whispered rapturously.

He pulled her nearer and suddenly

kissed the warm, sun-browned hollow in her throat.

'Crazy child,' he said unsteadily. 'You really had better go away. I'm more than ten years older than you are, and I ought to know better, but you're driving reason and sanity away from me, Terry.'

'If you're going to be divorced — for me — what does anything matter?'

'Dear!' he said. 'You're a distracting little temptress. An hour ago I thought life had ended for me. Are you seriously offering to make it worth while for me to start again?'

'Fate has rather thrown in our lot together, hasn't it? But I don't think I shall mind anything if I can stay with you.'

'You might regret it — you're so young.'

'I'm not, really. But perhaps I couldn't make you feel that life *is* worth while.'

'God, yes, of course you could. But you're not going to be allowed to make up your mind on the spur of the moment.'

'What are you going to do with me, then?' she whispered, her heart beating frantically fast, her shining eyes fixed on him.

He leaned down for an instant and touched her smooth young forehead with his lips.

'I can't send you back to your family, can I?'

'No — no — please let me stay with you.'

'Terry — Terry — '

He stammered her name, body and brain confused by her sweetness and eager for the exquisite consolation of the gifts she offered. But he asked himself if she were not merely stirred to it in this blind moment of generosity and emotion; told himself that he would be criminal not to give her time to think; to weigh up the whole situation.

'Listen, my dear,' he said. 'If you want to stay — you shall. The die's cast

279

since you've come down to me like this so openly. You know what everybody will think. You say you prefer that to the humiliation of an attempt at defence in the courts. Are you absolutely certain about that, Terry?'

'Absolutely,' she answered without hesitation.

'You really care enough about me?'

'Yes.'

'It's amazing,' he said under his breath.

'It's rather marvellous, really.'

'You sweet thing!'

He lost his head for an instant, and bent to the generous red mouth she lifted to his, and kissed her. It was not the light caress he had intended. Her young, slender arms curved about his neck, and her eyelids closed in rapt surrender. The kiss was long and deep and infinitely satisfying to them both. It seemed to Blaise Farlong that there must, after all, be such a thing in life as the law of recompense. He had tasted the dregs of bitterness, of suffering, and now this amazing and unexpected cup of rapture was lifted to his lips by this girl, this child who was accused with him.

She, body, soul, and brain on fire for him, thought:

'Now I know that I love him — *terribly*. Now I know what it is to be in love.'

Blaise lifted his head and looked at her hungrily.

'Darling thing,' he said in a shaken voice. 'You've driven all the common sense out of my head.'

'Good,' she whispered, and hid a burning face against his arm.

'But I've got to be sensible, and so have you.'

'Tell me you want me to stay — Dr. Blaise.'

'You know that now. And surely it's Blaise, without the prefix, isn't it?'

'Blaise,' she said, and added: 'It's an awfully nice name.'

'What a child you are,' he said, laughed unsteadily, and released her.

'Terry, my dear, I must smoke.'

'According to the rules of books and plays, a cigarette is required in moments of great emotion,' she laughed back at him radiantly.

A little sadly he looked at that radiant young face and lit his cigarette.

'The most adorable thing about you is your sense of humour at all moments, dear,' he said. 'But I'm such a broken reed, I feel I have no earthly right to take what you offer and spoil your life.'

'It will spoil my life if you don't take me, Blaise,' she said seriously. 'I really do love you.'

'It's incredibly sweet of you, darling.'

She loved the way he said the 'darling.' Somehow it fell from his lips so naturally. She said:

'And you're not to call yourself a broken reed. Thirty-two is no age.'

'Ten years older than you, Terry — and I've had months of rotten health.'

'But you're better now.'

'Much.'

'Then all you want is somebody to keep you better, and look after you and make you forget you've been so unhappy.'

He looked at her through the cloud of smoke.

'You've made me forget too much, my dear.'

She flung back her head, and half shut her eyes in an ecstatic way.

'Oh, Blaise, I'm so happy — and when I came tearing down to you I was *miserable*.'

'Are you sure you won't wake up tomorrow morning and feel more miserable?'

'I know I shan't — if you care about me, Blaise.'

'I care a great deal, little Terry. But I want you to help me keep my head — just for a bit longer.'

She swallowed hard. Looking at him, she was immeasurably thrilled by the thought that he was her lover and that he needed her. All other thoughts seemed to fly from her brain.

'I'll do whatever you want, Blaise.'

He began to walk up and down the room.

'Listen, dear. Stay here tonight, of course. Tomorrow you must go away. I can't keep you here, where you'll be open to insult. It goes against the grain altogether for me to allow you to throw in your hand like this and leave the case undefended. But you've put such a different complexion on the whole show tonight — haven't you?'

'I suppose I have,' she said, biting nervously at her lips. 'I certainly don't want to defend now. So much harm has been done to us both already — much more will be done by the publicity of the case, either defended or undefended. And if you don't mind facing things with me, I'll be perfectly brazen and say — I'd just adore to stay with you.'

'Oh, you darling,' he said. He felt suddenly like a man drunk with strong wine. There was something altogether intoxicating about this hazel-eyed girl with her sweet, tanned face and frank, unashamed betrayal of her feelings. He thought of the years of misery, of bitterness and friction, with Ruth. To think of Terry in Ruth's place was certainly an intoxicant.

'But listen, my dear,' he added. He came up, put an arm about her shoulders, and held her close to him. 'Do you realise what we'll have to face now? We'll be giving them all the right to sneer — to condemn.'

'They think they've got a right to sneer and accuse as it is,' said Terry, feeling astonishingly cheerful about it.

'Very well. Then there's the financial question. I'm so damned hard up, Terry. You've been used to having everything — '

'And to being miserable. Oh, *God*! how I've hated my life at Wimbledon, and all the parties and dances and society cats!' she broke in passionately. 'You know it. I told you — long before this happened.'

'That's true,' he said, knitting his brows.

'I'd rather be poor — and happy.'

'You're young, dear, and enthusiastic, but I've had experience — I want to wipe out the romance for a moment and make you see the grimmer side to the question.'

She looked up at his thin, tired face, and knew that she adored him.

'Darling Dr. Blaise, you'll never wipe out this romance for me,' she whispered. 'I'm quite practical — I know there's a grimmer side. But I shan't mind. Only — perhaps it won't be worth it — for you.'

'I'm beginning to think any amount of trouble and difficulty will be worth while if you're as nice to me as this, darling child.'

'Then let's face it together — please.'

He pitched his cigarette-end into the grate and took her wholly in his arms.

'You make it hard for me to refuse, Terry, my dear.'

She wound her arms about his waist

and hugged him.

'Good,' she said happily.

For an instant they clung to each other. His lips were against her mouth, and she could feel his heart's frantic beating and felt her own throb in breathless surrender.

When that long kiss ended, she said, in a hushed, rapturous voice:

'Mother said she supposed I was coming to my lover. It was truer than I ever imagined.'

He put her away from him and walked to his desk. The weariness had been wiped from his face. He looked blindly at the scattered papers in front of him, and thought:

'How could I have ever dreamed it would end like this — that I should find myself in love with this child — madly and crazily in love! Ruth tried to do me a bad turn, but perhaps she has done me a good one.'

'Blaise,' came Terry's voice rather shyly. 'Are you shocked with me?'

He turned to her.

'Shocked? Lord, no. Why?'

'I've rather flung myself into your arms, haven't I?' she asked, with a shaky laugh.

'Arms pretty ready to receive you, darling.'

'How awful it would have been if you'd coldly rejected me.'

He shook his head at her.

'You drive good sense clean out of my head when you look at me and talk to me like that, Terry. Darling, I want to be practical. I must be. Listen — you must go to bed. It's nearly midnight. You were exhausted when you came.'

'I'm all right now.'

'But you've got to go to bed. I'm going to reject you quite coldly now.'

She grimaced and rose to her feet.

'All right, Dr. Farlong.'

'And remember this.' He put two hands on her shoulders and looked earnestly down into her shining eyes. 'For the time being — we've got to be good, Terry.'

Her cheeks burned.

288

'I don't care what happens — I'll obey you blindly, Blaise — so long as you don't send me away.'

'Tomorrow — you must go.'

'Where?' she asked, crestfallen.

'To friends — somewhere — until you've had time to think it all over sanely, darling, and can make up your mind that you want to stay with me — always.'

'I know it now, Blaise.'

'But I won't let you throw your cap over the mill in two seconds, my dear.'

'Very well. Let time show. It will. I know that I love you.'

'Bless you, sweetheart,' he said unsteadily.

'Perhaps you need time to make up *your* mind, Blaise. Perhaps you don't love me.'

'I think I could very easily love you very much, dear. But I've been married for six years — and lived half my life — and I know what I'm doing. You must, definitely, think things out quietly before you take the final plunge.'

She bit her lip and looked sideways at the fine, sensitive hands on her shoulders.

'Very well, I will. But Lord knows where I'm going.'

'We'll talk about it tomorrow. I'm selling the practice and the place — at once.'

'Oh, Blaise, your garden — your flowers!'

'Pretty damnable,' he said. 'But what you've done for me tonight has made everything so much less hard.'

She suddenly took his hands and pressed her lips to them.

'I'm so glad, my darling doctor. Oh, Blaise, now I know why I've always liked doctors. It's because I was going to love you.'

He flushed like a boy and took her in his arms and hugged her. He found himself wishing with desperate sadness that he had not lived so long with Ruth and grown tired and bitter. He would have liked to have given his youth, his first ideals, to this girl, with her marvellously youthful outlook, her fervent unspoiled body and mind.

'Won't you let me help you make another garden one day?' she whispered, in his arms.

He whispered the answer against her lips:

'Yes, yes, a thousand times yes, my dearest — if you want to — when this damned business is all over.'

'It won't seem so damnable now — will it?'

'God, no!'

This time it was she who drew away from him — breathless, dewy-eyed.

'I'll go to bed now. You want me to.'

'Yes, you must. Listen, dear. There's nobody in the house — nobody to look after you.'

'Except my doctor.'

'Your doctor is better at giving prescriptions than dealing out linen and making up beds.'

'I'll do that. Tell me where the linen cupboard is and which bedroom I'm to sleep in.'

'The spare room,' he said.

In a queer way he did not want Terry to sleep in the room that had been Ruth's . . . and was still inevitably pregnant with memories of their life together. A life he wanted to forget, to wipe out utterly.

He took Terry's arm and walked with her upstairs to the first landing.

They found sheets and pillow-cases in the airing-cupboard. Together they made up one of the twin beds in the spare room.

She found a curious delight in those few domesticated moments. When he took her in his arms and bade her good night, she drew his face down to hers for an instant and pressed her cheek to his.

'I'm so happy,' she whispered. 'I want you to believe that.'

'I will,' he said. 'But I want *you* to think well these next few weeks, my darling.'

'And if I'm still of the same mind, will you want the co-respondent in the divorce case to stay with you — always?'

'Yes,' he said huskily. 'I shall want the co-respondent to stay with me — always.'

He kissed her hands and left her, shutting the door behind him. Terry walked slowly to the bed and began to unpack her suitcase. Her heart was racing and her cheeks were on fire. She felt like one in a dream. Yes, the nightmare of the last few days had changed tonight, mysteriously, gloriously, to a dream. It was like a miracle; that such an ugly, sordid thing as Ruth Farlong had done to them both could be transformed into so much beauty; into this ecstasy.

How strange that she and Blaise Farlong should have been thrust into an unjust and shameful situation — to discover in the end that, even though it remained unjust, they need no longer feel ashamed. Love had cast out shame; love that had sprung delicately, like an exquisite flower, out of a bed of rank and ugly weeds.

She recalled the hateful, humiliating scene in the Colroyds' house; her mother's horror; that last wretched scene at home. She had fled from it all in deep misery. But the misery had passed from her. She felt absolutely fearless, and ready to face whatever difficulties life had in store for her. She loved Blaise. He would love her — he had said so. He had said: '*I shall want you to stay with me — always!*'

Terry suddenly knelt beside the bed that he had helped her make, put her face in the curve of her arm, and wept. But this time not for sorrow — only for happiness.

12

Terry and Blaise breakfasted together that next morning just as they had done on the fatal day when Ruth Farlong had returned home and discovered them.

But this time there was no one to discover them except the gardener's wife, who came to prepare the doctor's breakfast. She was a good woman, and, like her husband, who had worked with Blaise in the garden, adored him. She had been one of his most loyal champions down in the village, where tongues wagged freely subsequent to Mrs. Farlong's departure and Mrs. Clarke's story.

To find a young girl in the doctor's house this morning was apt to shake the good woman's faith somewhat, but a few words with the doctor settled her doubts.

Blaise went straight into the kitchen and told her everything.

'I ask you as a personal favour, Mrs. King,' he finished, 'to tell nobody that Miss Manstone was here when you came this morning. Quite enough has been said as it is. I'm not going to pretend that the divorce won't go through. I daresay it will; I daresay many things will happen to confirm the suspicions against us. But the less chatter there is the better.'

Mrs. King, no longer young, and a motherly soul, looked at the doctor with kindly eyes. He was as straight a gentleman as ever walked the earth, she was sure. She was not going to judge the doctor, anyhow, let the rest of Rossdown say what it would.

'You can rely on me, sir,' she told Blaise grandly.

She served up a particularly good breakfast on the face of it. Blaise told Terry about her during the meal.

'It's rather marvellous to feel you've got a friend in a woman like that — a sterling creature.'

'She's the first woman of wisdom I've

met in this village,' said Terry. 'She knows what's nice.'

Blaise looked across the table into a pair of mischievous hazel eyes and shook his head at her.

'You can't flirt with me early in the morning, my child, I'm much too elderly for that.'

'All is over between us if you're not going to be nice to me with my eggs and bacon,' said Terry.

He was astounded that his heart could beat so fast when he looked at her. The sun streamed in through the french windows of the dining-room and turned the brown bobbed head to shining bronze. A good night's rest had taken the shadows of exhaustion away from her eyes. She was young and lovely and radiant, and it did his heart good to see her.

'I don't know what I've done to deserve all this, Terry,' he said in a low voice. 'It's a miracle that my lot should have been thrown in with anybody like yourself.'

'That's exactly what I thought after you left me last night,' she said.

'Nevertheless, we can't gloss over present difficulties, Terry. Now where can you go? Because you must go quickly.'

'I'd much rather not.'

'Nothing would induce me to let you remain here and let you be open to all the damnable gossip.'

'But I shall hate you to stand it all alone.'

Packing his pipe, he let his gaze rest on her, shook his head, and smiled.

'It's absurd and adorable for you to be so maternal about me. What the hell do I matter? It's you, my dear. I don't want you to have to stand anything unpleasant. To please me, try and think of someone you know to whom you could go for the present. I suppose your mother — '

'Nothing will induce me to go back to my mother,' she said quickly, with heightened colour. 'Even if she took me in because she thought it her duty, my life at home would be absolutely impossible. She and Barbara treating me like a pariah — feeling that they were disgraced by my mere presence in the household. No, Blaise, I've left home for good.'

'It's so rotten — ' he began.

She rose from the table, went quickly to his side, and laid a hand across his mouth.

'Don't! We had that all out last night. We decided that the rottenness wasn't going to matter now — it doesn't matter to me any more and please say you feel the same.'

He kissed the hand against his mouth.

'You know you've changed things, dear, but you'll never make me stop regretting that there should be any slur on your name through my wife.'

'I'm jealous of the thought that she was your wife, now.'

'You needn't be,' he said grimly. 'There isn't an atom of love left in my heart for Ruth. And in six months' time she will no longer be my wife.'

'It's her loss,' said Terry.

'Darling child,' he said. 'You fill me with confusion — I can't imagine why you're so nice to me. You're quite distracting. But be good and tell me where I can send you.'

'There's only one possible person I can go to,' said Terry. 'That's my friend Gage Thornton. We were at the finishing-school in Paris — she was a sort of pupil teacher there, and older than I, but we got on awfully well. She's been in Paris with her husband lately, but if they're back in England I know they'd put me up for the time being.'

'What a queer name — Gage.'

'Isn't it? She's rather a darling, and Tony, her husband, is a perfect dear. They're the happiest couple I know, and they've got the most glorious house in Sussex — at the foot of the Downs, not far from Ditchling.'

'Well, that's within easy distance of Rossdown Forest,' said Blaise.

'You'd love Frog's Hall,' said Terry.

300

'Isn't that an attractive name? It's a sixteenth-century farmhouse, and used to be called Frog's Farm. I know you'd like the garden, and Gage and Tony would love you.'

'I doubt that,' said Blaise wryly. 'But your friends sound nice to me. Now for heaven's sake, Terry, get through to them on the phone at once, and see if they're back.'

Terry lost no time in putting that telephone call through to the Thorntons' house. She was surprised and relieved when Gage herself answered the call.

'How are you, Terry dear? Tony and I only got back from Paris last night. We flew back — wasn't it extravagant? I was quite petrified, but Tony adored it. Are you speaking from Wimbledon?'

'No,' said Terry. 'Very much not. I'm speaking from a house not far from you — Rossdown Forest.'

'What are you doing there?'

Terry's cheeks went pink and hot, and she glanced over her shoulder at

301

Blaise, who was standing behind her, solemnly puffing at his pipe. With a queer little feeling of panic, she put out a hand, and Blaise took it and held it while she continued her telephone conversation.

'Something rather desperate has happened to me, Gage. I've left home for good.'

'That's quite the most cheering bit of news I've had for years,' said Gage. 'Whatever gave you the pluck?'

'I can't tell you on the phone — it's all so amazing — '

'Don't tell me it's an affair,' said Gage, with her pretty, familiar laugh.

'Yes,' said Terry.

'Oh, my dear — who — where — since when?'

'Only since yesterday, really,' said Terry. 'But I must see you and tell you everything. The point is, I'm adrift on this wicked world. Could you and Tony bear to shelter a fallen woman?'

Blaise looked down at the brown bobbed head and his face creased into a

broad smile. She was incorrigible
— and adorable — and he knew that he
loved her very much indeed, and that
he could not possibly part with her for
too long.

'It sounds too thrilling for words,'
Gage Thornton said to Terry. 'I've never
been so intrigued in my life. But of
course, come to Frog's Hall for as long
as you like. Tony and I would love to
have you.'

'May I come today?'

'This minute, if you like.'

'Then I will, Gage, and thanks
awfully.'

'How will you get here? Would you
like me to fetch you?'

Terry looked up at Blaise.

'Shall I let her fetch me?'

'Perhaps you'd better. I must do a
spot of work.'

Terry spoke into the telephone.

'If it wouldn't be a fearful curse to
you, Gage, I'd love you to fetch me. You
know Rossdown? Well, go straight
through the village, a mile and a half

down the Crowborough road, and you'll see a house with nice yew hedges and an iron gate — it's called Russet Place. You'll see a brass plate up with the name Dr. Farlong.'

A sudden tinkle of laughter from Gage.

'Don't tell me your incurable passion for doctors has been satisfied. You always were quite impossible about anything with an M.D. or F.R.C.S. after its name.'

Terry squeezed Blaise's hand very tightly and answered:

'My incurable passion for doctors is quite definitely satisfied.'

'Wonders never cease,' said Gage. 'I've often thought of you while I was in Paris and imagined you brooding under mother's wing. I'm very intrigued, darling. Tony's in his studio. I must go and break the news to him. Then I'll get out the Sunbeam and I ought to be with you within an hour.'

Terry hung up the receiver.

Blaise had put down his pipe. He

drew her into his arms and held her close.

'Wicked child — what have you been saying?'

'What you heard.' She stood on tiptoe and touched his chin with her lips. 'Gage knows I've always adored the medical profession. She asked me if my incurable passion was satisfied, and I said definitely 'Yes.''

He drew a deep breath. What an enchanting mixture she was of child and woman — the most fascinating person he had ever known — like an April day swinging lightly from tears to laughter. An almost mischievous twinkle in the limpid eyes — and the promise of amazing passion in the full, sweet lips. It struck him suddenly that if she were to wake up and regret this sudden madness, life would indeed be over for him. He was frightened. Fate had such a hideous way of offering something with one hand and taking it away with the other.

'I hope to God you won't find me

unsatisfactory as time goes on,' he said, with his lips against her hair.

'I know I shan't — because we have everything in common. We love the same things, don't we?'

'Yes, we seem to do that.'

'Do you know what I want more than anything in the world?' she asked in her quick, impulsive fashion.

'What, dear?'

'To start a new garden, with you to teach me how to grow all the flowers that we both like. To make you terribly, terribly happy — to make you feel that you simply hate your long list of patients because you can't get back to me as soon as you'd like to do.'

'Oh, my sweet, don't say things like that and expect me to remain sane. I think you're the most adorable person God ever made.'

She sighed and pressed her cheek to his shoulder.

'Isn't it funny that I don't care what anybody says or thinks — so long as you love me this way?'

'This is where the elderly doctor has, very much against his will, to cast aside romance, and consider realities. You're promising me heaven, Terry, and God knows the later years of my marriage with Ruth have been hell. I ask nothing more of life — providing you still feel the same when the divorce is through — than to have you for my own and to start afresh with you in the way you describe. But it seems more than I deserve.'

'I think I'm rather lucky — I might have had to stamp on my passion for doctors and marry a pork butcher,' she said.

'The pork butcher might have been a better proposition from the financial point of view, my dear.'

'I hate money,' said Terry blithely.

'Oh, you baby! But one has to live, you know.'

'Doctors can always make a little, can't they?'

'It may not be so easy, sweetheart. This doctor's reputation won't be too good when the divorce court's through with it. That's why I want you to be serious and to think well before you finally link your life with mine. It'll be uphill work for us, Terry. Fighting down disgrace — even though we have done nothing disgraceful.'

'I know all that, but I'd rather fight it down with your arms around me.'

He held her closer.

'I think I shall find it very easy — with you to hold.'

She breathed quickly and lifted her lips to his kiss. Then, when he lifted his head, she gave a queer, broken little laugh, and moved away from him.

'I think it's just as well Gage is coming to fetch me away. I feel quite disgraceful.'

'I think it's as well you are going, darling.'

'But I shall see you soon, shan't I?'

'But of course. I'll come and see you.'

'Then I shan't mind what happens.'

'We'll just have to await developments.'

'I suppose your — your wife' — she grimaced over the word — 'will be surprised that we don't defend?'

Blaise shrugged his shoulders.

'I don't think she'll mind so long as she gets her freedom.'

'I can't stay with the Thorntons very long — but Gage is a marvellous friend, and she'll suggest something.'

'What will you say to your mother now?'

'I shall write and ask her to send on my things to Frog's Hall. She and Barbara can think what they like. They've been beastly to me — I honestly can't say I'm sorry we're through.'

Blaise looked at his wrist-watch.

'Heavens, child, I must go. I still have a list of patients — though doubtless a few more doors will be shut today. I want to see Beggland about the practice, too, and then let Heslop know that I don't mean to defend.'

Terry watched him put some instruments into a case. She found it rather exciting to watch him. She thought:

'How marvellous it will be when I'm his wife — when I can help him clean those instruments and get things ready.'

Blaise, folding up a stethoscope, saw her rapt gaze fixed on him, and a smile lit up his face.

'Why are you looking at me like that, most engaging person?'

'I was thinking,' she said shyly, 'how thrilling it will be when I can help you with your work.'

He went on smiling a trifle sadly. He seemed to hear an echo of Ruth's hard voice, sneering at him because he liked to amuse himself in the winter evenings by cleaning up his surgical appliances — making little experiments with splints — interesting himself in his job.

'It's all such a bore,' she had said. 'Why can't you shove the damn things into a drawer and come out and play Bridge?'

He snapped the lock of his case and looked at Terry earnestly.

'Do you like Bridge, Terry?'

'Loathe it,' she said. 'Can't play — I simply refused to learn, because I dreaded being dragged into Mummy's Bridge-parties.'

Blaise raised an eyebrow and grinned like a boy.

'We're certainly a pair, my child. Well, I must be off, but I'll see you soon. Don't forget to weigh up all the pros and cons, and when I see you again — '

'When you see me again I shall just tell you again that I don't want to leave you,' she whispered.

He kissed her with almost desperate tenderness.

'God bless you, my darling. I can't believe my luck yet — but you've changed the whole world for me.'

She saw him off at the gate, and, because there was a frantic little desire in her heart to step into that car and go with him, she sought refuge in flippancy. But she thought how awful it would be if, when they met again, he no longer had any use for her.

311

'Good-bye, nicest of doctors. I don't mind you giving all your lady patients heart-failure — but don't let any of them affect *your* pulse-beats.'

He switched on the engine, leaned out of the car, and gave her a long, passionate look.

'There won't be any increase in the tempo of my pulse-beats until I hold you in my arms again, Terry.'

She waved to him as he drove off, then turned slowly and walked down the flagged path, along the herbaceous border, and looked at his delphiniums through a mist of tears.

13

Terry dined that night with the Thorntons at Frog's Hall in a condition of complete content. That was what love had done for her. She felt that she was soaring up toward the stars. The trifling worries of a mundane world were left behind her. Certainly nobody would have dreamed that she had just been disgraced in public, run away from home and was about to face the ordeal of being cited in a divorce case.

Nothing seemed to matter now that Blaise Farlong had need of her. She was conscious of a pure, unstinted pleasure in that thought and in the knowledge that he was the one man on earth for her.

She sat at the long refectory table with her friend, Gage, on one side of her and Anthony Thornton on the other. Friends, both of them. They had listened to her story and believed it.

'It may sound incredible — and undoubtedly is most extra-ordinary,' Tony Thornton's verdict had been, 'but I'm prepared to believe that what you say is true, because my experience of life tallies with the old saying: 'Truth is stranger than fiction.' And a jealous unscrupulous woman will do any dirty thing. It was an excellent chance for Mrs. Farlong to get rid of her husband.'

Gage had said:

'So long as he cares for you, Terry, and is going to make you happy, I don't see what it matters about the divorce. Fiddle-sticks to the reputation and disgrace. I'm just like you. I'd have gone through anything to be with Tony, only luckily for me he was free and unattached when we met.'

Tonight for the first time since she had started out on her walking-tour Terry knew what it was to feel at peace. It was such a blessed relief to be away from the suspicion and resentment which had been cast upon her by her mother and sister. She could well imagine the atmosphere at home at this moment — her mother overcome with horror at what had occurred, and Barbara wailing about her prestige with Francis and the Colroyds.

Terry would have been sincerely sorry for them, and more remorseful that she should be the unwilling cause of casting a slur upon the good name of the family, had they been a little kinder, a little more charitable over the affair. But she knew that both her mother and Barbara were thinking more of themselves and their reputations than of her own welfare. So she hardened her heart toward them.

She had written to her mother this morning and asked that her belongings should be sent to her at Frog's Hall. She had said that she would not trouble them again and that she hoped the divorce case would not affect their lives too seriously.

A little wistfully she wondered if life held for her such happiness as these two, Gage and Tony had found together. A more admirably matched pair she had never known.

Gage Thornton was slender and graceful, with a delicate, sensitive face, curly brown hair, and large eyes almost as blue as forget-me-nots. A woman of twenty-six — but absurdly young for that — with swift, bird-like movements and a trilling, infectious laugh. She had known hard times. She had worked for her living. In Paris, Terry remembered how hard Gage had worked. But always with that gay courage and ready laugh which was what had first endeared her to the heart of Anthony Thornton when he had met her abroad.

They were so beautifully mated, Terry thought, looking with affection from one to another. Tony was as dark as Gage was fair — finely built, brown as an Indian, and with a sense of humour as unlimited as hers. They seemed to laugh their way through life together. And life for them was a glorious adventure. Tony had a little money of his own and was going to make a lot. His portraits were successful. The critics thought him one of the most brilliant young painters of the day. Of course, he had painted his wife a dozen times — he was never tired of using her as a model. Terry had promised to sit for him. Her suggestion that she should only stay at Frog's Hall a few days had immediately been downed by both husband and wife. Their house was open to her for as long as she needed a home, which, Gage declared, was until the divorce was over.

'Of course you must stay with us,' Gage had said. 'We'd love you to, and you're such a babe still, Terry, you want looking after — until your doctor can take on the job for life.'

Terry felt certain she would not need much persuasion. She adored Frog's Hall. It was so full of beauty. Both of them artists, the Thorntons had decorated and furnished the old house with perfect taste and judgment.

Tony himself had planned the structural alterations. Frog's Hall had been an old farmhouse in a dilapidated condition when they had first taken it. Now it had all the comforts of modernisation combined with the old-world charm. And, as Gage told Terry, they loved every stick and stone of it.

It was a rare thing, all this perfection and happiness; two attractive people who adored each other and who had a genius for creating loveliness and happiness about them.

She allowed her thoughts to wander to the possibilities of her own future. There would be nothing like this for her and poor old Blaise. Poor darling struggling doctor — he had no money and she had nothing. There would be no Frog's Hall for them. Had he not warned her that they would be poor — that they would have to live down disgrace and have an uphill fight? But she was undaunted by the prospect. It seemed to her that love can surmount any difficulties.

When she had first stood in the circle of Blaise's arms and received his first passionate kiss, she had known that as long as she lived she could never love or belong to any other man. If they were to be poor, it did not matter so long as they possessed that priceless jewel of mutual passion and understanding. Once upon a time she had envied Gage. But now she envied nobody in the world, because the man she had chosen for a lover had told her that if she did not change her mind he wanted her with him — always.

'You're very quiet, Terry.' Anthony Thornton's voice interrupted her reverie. 'Have a grape.'

'I'd love one,' said Terry, 'and if I'm quiet it's just because I'm thinking how marvellous life is at the moment.'

The dark, very handsome eyes of Tony Thornton cast a whimsical look at the girl on his right and then rested on the dainty figure of his wife sitting at the other end of the long table. Gage looked rather like a Goya picture, he thought, in the new evening dress which she had just brought back from Paris. Black and white lace, tight waisted, with a long full skirt and red roses pinned on the narrow strap across one white, slender shoulder.

'Darling,' he said, 'I fear your girlfriend is shockingly unmoral. She ought to be brooding in sorrow over her sins, instead of which she sits and thinks how marvellous life is.'

'But she hasn't committed a sin, poor child,' said Gage.

'But the world thinks so, and you *know* the world is always right,' said Tony.

'Don't be so absurd,' said Gage, with her bird-like laughter.

'I'm beginning to wish I *had* sinned,' said Terry, 'since I get all the blame.'

'Now, Tony,' said Gage, 'this is all your doing. You've done nothing but encourage Terry to forget that she's a nicely brought-up child since she arrived.'

'I don't like nicely brought-up children,' said Tony. 'I loved you, darling, because you'd been dragged up.'

Laughing, they all three rose and wandered into the drawing-room for coffee. Later, Tony wandered off into the garden to take his wife's two Cairn terriers for a look at the rabbits.

It was a lovely summer's night. Terry and Gage sat on the window-seat, the green brocade curtains drawn back and the windows wide open, so that they could see the moonlight on the lawn. They could see, too, the reflection of the moon and stars in the lily-pond in the sunken garden just opposite the house.

Terry leaned her head back, half closed her eyes, and drew a long breath of her cigarette.

'Oh, Gage, the peace of it here.'

'Poor dear — you must have been through purgatory at home.'

'It's been pretty bad. Gage, when we last met, who would have thought such an astounding thing would have happened to me?'

'It *is* astounding, but, if good has

come out of the evil, what does it matter? If this doctor had been a swine or a fool and you hadn't liked each other, how much more difficult it would have been.'

'Yes,' said Terry in a low voice. 'I don't know what would have happened. I could have defended, but the slur would have stayed, and mother and Barbara would never have let me forget it.'

'You've never been happy in your own home, Terry. You were always so different from the family. This is the best thing that could have occurred. Am I going to like your doctor? Will he really make you happy?'

She asked the question with her gaze fixed earnestly on her friend. Terry was so much younger than she was, but so much in sympathy with her. She loved Terry. Neither of them had swerved from that devotion which had commenced in Paris in those days when Terry had been a shy, reticent child out of her element in a crowd of girls who thought only of clothes and affairs; and Gage had been a hard-working pupil teacher adoring her art and hating the hack-work of her profession.

She saw a light in Terry's hazel eyes which convinced her that this Dr. Farlong, whatever he was, had awakened in Terry the same intense feeling that Tony had roused in her — something rare and fine and deathless.

'If Blaise marries me when the divorce is over, I shall be the happiest woman in the world,' said Terry. 'And I know you'll like him, Gage. He's utterly different from Tony. Your Tony is handsome and brilliant and witty — and successful. Blaise in the eyes of the world is rather a failure. He has the sort of face I like — strong features, wonderful eyes — and he's clever; if his health hadn't been so groggy since the war he would have been in a far better position than the one he's in now. But he's had a lot of illness, and I should think that woman Ruth must have given him hell. He's sad and tired. I want to mother him. We can joke together — he has a store of humour, only it's been crushed by that woman. And his flowers — oh, Gage, you can't think how wonderful he is with a garden. You know I worship gardens — we have all that in common and something more.'

'He sounds a dear,' said Gage, 'but, whatever you do, don't let yourself be swayed by pity. It's no good marrying a man one's just sorry for.'

'Of course I shan't!' said Terry quite heatedly. 'I'm not at all swayed by pity. I'm desperately in love.'

'Then I'm glad, darling,' said Gage, 'and long may it last.'

'Yours is lasting.'

'Yes, Tony and I adore each other, and always will, I think. But life has been particularly kind to us.'

'It may be kind to Blaise and to me,' said Terry. 'And I honestly don't mind having to fight for it.'

'That's typical of you, my dear. You always had courage, and, as Mr. Henley said, 'It isn't life that counts — it's the courage you bring to it.''

Tears suddenly burnt Terry's eyelids. She looked out at the starlit garden and felt an overwhelming desire for the presence of her lover.

'It's funny,' she whispered, 'that Mrs. Farlong tried to do me the most dreadful harm and she's given me this happiness.'

'All the same, the woman ought to be boiled,' said Gage.

'Yes, it was a pretty shoddy thing for her to do.'

'It'll be a change for your doctor to have somebody like you for a partner, my dear.'

'I only hope I shall be all that he wants,' said Terry. 'But there's a long wait ahead of us, Gage. It'll be six months before we can be together.'

'If you mean to wait for the divorce.'

Terry bit her lip.

'I've got to leave that to him.'

'Would you go and live with him if he asked you to?'

Terry raised brilliant eyes.

'Yes.'

'I'd have done the same,' said Gage, 'if I'd been in that position with my Tony. When will you see him again?'

'Perhaps he'll come over tomorrow — he said he'd try. And then you'll understand why I'm so happy in spite of this *débâcle* at home.'

Gage Thornton did understand, very clearly, when she met Blaise Farlong that next day. He telephoned to say that he would be over directly after lunch and reach Frog's Hall just before three. Gage, not having seen him before, was immediately struck by the thought that he looked very thin and gaunt — old for his thirty-two years. But Terry was infinitely satisfied to note that he looked better than he had done since the trouble commenced. Gone was that miserable, ashamed expression which had lain in his eyes hitherto when he faced her. There was a new understanding between them — a deep and lovely one — and it looked out from his eyes when he greeted her after he had shaken hands with Gage.

'It's more than good of you, Mrs. Thornton, to let me come,' he said.

Gage knew then, at once, that she liked him, and understood the attraction that he had for Terry. A charming person with a charming voice and smile; and no fool. It was very important to Gage that one should not be tied up to a fool. For, after all, boredom is the greatest evil in marriage. With Tony one could never be bored — and with a man like Blaise Farlong it would be the same, providing that he had an intelligent companion. Ruth Farlong was obviously a woman of no intelligence and little sense.

'I'm very glad to meet you. I've heard so much about you from Terry,' said Gage, when they were seated in the drawing-room. 'Terry and I are very old friends, and the man whom Terry marries must also be a friend of mine.'

Blaise coloured a little self-consciously, but he thought her most gracious and attractive.

'It's awfully nice of you,' he said. 'I hope we shall be — very good friends. Of course you know everything. I'm afraid it's rather a beastly business, and I'm terribly grieved that this child' — he put out a hand and took Terry's — 'should be involved in it.'

'This child doesn't seem to mind very much,' said Terry, and felt a wild thrill of the pulses at the touch of Blaise's long, fine fingers against her wrist.

'I'm quite sure,' said Gage, 'that the beastliness, as you call it, won't affect Terry much. She seems quite happy in spite of it.'

'It's all amazing,' said Blaise. 'We little thought things would work out this way.'

Gage, with exquisite discretion, suddenly remembered an appointment and disappeared. Terry sat still, her heart beating very fast, her eyes fixed on the Persian carpet under her feet.

Blaise looked round the beautiful room. Sunlight streamed through the tall windows. The green brocade curtains shimmered in the glow, and a huge vase of delphiniums standing on an old walnut table caught his attention. But only for an instant. Then the beautiful room was forgotten and the brown-haired, hazel-eyed girl in it drew his whole attention. He stood up, walked to her side, took her arms, and drew her on to her feet.

'Terry,' he said.

She looked up at him, and found herself trembling ridiculously.

'Yes?'

'I can hardly believe that it's true,' he said.

'What?'

'That you really care like this about me — enough to forget the ugliness of what's happening to us.'

'It's true, all the same.'

'My dear,' he said, 'when I woke up this morning I was happier than I've felt for years. I even found it difficult to regret anything — because it had given me you.'

She looked up at him, her lips quivering into a smile.

'It sounded so queer when Gage spoke of you as the man I was going to marry. Am I?'

'God, yes, if you'll take me,' he said.

Then she was in his arms and her small hands were locked about his neck.

'Oh, my darling!' he said, and kissed her. For a moment they stood in a close embrace while the moments sped by, and there was no sound save the song of a linnet in the trees just outside, and the hum of a bee which had found its way into the drawing-room by mistake and buzzed inquisitively round the flowers which stood by the open window.

'I suppose,' said Terry — a flushed and breathless Terry when he released her — 'that we're no further ahead?'

'Not much, darling. Heslop has been told we aren't going to defend, so now I've just signed the petition for divorce and sent a note to my wife through

Heslop to tell her to go ahead and get it over as soon as possible.'

'And your practice?'

He lit a cigarette and began to walk up and down the room. She followed him with her gaze, familiar now with that restless way which he had of walking up and down; one hand in his pocket and the other lifting his cigarette to his lips.

'I had a chat with Beggland this morning. Of course he'd heard — everybody in Rossdown has heard about the divorce — and he was inclined to be stuffy with me. Just wanted to show me he didn't approve, don't you know.'

'Isn't it queer,' said Terry, 'how anxious people are to disapprove?'

He gave her a whimsical smile.

'Well, my sweet, we must give the devil his due. We happen to know we're innocent victims, but these people don't know it, and if they're outraged it's according to their lights. We mustn't lose our sense of proportion over it.'

'No, I suppose you're right,' admitted Terry. 'Well, what did he say?'

'He just advised me to get rid of the practice as soon as I could, and he happens to have a young cousin who has just been qualified and wants a small country practice. It's quite possible he may buy mine.'

'Then you might leave Rossdown quicker than you think.'

'I hope so,' he said grimly. 'It isn't too pleasant there at the moment. One good lady who used to bring her schoolgirl daughter to me wrote yesterday to say she was finding another medical adviser. I'm not fit, you see, to be the doctor of an innocent young girl after my behaviour with you.'

There was no laughter in Terry's eyes now. She clenched her hands and looked red and resentful, like an angry boy.

'It's hateful! It's so insulting.'

'It isn't pleasant, but that's what we're in for, Terry. Are you sure you understand that, my dear? You'll be insulted, too.'

She moved impulsively to his side, took his arm with her two hands, and pressed her face against it.

'Of course I understand. I was only angry for your sake — it's so unjust when you're so utterly to be trusted with any girl. But I know we're both open to insult, and I'm ready for it — so long as you love me.'

'I'm beginning to love you more than I thought possible,' he answered, and kissed the brown, bent head passionately.

'I can't bear not to be with you all the time.'

'I feel like that myself. I missed you like hell when you'd gone yesterday.'

She raised a flushed young face to his.

'Blaise, when you leave Rossdown, you're going to look for another practice, aren't you?'

'Yes, I must.'

'Where will you find it?'

'Heaven knows. But I shall have to get away from everybody who has ever known me — go to some other part of England.'

'I must go with you.'

He put an arm about her and pressed his cheek against her hair.

'Darling child, I shall want you with me, but I can't let you come until I'm in a position to marry you.'

'But, Blaise, in cases of divorce, do people wait till they are married? I always thought they went off together.'

'Oh, my sweet, but that can't happen to us. How can I let it happen? I feel so responsible for you now — I'm a married man and you're so young — '

'Blaise!' she broke in. 'You'll drive me quite crazy if you go on saying those things. I'm twenty-one — and I love you. I won't be treated like a piece of Dresden china that has to be wrapped up in cotton-wool.'

He put her away from him with hands that shook a little. He had been through much, suffered much, and the desire to take all that Terry offered was terrific. After all, their names and lives were irreparably linked, and under ordinary circumstances she would without doubt have gone away with him before the divorce. Six months was a long time to wait. Why should they — if she didn't want to? He wanted her — there was little doubt about that in his mind and heart. But it still went against the grain with Blaise Farlong to take advantage of this position. He was sorely tempted, and he tried to argue; to resist her.

'My dearest, you must help me to keep my head or I shall certainly lose it. It may mean the divorce won't be through until the winter — you'll have to stay with friends or arrange something of the sort, and I must be by myself and hunt for a job and gather my fallen fortunes together. Good God,' he added, knitting his brows fiercely, 'how can I ask you to share all those difficulties — to come to me before I have any sort of home to offer you?'

Terry, white now under her tan, and shaking, looked him straight in the eyes.

'Blaise, I may be all wrong, but I think it's you who are wrong. It would be ten times worse for us to stand the misery of the next six months apart from each other. I have no friends to go to. I can't accept charity anyhow, even from darlings like Gage and Tony. It means I shall have to get out and get a job. Live alone in London. I should go quite mad.'

He looked at her with troubled eyes.

'You can't do that, of course.'

'And you,' she continued, 'would drag out a miserable existence by yourself! No; we're letting the divorce go through — we're letting the world think we're lovers. Why shouldn't it be true? Just because you're decent and good and don't want to hurt me, you're hesitating. But I want to come with you, Blaise. I want to stand by you in all the trouble — hunt for work with you — *anything* — but don't leave me alone!'

She was crying now. Dismayed, he caught her close to him and covered her face with kisses.

'My little love, you musn't cry! Terry — darling child — if you feel as badly about it as that, I won't leave you alone.'

She trembled against him, pressing her wet eyes against his shoulder.

'Don't you want me?'

'You know I do, but I didn't think it right — '

'It must be right if we love each other — if we mean to marry when we can.'

'The moment the decree is absolute, I want to make you my wife, Terry,' he said hoarsely, 'but don't blame me, darling, if I'm afraid of hurting you — of ruining your life in any way — of letting you do a thing like this on impulse.'

'You're a dear, Blaise,' she whispered, 'and it's like you to look at it that way. But I do know my own mind. I can stay with Gage until you've got rid of the practice. Then, when you leave Ross-down, let me come with you — please!'

The desire to take her was too strong

for him. He felt like a starving man who sees bread and wine laid before him. He knew that Ruth had never roused in him the passionate tenderness that this slim, brown-haired girl had power to stir from the very depths of his being.

'I hope to God I shan't be doing wrong,' he said hoarsely, 'but I don't think I can help taking you when I go. I love you so much.'

A knock on the drawing-room door made them fly apart, he to light another cigarette, she to smooth back her tumbled hair. A maid entered with a letter on a salver, which she handed to Terry.

Terry, breathless, wildly excited, looked at the handwriting and grimaced at Blaise as the maid retired.

'From my mother.'

'Oh, Lord,' said Blaise.

Terry sat down on the window-seat, drew him beside her, and opened her letter.

It was not very long. And it had no beginning, and started straight away with the words: 'I am sending your belongings, as you desire, to Mrs. Thornton's house.' It went on to say that both she and Barbara were stunned by the whole affair; she, her mother, found it impossible to forgive or condone her outrageous conduct, and the doors of her home would be closed to her in future.

'You have always been an unsatisfactory daughter,' the letter concluded, 'but you might have considered the mother who did her best to bring you up decently, and avoided bringing public disgrace upon her and your poor sister. Barbara shares with me the feeling that she would rather not see you any more. We shall find it difficult enough to live down the scandal. No doubt your punishment will come when you wake up and realise that this married man to whom you have gone is a blackguard and a brute. For your father's sake I feel it my duty to say that if you are in financial need you can apply to me for money, but under no circumstances do I intend to help support this disgraceful man who has helped to ruin you.

'MOTHER.'

Terry's face was set and hard when she finished reading the letter.

'What do you think of that?' she asked Blaise with a quick, nervous little laugh.

Blaise Farlong's face was a dull red, and his hands were clenched.

'My God, she must have a heart of stone. Your own mother — it's incredible!'

'No,' said Terry. 'She's never cared for me. It was always Barbara. And you must try and understand that my mother is a woman of strict convention and rigid principles, and, on the face of it, I have caused a horrible scandal and disgraced the family name.'

'It strikes home what a damnable thing it is,' he said in a low voice.

340

'I like the bit about not intending 'to support this disgraceful man,'' said Terry with a broken laugh. 'She needn't worry. I wouldn't take a penny from her after this — not if I starved; neither would you!'

She suddenly tore the letter in half, crumpled it in her hand, and flung herself into his arms.

'I don't care! I don't care, Blaise. You see — what we've both got to face. But it doesn't matter to me if you love me as much as I love you.'

He held her fiercely and looked down at her, his grey eyes warm and bright.

'Then that settles it, my sweet, my lovely one. We'll face it together. I'll take you with me — look after you now and always!'

14

At half past two on the first day of September, Blaise Farlong's black fabric car pulled up outside the wrought-iron gateway of Russet Place.

Blaise stepped out and gave his hand to the girl who sat beside him.

'For the last time, Terry. I must have stopped outside this gate thousands of times. Queer to think that this will be the last.'

'There's something rather tragic about it, Blaise,' she said.

'No. You've brought me so much happiness, my darling, that there isn't much tragedy attached to it — only a pang because I'm leaving the garden. I wanted to come and look at it once again before the new man takes over. It will never look again just as I have left it — so few people have the same mind about gardening.'

'Thank goodness you and I have,' she said happily.

He took her hand, and, like very young lovers, they walked together down the flagged path and turned across a wide sweep of lawn toward the herbaceous border. While they walked slowly along, Terry turned her thoughts to the first day when she had strolled down this same border with Blaise; that first summer's morning when he had shown her his flowers and they had been strangers to each other.

Since then, how completely and absolutely things had changed! Barely two short months had elapsed and today they came here to say farewell to this garden, strangers no more. Lovers, passionately in love and about to set forth on the great adventure of life — the life they were going to lead together.

So much had been crowded into those eight weeks. Terry had stayed at Frog's Hall with the Thorntons while Blaise settled up his affairs. But he had not let a day pass without driving over to see her. And now they knew each other so well. Familiarity had bred no contempt; only respect and that certain knowledge that in most things they saw eye to eye. On the firm rock of complete sympathy about the little trifling things that matter so much more than most people imagine, they were going to build their house of love. He had had his experience — a bitter one. She had had none. But neither of them doubted that that house which they would build together would stand unshaken.

Neither of them had any illusions about the difficulties which they were about to face. Blaise, who had been through the mill, was bound to be a little sceptical — less wildly romantic than Terry, who had the flaming optimism of youth to back her up. But his fears were for her and not for himself. Again and again he warned her — begged her to think well before she took the step she wanted to take. But she never wavered in her determination to stand beside him and fight with him, so on the face of it he must needs take her at her word.

His practice at Rossdown had dwindled pitifully during those two months at Russet Place. Only a few staunch friends and admirers of his work continued to call in a medical man who was said to have committed adultery with a young girl under his own roof while his wife was away.

All the rebuffs, the disdainful looks thrown at him in the village, the icy scorn behind the courtesy of such people as Dr. and Mrs. Beggland, hurt Blaise badly. He was a man of honour, and even the armour of Terry's marvellous love and sympathy which she had cast about him could not be proof against all the shafts.

On more than one occasion when he came to Frog's Hall with a tight, grim look about his mouth she had guessed that he had suffered some fresh humiliation. It had taken all her sweetness, her gallant humour, to charm away the demons of resentment which were fighting inside the man's soul.

Now those days had passed. The practice had been sold, purchased with the house and furniture by Beggland's young cousin, Dr. Harrison. Harrison was unmarried. His one passion and hobby outside his medical work was photography. He had come down from town to talk business with Blaise, and had looked at the garden only from the photographer's point of view.

'Quite a good study for the camera,' he had called it.

But he had frankly admitted that he would have neither time nor patience to work in the garden himself. Blaise knew quite well that within a few short months the loveliness would become a neglected wilderness. Thorns, brambles, and weeds would spring up among the tender plants that he had cherished — choke them out of existence. That wrenched his heart a little. But Terry had made everything so easy to bear. He was amazed at the change she had wrought in his life.

The divorce was going through — taking its normal course. What Ruth was doing he did not know and did not care. But sometimes he wondered grimly what she had thought when she had heard through his solicitors that he was not defending the case. But, whatever the thoughts, she showed no inclination to alter her mind over the affair.

There had been a lot to do settling up the business. But now it was all done. Various bits of furniture, some pictures and ornaments belonging to Ruth, had been sent to her at her brother's house. Everything else Blaise had sold with the practice to young Harrison. He regretted nothing. He did not want to keep anything that would remind him of his disastrous life with his wife.

A few days ago Gage Thornton had driven Terry over to help him make a final clearance. Then for the first time he had spoken to her at length about Priscilla. He had shown her the little nursery where Priscilla had laughed and played for such a brief spell. There he had collected a small chair and a few toys that had belonged to her.

'I want to put these in store with some of the personal belongings, such as my silver and linen and a few bits and pieces that belonged to my mother,' he told Terry. 'Do you mind, dear?'

She had looked at the little chair and picked up a pathetic woolly toy, and before she could control herself she had burst out crying.

'Your poor, *poor* little baby — it must have been so dreadful for you! Blaise darling, of *course* you must store these things. I want you to. I wouldn't have you forget your little girl for *anything*.'

With his arms about her he had told her much about Priscilla. It had gone to the depths of her heart to realise the

348

love this man had borne the child that he had lost. He adored children, and Priscilla had been the loveliest thing in his life with Ruth. Terry, loving him desperately, shared his grief and the tragedy of his memories. That moment between them had forged another link, and made her, if possible, dearer to him. Before they left that nursery, in her generous, impulsive way, Terry had put her arms about his waist and hugged him. With her cheek pressed against his arm she said:

'I want to make up for everything. One day, Blaise, there must be another Priscilla; that's something I can and will give you — one day!'

He had held her close to him, speechless for a while. Then, kissing her eyelids and the soft tan of her cheeks, he had whispered:

'That will be something heavenly to look forward to. I only hope to God things will turn out all right for us, sweetheart, and that we shall have a spot of money. I'm not going to let you bear me children in poverty. But the thought of you as the mother of my child is simply glorious.'

Today the house was shut and locked, waiting for its new owner. When Blaise and Terry came for their farewell visit, there was nobody there except old King, the gardener whom Harrison was keeping on to cut the grass.

King touched his hat as Blaise and Terry passed him by, then looked after them, shaking his head gloomily. The doctor was the nicest gentleman he had ever worked for, and his departure was a personal loss to the old gardener.

It was a warm afternoon. The soft September sun drenched the garden with mellow light. In the long borders there were great masses of Michaelmas daisies in full bloom, a pale purple background for the bronze and red and yellow of the chrysanthemums. There were white daisies, too, like bright stars, and the shimmer of golden rod, and at the back of the house a wonderful show of roses — the second crop this year.

Arm in arm, Blaise and Terry looked at everything, then came to the place which Blaise called his nursery — the beds wherein he planted his delphinium seedlings.

Terry was filled with melancholy because those glorious delphiniums had come to an end of their blooming and the tall exquisite spikes were withered and dead.

'I hate them all to be dead,' she said in a grieved voice.

But Blaise stooped and touched a seedling which was still in flower; a fragile thing of azure blue and lavender with a pure white heart.

'This is still alive,' he said, 'and going to be rather a beauty. I hadn't named it. But I shall name it this minute — Teresa Mary, after you.'

Terry shook her head sadly.

'But Teresa Mary is going to be left behind. I can't bear it.'

Blaise stood up and turned to her with his swift wide smile.

'Cheer up, darling. I refuse to be

depressed today. Without you it would have broken me up to leave all my flowers. But having you makes such a difference, doesn't it?'

'I'm not half as nice as a delphinium.'

'Thank God you're more solid and lasting,' he laughed, and caught her hand and kissed it. 'I assure you, my child, a delphinium would be no wife for me. I'm a man who likes a few home comforts.'

She joined in his laughter.

'Then you're going to have an awful time. I'm a rotten cook, and the delphinium would be more decorative in the drawing-room.'

He laughed again and glanced at his wrist-watch.

'We mustn't spend too much time here, darling. We want to be in town by about six, don't we?'

She wrinkled her nose at him.

'Think of London — on this glorious day. Partridge-shooting begins today, Blaise.'

'I know,' he nodded. 'Neither of us is

going to like London much. Look here, shall we change our minds and steal a real honeymoon in Devon or Cornwall — or even Sussex?'

She was tempted, but she shook her head. They had made their plans and must be firm about it. They had both agreed that it would be foolish to waste money when it was so scarce. They must consider every penny. Only a half of Blaise's patients had settled their accounts, and every penny of the purchase-price that Harrison had given him for the practice and Russet Place must be put by — with that sum he would buy a new practice. It meant their livelihood. There was little enough cash in hand after Blaise had settled all the liabilities attached to his former life.

Terry, of course, had nothing of her own. Her mother had written to her once again, troubled, no doubt, by conscience, and offered her an allowance. But Terry had replied coldly and firmly that she required nothing, and that she hoped to be married to Dr.

Farlong as soon as the divorce was through and the decree made absolute. Since that they had not communicated with each other.

The kindness and sympathy shown to them by the Thorntons was unforgettable. Gage, herself, had insisted upon giving Terry the new charming dress and coat of green tweed, and little green cap to match, which she wore today. And Gage had slipped one or two very pretty silky things into Terry's suitcase when she had packed it this morning.

'Tony and I think you're very sensible not to wait and languish until the divorce is over,' she had said. 'We love your nice doctor, and we're quite certain you're both going to be very happy. That's all that counts.'

To Terry, as she walked back to the car with Blaise, it seemed, indeed, that that was all that counted — the knowledge that they were going to be perfectly happy, no matter what they had to face.

It was inevitable that she should regret that she must wait so many months before she could become his wife; she felt that they were stealing a happiness to which they had no real right. But he needed her and she wanted to go with him, and this mutual feeling had given them the right — that and the circumstances which had thrown them so remarkably together.

The fight for existence was to begin at once, as soon as they got to town. They were going up to a small quiet hotel, and tomorrow Blaise would start the earnest search for a new and suitable practice in some remote part of England. The farther away from Sussex the better, because of the publicity to which they were both subjected, and Terry did not care where she went so long as she was with him.

'We shall start life right away as Dr. and Mrs. Farlong,' Blaise had told her at Frog's Hall last night when they had made their final arrangements. 'And one day — may it come soon — we'll just slip away and make it all legal. But nothing can make me feel that you don't belong to me now just as much as though the registrar had confirmed it.'

Terry felt strangely like that, too. A narrow gold band shone on the fourth finger of her left hand. Her wedding ring. And this was like her wedding day. It made her smile to think of the ceremony that might have been had she never met Blaise, and been forced by her mother into a typical society wedding.

She had always had a horror of display. Let Barbara delight in white satin, orange blossom, wedding-bells, a crowd, a reception, cameras clicking, and the strains of 'O perfect love' to qualify it all.

Blaise had stopped the car on Ditchling Common, coming away from Frog's Hall, and had slipped that wedding ring on her finger.

'"Till death us do part," Terry, my darling,' he had said, and kissed her.

And that had been their wedding

— just that brief moment out there in the sunshine, with the green sweep of the Downs behind them and the blue of the sky above them and a solitary thrush to carol a hymn. Blaise opened the gates of Russet Place to let Terry pass through.

'What I do regret,' he said, 'is that we haven't a cottage and garden to which I could take some of my plants. This is just the time to transplant seedlings — and it would have been nice if we could have taken 'Teresa Mary' with us.'

'Well,' said Terry, 'when we get our new practice, don't you think Dr. Harrison might allow you to come and take a few of the plants?'

'I daresay,' said Blaise; 'but I don't think I ever want to come back to this place after today.'

She snuggled near him in the car and put a hand over his knee.

'My poor Dr. Blaise — scorned as the bad man of Rossdown.'

His grey eyes twinkled at her. It was

very satisfying to her to reflect that those kind, clever eyes twinkled so often these days, and that all the humour, the boy, had been reclaimed in him. There was scarcely anything left to the bitter reticent man Ruth had left behind her.

'Don't you be so free with your remarks about the bad man,' he said. 'You're a bad woman yourself.'

'My dear mother would die of horror,' said Terry. 'But if this is being bad, then I wish I'd never been good. I'm so happy that I want to jump out of the car.'

'Well, for Lord's sake don't do that,' he said as they drove down the road toward London. 'It wouldn't suit me at all to have to stop and pick you up mangled or concussed or something.'

'That would be all right,' said Terry cheerfully. 'You're a good doctor.'

'I thought you said just now that I was a bad one.'

'How dare you argue with me, when I've only been married to you an hour?' said Terry.

He slowed down the car. For a moment they were alone on the white, sunlit road. He kissed her swiftly and warmly on the lips and throat.

'Angel! I love you so. I only wish to God you were my wife.'

'It doesn't worry me that I'm not — that's how bad *I* am!' she said dewy-eyed, cheeks flaming like the roses they had left in his garden.

Blaise returned to the wheel.

'This won't do. You're quite intoxicating, darling, and I shall drive you straight into the ditch if I don't calm down.'

His heart was singing within him. Life seemed glorious indeed. This was what he had always wanted — hoped for: somebody with whom he could share everything — sorrow and joy, work and jest. After the long years with Ruth, nagging, complaining, sulkily criticising him, Terry was as stimulating and refreshing as wine to a thirsty man.

She, silent a moment while the car sped on its way through the country, looked at the trees, which were poems of red and bronze and gold in the September sunlight, and felt that all her dreams had come true.

The old life at Wimbledon with mother and Barbara seemed to have faded into a sort of dim background which meant nothing at all. She could even laugh now at the horror which had first been hers when she had found herself involved with the Farlongs in a disgraceful divorce.

Today she was passionately glad that it had all happened. She knew not a single qualm at the thought that she was setting out this moment to begin a new, intimate life with Blaise. She wondered if she were shameless, but told herself that there could be nothing shameful in it. They loved each other. They understood each other. Everything that had happened to them before had been as tributaries which finally joined this great river down which they rushed fearlessly, gloriously, today.

In spite of all the plans, the vows of strict economy, the feeling that they must at once get to London and to work, they never reached town that night. Tea-time found them at a tiny cottage just off the London road somewhere on the borders of Sussex. An inviting board which said:

VICTORIA'S COTTAGE
TEAS: HOME MADE-CAKES

and a sign fashioned like a little Victorian lady in a crinoline, swinging in the breeze, had induced them to turn off the main road and drive a few yards down a lane until they found it.

It was an enchanting place, with diamond-paned windows, a crooked roof covered with stonecrop and lichen, and with masses of honeysuckle and creeper hiding the whitewashed walls. The tiny garden was vivid with the same sort of flowers that Blaise had left in his garden. A solitary delphinium, deeply blue, struggling against decay, quite close to the doorway, decided Blaise.

'Of course we must stay here — if there's such a thing in the cottage as a room — we must stay here tonight, Terry.'

'It would be too heavenly,' she said. 'I was dreading London. Do ask them, Blaise.'

Blaise found the owner of Victoria's Cottage. She was a widow of Devonshire extraction, with a soft Devon burr in her voice and a gentle smile. She and her seventeen-year old daughter had been serving teas here for the last two summers, and were going to continue it because it paid. People liked the garden and the old-fashioned Victorian atmosphere of the cottage, and the home-made Devonshire teas.

At first the woman, Mrs. Parcoombe, smilingly rejected the idea of putting the doctor and 'his wife' up for the night. But Blaise had an engaging manner, and Terry was so ecstatic about the place that the woman said she

362

would talk it over with her daughter.

The result was successful. Mrs. Parcoombe told them that there was one spare bedroom in Victoria's Cottage — very tiny — if they cared to have it, and offered it to them for the night.

So, for a few hours, London and the search for a practice and the difficulties attached to lack of means was spared these two who were setting out to make the best of life together. Victoria's Cottage became a paradise for lovers. In the enchanted surroundings of the attractive, pretty little place, so remote from the world although so close to the main London road, Terry took the final step across the boundary line.

The September night was warm and starlit. For some time after the simple but excellent supper served to them by Mrs. Parcoombe they sat out in the garden.

'The smell of flowers and warm earth and your cigarette are most ravishing,' Terry told him.

He, with his arm about her, threw

away the cigarette and put his lips against her hair.

'And you smell nicer than anything.'

Then she became suddenly grave and ceased her jesting. Her brown young face looked pale and pure in the moonlight. Her eyes were ecstatic.

'There isn't a soul on earth that I envy, Blaise,' she said in a hushed voice. 'But every other woman on earth would envy me if they knew how happy I was.'

'God knows I'm happy, myself,' he said.

Just for a fleeting instant his mind reverted to another night, many years ago — the first night of his honeymoon with Ruth. And the difference between that night and this was inconceivable. He had been happy — yes, he had been young and in love with his wife. But it had been a different sort of happiness. A far more conventional and ordinary kind. And of course anything shared with Ruth had been conventional. They had not sat in a tangled garden of flowers outside a humble cottage. In full evening dress, they had danced at the Grand Hotel at Eastbourne, which Ruth had chosen and to which he had taken her.

Deliberately he shut his brain upon the past and turned his thoughts wholly to the present. Here was something so much more enchanting — and because of its very simplicity so much more likely to endure.

'I'm glad we like the same things, sweetheart,' he said.

'So am I,' she said. Then, with a funny little smile, she added: 'I'm a stupid, but I've got a funny feeling that I want to pick that delphinium by the door and take it up to our room and put it in water there, where I can see it.'

It was for those foolish fancies that he adored her. He said:

'We'll ask Mrs. Parcoombe.'

That good woman was only too willing that the delphinium should be plucked. She cut it and gave it to the young lady who seemed so anxious to have it.

'It's drooping a bit, madam, but

please to have it if you wish.'

So Terry carried it off to the tiny bedroom where there were only two candles to flicker bravely in the darkness and cast enormous shadows on the white-washed ceiling and walls.

Blaise watched Terry while she carefully trimmed the stalk and then placed the tall spike in the earthenware water-jug on the old-fashioned corner washstand. It was immediately reflected upon the ceiling. They both looked up and laughed.

'What a giant bloom!'

Arm in arm they stood a moment looking at the blue delphinium. It was a lovely thing, nodding from the commonplace brown jug in the corner. Then they examined the rest of the room with some amusement. It was so small, there was only just room to walk round the huge old-fashioned double bestead with its white spread and clothes turned neatly down. Over the mantelpiece was a motto in a frame:

Suffer Little Children To Come Unto Me.

Blaise looked at it and then suddenly took Terry in his arms and hid his face against her soft young breast.

'Oh, Terry, Terry, you're such a child, yourself. I'm so much older. God forgive me if I'm doing wrong in letting this happen. It's going to mean all your life — and no drawing back tomorrow.'

'I don't want to draw back, and I want it to mean all my life,' she said. 'I love you, Blaise.'

He stroked her hair with one hand and with the other drew aside the faded cotton curtains which hung across the tiny casements. The September moon, big and yellow, shed a mellow radiance over the tiny garden.

He pulled the curtains again and looked down at the girl in his arms.

'I'm going to have one more cigarette and one more turn round the garden.'

He left her, and she turned blindly to the dressing-table, took off the green

367

beads which were twisted around her neck, and began to undress. She could not still her heart's frantic beating, nor had she any wish to stem the surging tide of emotion which was drowning her now. She only knew that she loved this man with whom she had come and for whom she had burnt her boats, and that to give herself to him wholly was a physical consummation which would perfect an already well-nigh perfect union between them.

When Blaise returned, there was only one candle burning on the chest of drawers, and in the huge bed lay Terry in blue silk pyjamas which Gage had given her — looking very small and sun-browned, her hair tumbled over the pillow.

Blaise sat down beside her and without a word gathered her close to him and put his lips to her eyes, sealing them with his kisses, then more fervently found her lips and stayed there for a long moment of breathless passion.

One blue petal dropped suddenly from the delphinium in the corner, fluttered softly to the floor, and lay there unnoticed in the warm, fragrant darkness.

Part Two

1

One cold February morning the following year, Mrs. Manstone sat alone at lunch in the dining-room at the Cedars; exchanged her pince-nez for her reading-glasses and looked through a letter which Davis had just brought to her.

When first she had seen the round familiar handwriting of her youngest daughter, she had decided to burn the letter unread. Not since Terry acknowledged the receipt of her luggage over six months ago had Mrs. Manstone received any communication from her. If in her heart of hearts she had sometimes felt a pang of anxiety, and an even bigger one of curiosity to know what was happening to Terry, she had refused to give way to the sentiment. Terry had behaved disgracefully and caused a terrible scandal.

Mrs. Manstone could not bring herself to pardon and condone the offence.

For some time after that paralysing scene in the Colroyds' drawing-room, Mrs. Manstone had been terrified that Francis might break his engagement with Barbara. However, last October, Barbara became Mrs. Francis Colroyd, with all the flourish of trumpets necessary to Mrs. Manstone's happiness. The unhappy subject of Terry and her lover had only been mentioned between Mrs. Manstone and her friend Margaret on one occasion. And then Mrs. Manstone had writhed under the other woman's sympathy.

With both her daughters gone, Mrs. Manstone had, of late, found this big house a little lonely and depressing. Perhaps it was that very feeling of loneliness which made her change her mind and read Terry's letter instead of burning it.

Terry wrote from an address in Devonshire: 'Thornbank, Chenwood, near Barnstaple.' The letter said:

'My dear Mother, — You may or may not wish to hear from me, but I thought that you might like to know that the decree was made absolute on the 2nd of February, and Blaise and I were married yesterday.

'According to the world, I suppose we have been 'living in sin' until now, but our legal marriage cannot make us any happier than we were.

'Blaise bought this practice just before Christmas. It's a very tiny one, but our perfect happiness makes any struggle worth while.

'I read about Barbara's wedding and wrote and wished her luck, but she didn't answer. I suppose you both find it impossible to forgive me. But here I am if you ever want to see me again.

'TERRY.'

When Mrs. Manstone reached the words 'living in sin' her cheeks became pink and she breathed quickly. She folded up the note, put it in her bag, and continued eating her pudding.

She had tried not to think about Terry and this doctor for whom she had wrecked her life. It was beyond her nature to understand or sympathise with such a state of affairs. And of course Terry's conduct had proved indisputably that she *had* been the cause of that divorce. All Mrs. Manstone's sympathies were with Ruth Farlong — the wronged and suffering wife.

She was undoubtedly relieved to think that Terry was now legally married to this man. And the natural maternal affection, still feebly flickering in her, was satisfied by this first-hand knowledge that the girl was all right. That she should be so happy seemed difficult to credit. Although, of course, one's Bible taught one that the wicked prosper.

It seemed all wrong to Mrs. Manstone that Terry should be so content, for she had committed so great a wrong against herself — her family — the laws of decency; while, on the other hand, poor Barbara, who had always been a good girl, had had nothing but misfortune since her wedding.

Her honeymoon, spent in the South of France, had been spoiled by an attack of measles — such a degrading disease to develop on one's honeymoon! She had spent three weeks in a nursing-home apart from her husband, who returned to the City disgruntled. His fastidious nature revolted from any such distressing illness, and when Barbara finally joined him in England her hair and beautiful complexion had suffered; she had looked blotchy and even haggard; and she confided to her mother that Francis was 'not very nice about it.'

The marriage had, in fact, not been a success except from a social and financial point of view. The young couple were now living in a flat in South Kensington, and Mrs. Manstone saw her daughter frequently. Barbara was never without a complaint. Francis appeared to be an unsatisfactory husband. A coldness had sprung up between Mrs. Manstone and her friend Margaret, who complained that the girl her son had married was thoroughly selfish and egotistical, and that poor Francis, who had always been made a great fuss of at home, was very unhappy.

Naturally, Mrs. Manstone was not going to admit that the friction between the young pair was the result of Barbara's upbringing and temperament. She preferred to place the whole of the blame upon Terry's affair. The unfortunate publicity and scandal which must have leaked out in their circle of friends had undoubtedly affected Francis's outlook. He had married Barbara lacking his former enthusiasm. It was very unpleasant, he said, to have men at his club chipping him about his sister-in-law.

Barbara and her mother were both sure that if the marriage were a failure, the fault lay at Terry's door.

Mrs. Manstone finished her pudding and read Terry's letter again. She concentrated on the last line. '*Here I am if you ever want to see me again.*' Then, tightening her lips, she put the letter back into her bag and shook her head.

No! Terry need not expect to be forgiven so easily. She had no wish to see her or that horrible man. It was lucky for Terry that he had married her. She had heard through Margaret Colroyd that poor Ruth Farlong had led a most unhappy life with him for years.

After lunch, instead of taking her customary rest, Mrs. Manstone wrapped herself up in furs, for it was a bitterly cold afternoon, and went on the Underground to South Kensington. She had arranged to spend an hour or two with Barbara, and then they were going on to tea and Bridge with the Furnabys. Mrs. Furnaby was still friendly with the Manstones. But Mrs. Manstone had seen nothing of Lady

Carisdon since the newspaper reports of the Farlong divorce. That was a bitter pill for her to swallow. Lady Carisdon had faded out tactfully but quite definitely. And it was only one of many similar incidents which made it difficult for Mrs. Manstone to think kindly of her youngest daughter.

She found Barbara lying on the settee in the drawing-room of her flat — an expensively appointed apartment which looked as though it had been manufactured by furnishing experts; without a touch of individualism.

Barbara, with a rug over her knees and clasping a hot-water bottle, looked pale, peaky, discontented, and not nearly as pretty as she had been before her marriage. Her small, prim mouth was pulled down peevishly at the corners. She greeted her mother without enthusiasm.

'Sit down, mother. I'm feeling like death. Isn't it cold?'

'Bitter,' said Mrs. Manstone; unloosening her furs and settling herself in a chair beside the settee, regarding her daughter anxiously. 'You don't look at all well, darling. What is it?'

'Don't ask!' said Barbara darkly.

Mrs. Manstone stared.

'You don't mean — '

'I believe so,' said Barbara, in a voice of deepest gloom. 'It's simply sickening, but Dr. Ackroyd thinks so — in the summer. After my illness I should think it will kill me. And my nerves are so much on edge I shall never stand a screaming baby. Francis has been most unsympathetic. He says I needn't make a fuss — that it's perfectly natural.'

'Well, of course it is,' said Mrs. Manstone. 'But I think you need some consideration — I can't understand why Francis is so unkind.'

'He doesn't understand me,' said Barbara bitterly. 'And I don't see that the baby will make things any better. Francis has said already that he'll want it kept well out of his way until it's old enough to amuse him. It'll mean leaving this flat, too. My mother-in-law thinks we ought to take a house in the country, but I loathe the country. It's all very well for Francis — he'd have shooting in the winter and fishing in the summer. But I'd be bored stiff. Mrs. Colroyd only thinks of her precious boy.'

'It's a shame, darling,' said Mrs. Manstone. 'I'm so sorry'; then added with a bright smile: 'But it will be rather nice for you to have a little one. Dear me — you puss! — making me a granny!'

Barbara felt much too morose to joke.

'Any news?' she asked.

'Yes,' said Mrs. Manstone, her smile fading. 'I've had a letter from Terry.'

A fleeting spark of interest in Barbara's eyes.

'Have you?'

Mrs. Manstone drew Terry's letter from her bag and handed it to her eldest daughter. Barbara read it. Then, with a slight pink in her cheeks, she handed it back.

'Terry doesn't seem to have suffered much by what she did. She brought a lot of trouble and unhappiness to us, but she seems to be enjoying herself.'

'Hm! Of course, a lot of this may be bravado — one doesn't know how much is true,' said Mrs. Manstone. 'This Dr. Farlong must be a horrible character, and I don't see how Terry *can* be happy with him. But I'm a little relieved to think she's really married.'

'Yes. It hasn't been very pleasant, knowing that she was living with that man without being married to him. As I've said before, I think it had a very serious effect on Francis's love for me — and my mother-in-law's attitude too. She's always hatefully patronising. And when we had a row the other night, Francis brought up Terry's name. I was so ashamed. Are you going to see her, mother?'

'No. I have no wish to, and nothing would induce me to meet that vile man.'

Barbara sighed, flung her hot-water

bottle on the floor, and rose to her feet.

'I suppose I'd better make an effort and get dressed for this Bridge-party.' Then, as though suddenly struck by a terrific thought, she swung round and faced her mother. '*What* was that address on Terry's letter?'

'Some place called Chenwood, near Barnstaple. I haven't heard of it, but I suppose it's a remote village.'

Barbara stared at her mother.

'Chenwood — why, it's quite a well-known beauty-spot — one of these places full of thatched cottages. And what *do* you think? — going to the Furnabys this afternoon has just reminded me — the Furnabys are going down to Chenwood for a week at the end of the month. Rita told me so. Mrs. Furnaby has a sister who lives there.'

'Good heavens!' said Mrs. Manstone. 'Then if it's a tiny place, and Terry's — er — husband is the local doctor, they're almost bound to come up against each other. You know what Mrs.

Furnaby and Rita are like — they're very agreeable, but they've got tongues a yard long.'

Barbara shrugged her shoulders.

'There you are! That sort of thing follows you up all your life. The Furnabys have been very loyal to us, but Rita and Terry used to see quite a lot of each other as children, and it will be frightfully awkward if they do meet.'

Mrs. Manstone, to do her credit, was thinking not so much of her own viewpoint as of Terry's prestige.

'I daresay nobody in the village realises that Terry and this man were not married when they settled there. Do you think I ought to ask the Furnabys to keep their tongues quiet?'

'No,' said Barbara. 'I think it would be very unwise to mention it at all. After all, Mrs. Furnaby's sister may not know Terry's husband. I think it'll be better to keep quiet.'

'It's all very trying,' said Mrs. Manstone, 'and that saying is so true, 'Old sins have long shadows.' Terry has only herself to blame if the scandal finally leaks out, wherever she settles.'

'Do you think they've got any money?' Barbara asked curiously.

'Nothing except what he earns. Margaret Colroyd told me that. Of course, she's heard the ins and outs of it all from Ruth Farlong. It worries me a little — I *am* Terry's mother, after all.'

'I shouldn't let it worry you,' said Barbara. 'You did everything for Terry and she let you down. It's up to this man to look after her now.'

Mrs. Manstone sighed heavily, tore Terry's letter into pieces, and dropped them into the waste-paper basket by the writing-desk.

2

Terry Farlong, with a spade much too big and heavy for her, was engaged in the strenuous task of digging a new flower-bed.

She had been working out here in the garden since two o'clock, when Blaise had rushed in, an hour late, for a lunch which he had only had time to swallow before a telephone call took him away again to a patient five miles outside the village.

That was the sort of life Blaise had been leading since he had taken his practice at Chenwood. A small and not very enterprising one, but with a straggling district and a panel. The sort of practice which meant that he was on the go from early morning till late at night, and very often out in the middle of the night.

It was exactly the type of practice

which he had tried to avoid in the past because of his health, to say nothing of the fact that Ruth would never have tolerated such an existence. But there had been little choice for Blaise after he had left Rossdown. He had to take what he could get, and the farther away from old associations the better. This remote Devonshire village had seemed exactly the sort of place that he and Terry wanted. He had known from the first that it would be all hard work, with little or no scope for talent and development. But he had bought the practice and settled here quite happily. It was within his means, and the chance for him and Terry to begin life afresh.

Terry dug her spade into the ground, let it stay there, took off her gloves, and blew upon her cold hands. The short winter afternoon was waning. Her wrist-watch told her that it was a quarter to four. With any luck, Blaise would be back for tea. It was time to put the kettle on.

She stood a moment looking at her

home with the pride of possession in her eyes, although there was nothing beautiful or attractive about Thornbank. They had not been able to pick and choose. This was the local doctor's house, and they had taken it over with the practice — just as it was.

It seemed a little hard that they should have had to accept Thornbank in a village famous for its charming old thatched cottages. But here it was, a square, grim little house of rough grey Devon stone, with square windows and a square little garden around it.

Chenwood nestled at the foot of a hill, but Thornbank had been built almost on the crest of the hill, braving the bitter north winds in the winter and with little protection from the hot sun in the summer. There was no electric light in the village. Only the rich in the big houses had their own plants. But Terry and Blaise considered themselves lucky to have gas and a good old-fashioned range for cooking and hot-water supply.

They had almost despaired of the garden when they had first come here at Christmas-time. The last doctor who had lived in the place had been an elderly widower, with no interest out of doors. Everything had been neglected. In front of the house there was a strip of lawn, flanked by a gravel pathway, and a round bed, with a few forsaken plants struggling with the weeds, in the centre of the lawn. The whole was enclosed by an ill-kept privet hedge. The garden at the back had more possibilities. It had one good wall, a few nice trees, a kitchen garden, and what had once been a croquet lawn — about an acre in all.

After the beauty of Russet Place — all that loveliness which Blaise had created and cherished — Thornbank had presented a dreary and even hopeless spectacle. But Blaise, with the optimism which Terry's love had given him, had said:

'There's a devil of a lot to do, but it can be done, and we'll make this place sit up, between us. I'll bet you, Terry, there'll be quite a lot of flowers — and some good delphiniums into the bargain — next spring.'

Now, even after two short months, there was something to show for their arduous labours. The place looked cleaner, tidier, more cared-for. They spent all their spare time working out of doors. It was common knowledge in the village that the doctor and his young wife were 'gardening-crazy'. He was always to be found in old grey bags; shirt-sleeves rolled up, and a spade or a hoe in his hand, and Terry with him.

The bed on which Terry had been working this afternoon was for some of Blaise's new seedlings. They had not yet been able to touch the borders surrounding the croquet lawn. It was a wild and tangled mass. The walls were almost concealed by brambles and creepers, and the beds were still rubbish-heaps. But they were going to start on them next month.

Terry walked into the house, lit the

gas-jet in the kitchen, stoked up the little range, and put the kettle on to boil. They had one maid, a cook general; the only one they were able to afford. This was Thursday, her afternoon out, when Terry saw to the tea and supper. Far from hating Edith's day out, she looked forward to it. It was a special treat to be quite alone in the little house with Blaise. She liked to serve him his meals and look after him herself. She was never tired of seeing him come into that tiny kitchen; grin at her like a boy, and insist upon helping her wash up the dishes.

When she protested that he was tired, he said:

'I'm only tired of doctoring — but a little domestic work will be quite soothing. Besides, I adore you with Edith's check apron over your dress — and a smut on your nose.'

They were happy. So happy that sometimes Terry wondered how long it would last. It did not seem possible that two people were meant to be quite so ideally content as she and Blaise. She alternated between her supreme happiness and a very natural and human anxiety lest anything should happen to end it all.

Blaise might get ill; this panel practice and the night work were terribly trying for him. Or he might get smashed up in the car. Or catch some appalling disease from one of his patients. Of course, it was absurd to think along such lines, but how could she help it? He meant everything — everything in the world to her now, and she knew that to him she was the only thing that mattered.

While she moved about the kitchen preparing the tea, her thoughts wandered back through the last six or seven months. Time had flown amazingly quickly. It seemed only yesterday that she and Blaise had taken the final step across the Rubicon; only yesterday since that marvellous and unforgettable night in the funny little Victorian cottage that they had found.

Even now she could close her eyes and see that dear, queer little bedroom; the moonlight spilling through the open casements; the blue delphinium nodding in the brown jug; and the transfigured face of her lover close to her own.

The passionate fulfilment, the beauty of those hours, had given Terry a fuller and sweeter understanding of life. The laughing child had become a woman who laughed for love in the arms of her lover. And a woman who wept, too, because of that other one whom he had once held in his arms.

Close to him in the warm, starlit shadows of that tiny room, she had said again and again:

'Tell me you love me more than you did *her*.'

He had had only one answer against her lips:

'I do — I swear to God that I do. She never meant what you mean — it's all so utterly different.'

And she remembered how that next

morning they had seen the dawn break, looked out on the rose and opal of the sky and heard the first birds piping drowsily in the eaves. She had slipped out of bed and found beneath her feet a score of crushed blue petals which had dropped from the delphinium during the night. She had said:

'Oh, look, the carpet's covered with blue petals.'

Blaise had smiled at her and said:

'I've always thought delphiniums were the nicest flowers in the world — now I know that they are. That flower shed its petals for my bride to walk upon.'

She loved to remember all those exquisite trifles, because they are the threads with which a woman spins the web of her happiness.

There had been other lovely nights and glorious days — there were a thousand other memories to look back upon and laugh about and weep for, too, because anything so beautiful is in a strange way tragic as well.

But of course there had been prosaic and less lovely moments. The days spent in an unattractive cheap hotel in London. The rigid economising. The search for a suitable practice. The times when Blaise, depressed, dispirited, loathed his poverty and disgrace because of Terry, wanting passionately to give her things that he could not afford.

She, with her unfailing humour and that genius which she had for charming away his gloom, had managed always to make him smile again and see with her the light on the horizon.

Twice in succession Blaise had discovered what he thought would be a suitable practice. Each time, before anything was signed or settled, he had learned from the doctor in question that the story of his divorce was common knowledge in the place.

On the last occasion, the medical man — a decent enough fellow — had said:

'I don't advise you to come here, Farlong. I'm frightfully sorry, old chap;

I'm not at all narrow-minded myself, but — '

Blaise, tight-lipped, secretly furious, had to give up the idea and go back to Terry with his story.

Those were moments when it took all her tact and patience to cure him of his mental ills. But she never failed. He could forget his humiliation, his bitter resentment against the injustice of the whole thing, when her arms were about him and her lips whispered:

'Don't let it matter — don't let anything matter. I love you — isn't it worth it? It is — for me!'

He felt always that it *was* worth it. But for her sake more than his own he resented the intolerable position.

Then came this offer of the practice at Chenwood. In such a remote Devon village probably there were few, if any, who had heard of the Farlong divorce-case. The physician who sold them the practice had not heard of it, anyhow, and took it for granted that Dr. and 'Mrs.' Farlong were a respectable married couple.

'We'll have to cheat 'em for a bit,' Blaise had said, 'and hope for the best. Then we'll run away one day and get tied up by the law, and not a soul in Chenwood need know.'

That was what had happened. Feeling a little guilty, they settled at Thornbank, spent their first Christmas together, and found to their immense relief that nobody was the wiser.

It had been a wonderful Christmas. A very quiet one. Just the two of them in front of their own fire, and not even a turkey, because Terry had said they would never get through it. But they had had their bunch of mistletoe and made good use of that. Every time Blaise had come back from a sick-call he had called Terry out into the hall and insisted upon kissing her again, until finally they had laughed so much they were sure they scandalised their little maid.

A certain ironic amusement lay in the fact that most of the good women in the village had called upon the doctor's wife and she had received quite a number of invitations. But firmly, and at once, she had let it be known that she did not play Bridge, so after that the invitations fell off a little. But Terry did not worry about that. She wanted to spend all her spare time in the garden with Blaise, and neither of them found that their leisure was long enough.

She wondered what on earth the village would have thought if they could have seen what happened two days ago. She and Blaise, in the baby Austin, which, for economic reasons had succeeded the big car, had driven that morning early into Barnstaple. There, at the local register office, Teresa Mary Manstone had legally become Blaise Farlong's wife.

They had not even been able to steal that day for a second honeymoon. Blaise had to get back to Thornbank for his six o'clock surgery. But driving back to Chenwood, that cold, dark afternoon, they had had a lot of fun.

'Do you feel any different now that I have made an honest woman of you?' he had chaffed her.

Terry, with a huge bunch of violets pinned to her coat — the first of the year, and his present to her on this their wedding day — had answered:

'Yes. I feel too *terribly* respectable! I keep crackling my marriage-lines. In fact, now that I'm your wife in the eyes of the law I'm going to start hen-pecking you. I think I've been much too nice to you all these months. Tonight I shall move into the spare room.'

'Thank God there isn't a bed in it,' said Blaise.

'Then I shall put a mattress in the bath.'

'Are you refusing to sleep with me?'

'Certainly,' said Terry. 'We're married.'

He pulled the car up to the side of the road.

'Darling, you're only twenty-two, and I really cannot allow you to be so terribly cynical. There's only one thing left for me to do — I am your husband, and I shall enforce my rights.'

Then she was in his arms and he was crushing her, violets and all, close to his breast.

'Dear, sweet thing! You have been too nice to me all these months — much too nice! You'll never know what you've meant or how you've helped me. I was glad when the decree was made absolute — frightfully glad that I could marry you at last — but you've been a wife to me in every way all this time, my darling. I can't feel you any more mine.'

She put her cheek against his and shut her eyes, sighing.

'No, I don't feel I'm any more yours. I've been utterly yours ever since we went away together. Have you really been happy, Blaise?'

'You know that.'

She looked at him and was satisfied. There were tired lines about his eyes because he had been called up in the night three times this week, and broken sleep told on his nervous system, but he looked ten times better than when she had first met him. There was more flesh on his tall frame; his cheekbones were not so outstanding; and the harassed, repressed look had vanished completely. His was the face of a contented man.

While she prepared his tea today, Terry recalled all these things and was conscious of deep satisfaction. Sometimes she had felt a natural wish to see her mother and sister again. But that feeling rose, perhaps, more from vanity than anything else — she just wanted to show them how happy she was. And she felt no real distress because, so far, she had had no reply to the letter which she had written to her mother to tell her that she was Blaise's wife.

The telephone bell rang.

Terry stopped cutting bread-and-butter and ran into the tiny consulting-room. It was the one room on which they had spent a little money. It had been so cheerless before; so shabby.

Terry had chosen the restful green paper for the walls; made Blaise spend the money on building the bookcases for all his books and on the one good Persian carpet for the floor. His desk and chair, the couch and medical appliances, he had brought with him from Rossdown.

It was always with a very natural feeling of pride that Terry saw her own photograph in a leather frame on that desk where in former years Ruth's pictured face had looked at him.

She answered the telephone bell.

The call was from Little Chenwood, an off-shoot of their village, some four miles out. One of Blaise's panel patients was in labour, and the midwife was worried about her condition — wanted the doctor as soon as he could come.

Terry wrote the message on a pad and sighed. Gone were the hopes of a cosy tea with Blaise and an hour's rest for him.

He was late in coming back to tea.

She heard the little Austin stop outside the gate, and was at the front door to meet him. The cold wind made her shiver. Blaise came up the path with his case in his hand. It was quite dark now. The gaslight in the hall fell upon his face and showed her how tired he was. Her heart sank. But as he took off his overcoat and muffler he greeted her cheerfully.

'How goes it, darling?'

'It doesn't go at all,' she said despondently. She took his scarf from him and laid it over the hall chair. 'There's an urgent call waiting for you.'

Blaise rolled his eyes heavenwards.

'Ye gods and little fishes! What is it now?'

'You've simply *got* to have a cup of tea and something to eat first of all,' she said. 'You hardly had any lunch.' She took his hands and chafed them anxiously. 'And you're frozen.'

'It's a raw night — we ought to be getting some warmer weather this month,' he said.

He followed her into the consulting-room, and with an arm about her shoulder glanced at the message on his writing-desk.

'Damn! I've only just come from Little Chenwood. Why didn't I know? I'm running short of petrol, too. I shall have to fill up before I start off again. You know, Terry, that little blighter of a car is getting on my nerves. I want something bigger.'

'I know you do. You're so used to a big one.'

'We'll try and save up for a Morris or a Standard,' he smiled.

She followed him with her gaze as he walked to the fireplace and spread his cold hands out to the blaze. Not for the first time since he had taken on this practice she regretted for his sake that other, easier life which he had led at Rossdown. That hateful woman, Ruth, had at least been able to make things more comfortable for him. Those wretched attacks of colitis — his legacy from the last year of the war — had been recurring with more frequency this last month or two. It was due to the hard work, the irregular feeding, the cold. She knew perfectly well that he ought not to lead quite such a strenuous life. But a man in his position had no choice.

She turned, hurried into the kitchen, made the tea, and brought it back.

'Just a quick bite before you go off again, darling.'

Blaise, with his back to the fire, took out his diary and wrote in it.

'Mrs. Tiddy, 2, Barnham Cottages. The Lord knows where they are. Somebody in Little Chenwood will be able to tell me, no doubt, but I haven't been there before.'

Terry brought his tea and handed him a piece of bread-and-butter.

'I'd like to have had some toast for you, but I knew it was no good making it, as it gets all soggy, waiting.'

He was not too tired to bend down and kiss the little hand that had given him the tea.

'Sweet thing — you think of everything! What a marvellous little wife you are.'

'I'm very annoyed tonight,' said Terry, 'because you're looking worn-out. This practice seems to have grown since you took it on — it's shattering.'

'Never mind. I shall live through it.'

'You don't feel ill tonight, do you?'

'No. I'm better. Don't worry about me.'

Between mouthfuls of tea and bread-and-butter, still standing with his back to the comforting fire, he questioned her about her own day's work. He liked to see her in the old tweed skirt and jumper and to think of her working in their garden. This life agreed with her, anyhow. She was looking the picture of health, bless her; browner than ever; bright-eyed, and absurdly young.

He had shut his mind to the past because it did not bear thinking about, and yet sometimes, for sheer pleasure, he compared this life he led with Terry with the existence — and it had been only an existence — with Ruth.

Life had held more comforts at Russet Place, if one set much store upon a staff of servants and four-course dinners and a good deal of leisure and recreation. But Blaise would not have changed this new life, which meant exhausting work and strict economy, for that more luxurious one for anything in the world. What were all the material comforts worth if one came home to a woman who could only nag and criticise? Any sacrifice was worth while for the sake of this home shared with Terry. It was a real home and she was a real wife. He knew that her bright hazel eyes were fixed on him with anxiety — that she worried about his health. He wondered if she ever thought about herself.

'That bed for the new seedlings is nearly ready,' she told him proudly. 'Wait till you see it in the morning.'

He put down his empty cup, lit a

cigarette, and moved to his cupboard to collect the instruments he wanted for a maternity case.

'You're not to go at it with that heavy spade too hard, my dear,' he said.

'I'm strong as a lion.'

'Don't you argue with me.'

'Doctor's orders?' she laughed.

'Yes.'

He rummaged in the white enamel cupboard.

'Where did I leave my forceps?'

She walked to a drawer under the cupboard and pulled them out.

'You put them in here yesterday.'

'I told you that you think of everything.'

She put the instrument in his case and snapped the lock.

'I hope the poor woman will be all right.'

'I'll do what I can. I'd better nip along now.'

She fetched him his scarf and wound it round his neck.

'Get back as soon as you can. It's

only a cold supper, but there's some soup.'

'That sounds good on a cold night.'

She arranged the scarf carefully about his neck, then put up a hand, touched his cheek, and looked at him wistfully.

'I wish you didn't look so tired.'

'I think it's my natural face,' he laughed. 'You always say I look tired.'

'You nearly always do.'

'I'm amazingly happy in spite of it.'

She hugged him for a moment and then turned from him so that he should not see that tears had come suddenly to her eyes.

A moment later she heard the self-starter on the little Austin, and from the window watched the head-lamps throw a white shaft of light along the frosty road, then disappear down the hill.

A quarter past five. Surgery would begin at six. There was no hope of a rest for Blaise until seven or half-past.

Terry put some more coal on the fire

in the consulting-room; made up the kitchen range so that there would be plenty of hot water for baths; then found her way up the dark little staircase with which she was so familiar, and lit the gas-jet in her bedroom.

It was not the sort of room that either of them would have chosen had they been able to afford to decorate and furnish it as they would have liked. But they had agreed that it was foolish to spend money unnecessarily. All Blaise's small capital had gone toward the purchase of this practice, and it was not worth much more than £500 or £600 a year to them at the moment. They had decided that they could not and would not stand the old-fashioned floral wallpaper which had been in this, the best bedroom, at Thornbank, when they took over. So the walls had been distempered — a pale primrose yellow, which picked up all the sunlight. Terry, herself, had made the curtains — cheap cretonne, but of a pretty green and yellow design. They had found the inexpensive table of old oak which, with a mirror, served as Terry's dressing-table. The real extravagance in the room was a nice old oak cupboard which they shared as a wardrobe.

They had had to buy the laid carpet from the former owner, but fortunately it was an inoffensive brown. The big double divan bed had once had hideous brass rails at the foot and the head, but Terry had very soon had these taken off, and now the bed looked quite nice, covered with a charming old patchwork quilt which Terry's grandmother had made and bequeathed to her, and which Mrs. Manstone had dutifully sent with her other possessions.

The tiny room communicating with this one was Blaise's dressing-room. There were two more bedrooms in the house, one occupied by Edith, the cook-general, and the other a spare room which they had not attempted to furnish.

Downstairs there were three rooms

— the consulting-room, which led through to the surgery, which the last doctor had built on, rather shoddily; the tiny dining-room with a hateful fumed-oak suite, just as it had been left; and the drawing-room. Terry had despaired about the drawing-room. Impossible to make it attractive without spending money.

At the moment it revolted both her and Blaise. They always sat in his consulting-room. They could not bear that other room, with its pale pink paper and a carpet which had roses all over it; a fireplace made hideous by a shining white enamel overmantel and a varied collection of mahogany chairs and occasional tables, and only two armchairs which offered any comfort.

It was as they had found and bought it. Terry kept the door firmly shut unless she had a caller. But she and Blaise promised each other a holocaust of everything in the pink room as soon as they could afford to make what they wanted out of it.

Terry washed herself and changed her gardening clothes for a brown velvet dress with long, tight sleeves and a square neck in which she looked rather like a mediaeval page, with her brown bobbed head and sun-tanned skin.

Gage had sent her that dress. Gage had been a perfect dear to them ever since they had come here. A good many charming dresses hanging in Terry's cupboard had been sent from Frog's Hall. And many little things such as a crystal bowl, a Bristol jug; some lovely bits of china, which made the interior of Thornbank beautiful, had been sent by the Thorntons from time to time.

There was a standing invitation for Terry and her husband to go and stay at Frog's Hall. But, so far, Blaise had had neither time nor opportunity for a holiday.

Terry covered her pretty dress with a blue overall, then went downstairs to prepare her husband's supper. He liked her in her old clothes, but on principle she changed every night. At the Cedars

— heavens, how long ago that seemed!
— she and Barbara had been made to
change for dinner every night, and then
Terry had rebelled. But now she liked
to look her best and prettiest for Blaise
in the evening.

She found herself thinking quite a lot
about her mother and sister while she
mixed a salad-dressing in her tiny
kitchen tonight.

She wondered if her mother would
come and see her now that she knew
that she was properly married. She did
so much want her to meet Blaise —
realise what a dear he was.

The telephone-bell rang as she was
carrying the salad-bowl into the dining-
room.

Her lips tightened. If that were
another urgent call for Blaise, she'd tell
them he was dead and buried.

She answered the call. It was not,
however, a demand for the doctor. A
bright and friendly voice said:

'Is that Mrs. Farlong?'

'Yes, speaking,' said Terry.

'This is Mrs. Stanson.'

Terry knew and liked Mrs. Stanson. She was one of Blaise's best patients down here — the owner of the famous Manor House, which was one of the sights worth seeing in Chenwood. They kept three gardeners there. Terry and Blaise adored the wonderful grounds, and Mrs. Stanson had a soft spot in her heart for Blaise, with his unusual love for, and knowledge of, gardening.

'I want you and Dr. Farlong to dine on Saturday night,' said Mrs. Stanson. 'My husband and I would be so pleased. I have my sister and her daughter coming down for the week-end.'

'It's awfully nice of you,' said Terry. 'I'd simply love to, and I'm sure my husband isn't engaged.'

She returned to her duties in the kitchen, humming. Mrs. Stanson, although one of the Bridge-players of the village, and a great gossip, was a very cheerful amiable woman, and her husband, a retired Admiral, liked

416

Blaise, and generally carried him off for billiards. It was a game Blaise played well. Terry knew that Blaise liked a dinner at the Manor House.

When he came back from Little Chenwood, Terry imparted the news of the invitation.

'We're dining at the Manor House on Saturday, darling. Is that all right for you?'

'Yes — if you'd like to go, sweetheart. I rather like knocking a ball with the Admiral.'

'Mrs. Stanson said her sister and daughter are coming for the week-end.'

'I hope the daughter's young and pretty,' said Blaise.

'Oh, do you?' said Terry darkly. 'Well if you flirt with the daughter, *I* shall shut myself in the billiard-room with the Admiral. He thinks I'm a dear little thing.'

'Well, I think you're a horrid little beast,' said Blaise.

A bell pealed through the house.

Blaise and Terry, standing in the

consulting-room, grimaced at each other.

'Surgery begins,' said Terry. 'Kiss me quickly and tell me that you'll shoot the Admiral if he so much as looks at me.'

'So I will,' said Blaise, and held her tightly to him for a moment, kissing the soft hollow in her throat. 'You look lovely in your brown velvet dress, Teresa Mary, and I love you.'

'Oh, darling!' said Terry in an ecstatic voice, and shut her eyes.

The bell pealed again. Blaise let Terry go, went firmly into the surgery, and closed the door behind him.

3

Sometimes Terry went with Blaise on his rounds and drove the little car for him. He liked to have her with him, and said it made him feel important to have a chauffeur and was much less fatiguing than when he drove himself.

On the Saturday when they had arranged to dine at the Manor House with the Stansons, Terry drove her husband to his patients, feeling particularly cheerful because at last the weather had changed for the better.

The February morning was quite mild and warm, and, as Blaise had remarked to Terry when they took their customary stroll through the garden before breakfast, spring was in the air. They had even discovered a few snowdrops, and the small green crocus spikes were pushing bravely through the brown, caked earth.

Twelve o'clock found Terry in the quaint winding High Street of the village of Chenwood, sitting outside the baker's shop. Blaise was attending a patient who lived just over the bakery. Terry interested herself in a book.

The blare of an electric horn made her turn round. A big blue saloon car had pulled up just behind her, and three women stepped out of it. Terry recognised the big, stout woman in the blue cardigan suit, with a round beaming face and hornrimmed glasses. It was Mrs. Stanson. Mrs. Stanson saw the girl in the little red Austin and waved to her. She then turned, spoke to the two women behind her, and they all came up to the Austin.

Then Terry's heart gave an uncomfortable jerk. The book slipped from her fingers. Surely it was not — but yes, it was! Her mother's old and close friends, the Furnabys. Mrs. Furnaby, tall, stout, familiar, with bobbed grey hair and a florid complexion. Rita, who had played with Terry in their child-hood, and now, at twenty-two, looked several years older than Terry. A big, gawky girl, who did nothing but grow her hair and cut it again and seemed perpetually in the untidy between-stages.

Mrs. Stanson reached the side of the baby Austin and bent down to Terry.

'How are you, my dear? I must introduce you to my sister and my niece — you'll be meeting them up at the Manor House this evening.'

She turned to the others. 'May, my dear — Rita — I want you to meet Mrs. Farlong, our nice doctor's wife. They're coming up to dinner with us tonight.'

Terry wanted to open the door of the car and get out, but she felt too paralysed. With hot cheeks and a sinking sensation in her heart, she looked out and saw Mrs. Furnaby and Rita staring at her. They both had wide-open mouths and eyes round with astonishment. They exchanged glances.

Then from Mrs. Furnaby came the name:

'Terry — Terry Manstone!'

'Oh,' exclaimed Mrs. Stanson brightly. 'Don't tell me you two know each other.'

Across Mrs. Furnaby's face a very righteous look was settling.

'Oh, yes,' she said slowly. 'We know each other. Did you say this is — the doctor's wife?'

Then Terry roused herself. With a cold and trembling hand she opened the door of the Austin and got out. She looked frantically at the bakery. If only Blaise would come out and support her! This was almost as bad as that unforgettable night at the Colroyds' party.

'Yes, I — I'm married now,' she said stupidly, and added: 'Hallo, Rita, how are you?'

'Hallo,' said Rita Furnaby, because she could think of nothing else to say, and looked at Terry with fascinated eyes. There had been such a scandal at Wimbledon about Terry that Rita regarded her almost as she would have done a waxwork figure at Madame Tussaud's. Everybody at home looked upon Terry Manstone as something too disgraceful even to talk about. Rita, firmly chaperoned and never allowed to escape maternal vigilance, had often thought about Terry and been quite thrilled in her imagination. Terry was living with some man — in sin. Rita thought it disgraceful, but she was also a little envious. Nobody had ever wanted to make an attack on *her* virtue, which was depressing.

Mrs. Stanson, quite unaware of the tense atmosphere, chatted brightly for a few moments, and then Blaise, carrying his case, emerged from the bakery.

Mrs. Stanson's eyes brightened. She liked the young doctor who had taken the place of the last dull and elderly one. She thought him charming, and she was anxious to do what she could for these young things who seemed to have none too much money and were putting up a very good show.

'Here comes the doctor!' she exclaimed.

Mrs. Furnaby and Rita turned and looked with eyes of horror at the man who was commonly known at home as Terry's seducer.

Whatever Mrs Furnaby's feelings were, Rita became decidedly envious of Terry now. Dr. Farlong did not look at all wicked, but he certainly had a very nice figure and a delightful face; thin, brown, grey-eyed, keen.

'Hallo, hallo,' began Blaise cheerfully. 'How are you, Mrs. Stanson?'

'The asthma's decidedly better, thanks to you,' she said. 'May I introduce my sister, Mrs. Furnaby, and Miss Rita Furnaby, my niece?'

Terry could only stand there, galvanised, while Blaise raised his hat and bowed to the two women.

Rita mumbled: 'How do you do?' But Mrs. Furnaby, with an icy and almost imperceptible nod, turned her back.

'We shall be late for lunch, Agnes,' she said to her sister.

A minute later Mrs. Stanson and the Furnabys had returned to their big saloon and the chauffeur was driving them down the High Street. Blaise looked at Terry.

'What's the matter with you, darling? Why, you're quite white.'

'I feel a bit pale,' said Terry. 'My God, what a frightful thing! Do you know who that was?'

'You mean the big gawky girl whom I've got to flirt with, and the mother who rather handed me the frozen mitt?'

Terry sat down in the car, shivering in spite of her thick tweed coat.

'It's no joke, Blaise. Mrs. Stanson's sister is May Furnaby — one of my mother's oldest friends from Wimbledon — and the girl is Rita, who used to come to our house twice a week when Barbara and I were children.'

The smile faded from Blaise's face. He took the wheel, started up the little car, and glanced quickly at his young wife's face. He had not seen her look like that for a long time — wide-eyed, scared.

'Good God!' he said. 'They're old friends of yours?'

'Not my particular friends, but they've known me all my life and of course they know the whole story — about us. Just before you came out you should have heard Mrs. Furnaby — suggesting that she had not heard aright when I was introduced as the doctor's *wife*. It's too frightful, Blaise. Mrs. Furnaby is a very nice woman, but a fearful gossip, and of course she'll tell the Stansons everything. She'll be pouring out the story now. The Stansons will know that we weren't married when we first came to Chenwood. You can be quite sure Mrs. Furnaby will have heard from my mother that the decree was only made absolute a week ago.'

Blaise missed his gear as he changed down to ascend the hill to Thornbank — an unusual occurrence for him. He swore under his breath.

'God, what a damnable thing! Why in the name of heaven should this have happened? Why should Mrs. Stanson be related to a friend of your family's?'

'I tell you,' said Terry, 'there's no getting away from a thing of this sort. We chose the most remote village in Devonshire and yet here we are — cornered.'

'You mean Mrs. Stanson will let out — '

'I bet you it will be all round Chenwood in twenty-four hours. She's awfully kind and charming, but she's exactly the same type of woman as Mrs. Furnaby. She'll never keep her tongue quiet. She'll tell somebody as a confidence, and that somebody will confide in her best friend, and so on, until everybody knows about us.'

'Hell!' said Blaise.

Terry bit her lip.

'It *is* hell, darling. It's going to shatter things for us, and it will be frightfully injurious to the practice.'

Blaise stopped the car outside the

gates of their home. In silence they walked up the path and entered the house. In the consulting-room Blaise went to his desk and looked at the pad.

Edith had written down a message. Would Dr. Farlong be at Mr. Parker's, the dentist's, at half past two, to give gas?

Gloomily Blaise surveyed this message. Parker was a decent little fellow, and had lately given him one or two jobs of the kind. In fact, Blaise was doing very well at the moment — well enough for a small practice. But now what would happen? This disastrous arrival of the Furnabys at the Manor House must inevitably have the most deleterious effect upon his reputation.

He felt Terry's hand on his shoulder, and turned to her.

'This isn't any too good, is it, darling?' he said with a short laugh.

She had taken off her coat and hat and was pushing back the brown lock of hair that would fall across one cheek. Her small face was very grave.

'It's the most abominable thing to have happened,' she said.

'And I don't see what we can do,' he said, unless we ask Mrs. Stanson to be kind enough to keep quiet about it.'

'We might do that,' said Terry gloomily. 'The people who are nice to you when everything's all right aren't half as nice when something like this happens. The Furnabys won't put the best complexion on the story. The Stansons will believe, just like anybody else, that we were the aggressors. Nobody but those directly concerned in it know the truth.'

'And we rather burnt our boats when we went off together.'

Terry suddenly flung back her head.

'You're not to regret that — *I* don't, and *you're* not to!'

He put an arm about her shoulders and drew her close to his side.

'Darling child, how could I regret it? It was the most glorious thing that ever happened to me! But I don't much like the idea that you're going to suffer for it all your life.'

'Well, don't let's worry until we have to.' said Terry. 'It may be all right. All the same, I can't believe the Furnabys will keep quiet, and heaven knows how the Stansons will take it. The Admiral's rather a stickler for good form and the Englishman's behaviour and that sort of thing.'

'God knows why an Englishman should be expected to behave any better than a dago,' said Blaise.

That made Terry laugh, but the laughter trailed away quickly. She was feeling very anxious — not only for her own sake, but for the sake of this beloved man whose reputation was of such vital importance.

They sat down to lunch. Neither of them enjoyed it. The cottage-pie was singularly unattractive, and the caramel pudding not a success. Edith was no cook. Terry looked miserably at her husband's plate.

'You've eaten nothing.'

'Not hungry,' said Blaise.

The telephone-bell rang.

'I'll answer it for you, darling,' she said.

He nodded, and, frowning, pulled out his pipe and clenched his teeth on the stem. He was much more worried than he would have cared to admit, even to Terry. When she came back into the tiny dining-room he gave her a questioning look. Her cheeks were blazing red, and she looked as though she were going to cry.

She shut the door behind her and stood with her back to it.

'The blow isn't slow in falling,' she said in a suffocated voice. 'That was Mrs. Stanson's parlour-maid. Mrs. Stanson is so very sorry she must ask Dr. and Mrs. Farlong to postpone dinner this evening, as her sister is not at all well.'

Then Blaise sprang to his feet, his face flushing darkly, pipe in his hand.

'God!' he said furiously.

Terry fought with herself. She wanted to burst into tears. She told herself not to be a little fool. She had been crazy to expect their ideal happiness to last — mad to hope that the consequences of their conduct would not follow them here. No, not their conduct; Ruth Farlong's despicable lie. It was for that they must suffer now. Yet if those lies had never been told and that divorce had never taken place, she, Terry, would never have known any happiness with Blaise at all.

But she could hardly bear to see that dark, shamed look on Blaise's face. She made a gallant effort to console him.

'Don't take it too hardly, darling. Perhaps it's true — perhaps Mrs. Furnaby *is* ill.'

'You know it isn't true.'

'Then I suppose we must take it for granted that there will be an abrupt end to our friendship up at the Manor House.'

'And an end, also, to my attending the Stansons professionally. They can easily get a man out from Barnstaple if they want one.'

Terry stared in front of her blindly.

'I don't see how we can appeal to Mrs. Stanson now. She's nipped that in the bud.'

'One can't blame her,' said Blaise bitterly. 'They're well known County people — the Admiral and his wife won't want it said that they're encouraging behaviour such as ours. We cheated Chenwood, Terry. We won't be forgiven for that.'

'What else could we have done? We had to live.'

'Oh, I know!' Blaise began to march up and down the tiny dining-room, hands in his pockets, his pipe forgotten. 'This is only the beginning,' he added. 'It'll be a repetition of Rossdown. There'll be other people who won't care to know us when they're told we were only married a few days ago. It doesn't matter how decent we are — or how much we love each other — or how far circumstances were against us. Nothing will be taken into consideration. We shall just be boycotted. And God knows we can't live on the panel alone, if I lose my private practice.'

'Blaise!' said Terry in a low, breathless voice. 'Don't! You're frightening me terribly! It won't be as bad as that — it can't be; we've only just come, and things were beginning to look so bright.'

Blaise paused in front of the window and stared out at the small garden. It was looking quite attractive on this sunny February day. At the bottom of the croquet lawn was his new nursery — the beds where he meant to put his new delphinium plants. He felt suddenly physically sick. His mind was carrying him too far. In a lightning flash he was seeing the end of everything here — more disgrace — and this time he would not face it alone, as he had done at Rossdown. Terry would be involved. But he wasn't going to have Terry cut by these damned village cats — by God he wasn't!

Edith entered the room.

'Can I clear away, please?'

Terry and Blaise walked out and shut themselves in the consulting-room. There Terry crept into his arms and hugged him tightly.

'"We ain't got much money, but we do see life!"' she quoted with a choked laugh.

He pressed the brown head passionately to his shoulder.

'I love your pluck — I've always loved it. But, Terry, this is a frightfully serious thing.'

'We faced something like it before,' she said, 'and got through it, and found it worth while.'

'My sweet, I know. But we've got to live — this is our living.'

'Oh, don't let's start despairing. It might go no farther than the Manor House. It may be all right,' she cried against all her inner convictions.

The telephone-bell rang.

Blaise released Terry and picked up the receiver.

'Hallo.'

'Can you come and see Mrs. Taylor's baby?' said an uneducated voice which sounded some way away.

'Is she worse?' Blaise pulled himself together and asked the question.

'Yes, doctor, she's been took very queer again, and I'm speaking from the post-office.'

'I'll be there within the next quarter of an hour,' said Blaise.

Terry turned silently, fetched his scarf and coat from the hall, and brought them back to him. She smiled at him gallantly while she wrapped the scarf about his neck.

'Long way?'

'Couple of miles. Then I'm going on to give gas at Parker's. After that, two people at Little Chenwood, then I'll be home again.'

'Cheer up, my darling,' she whispered. 'Things may be all right.'

They kissed with more than usual tenderness. He broke into a smile as he looked down at her.

'Nothing seems to matter when I hold you in my arms like that, Terry. You're a wonderful little person.'

From the window of the consulting-room she watched him drive away. A hot mist of tears blinded her sight. It really was the most damnable thing to have happened, just when they were so happy. She knew how badly Blaise would take it if they cold-shouldered him here in the way they had done at Rossdown. He would find it intolerable. She wouldn't like it herself, but somehow as Blaise's wife she could endure anything. Men were different; men like Blaise, innately fastidious and proud, keen about their work, would not find a double dose of this sort of thing easy to swallow.

She was stricken with a sudden dreadful fear that it might make a difference to his attitude toward her — might spoil their ideal happiness. Ah, that would be intolerable to her. To see Blaise grow morose and bitter, turn from her — that would be more than she could bear! That mustn't happen. She wouldn't let it. She must give him everything that she had to give — make up for what he lost — if it were in her power to do so.

Fiercely she brushed her eyelids with the back of her hand, like a boy ashamed to cry, went into the hall, put on her old coat and gum-boots, and walked into the garden to find the spade and go on with her digging.

Up at the Manor House, after a late luncheon, the Admiral and his wife and their visitors were discussing the Farlongs while they lingered over coffee and cigarettes.

Mrs. Stanson and her sister had already discussed the story from end to end, inside and out. But they could not let it alone. It was a choice bone to worry, and both of them, priding themselves upon being most charitable and amiable creatures, adored a good scandal.

'I'm too grieved for words,' Mrs. Stanson was saying. 'I did so like Dr.

Farlong, and the little wife seemed such a nice child. It's incredible to think she behaved so badly.'

The Admiral, cutting a cigar, grunted:

'The fellow's to blame. Seemed a plausible sort of chap — sportsman and all that — but you can't tell; and he's a swine to have ruined that young girl.'

'Terry Manstone,' said Mrs. Furnaby, 'was always a wild, difficult sort of child. Her poor mother had no end of trouble with her at home — I can't say any of us were really surprised to hear that she'd thrown her cap over the mill. It was a most terrible thing for poor Mrs. Manstone, who's a delightful woman, and for Barbara, the eldest daughter, who married young Francis Colroyd. Barbara was absolutely different from Terry, wasn't she, Rita?'

Rita nodded.

'Barbara's frightfully nice.'

'I don't understand now how it all began,' said Mrs. Stanson.

'Nobody knows. It's quite a mystery,' said Mrs. Furnaby. 'Apparently Terry went on this walking-tour and just stayed the night with Dr. Farlong while his wife was away.'

The Admiral grunted again.

'Fellow's an out-and-outer — taking advantage of a young girl under his own roof.'

'That's a man's point of view, my dear Charles,' said his wife. 'Personally, I think women have the final say in these things — it was the girl's fault. She needn't have stayed with him if she hadn't wished to. I daresay Dr. Farlong and his first wife weren't very happy, and along comes a foolish, sentimental girl and throws herself into his arms — and that starts it all. I blame her more than I do him.'

'It's a disgraceful thing, anyhow,' said the Admiral. 'Settling down here, pretending they were man and wife.'

'I'm shocked beyond belief,' said Mrs. Stanson, her plump face puckered. She was disappointed as well as shocked. Of course, it meant that she couldn't know the Farlongs any more, and she had liked the doctor.

'Of course they are married *now*,' put in Mrs. Furnaby. 'Terry's mother heard from her just before I left Wimbledon. They got married as soon as the decree was made absolute.'

'I won't have 'em in *my* house again,' said the Admiral.

Mrs. Stanson sighed.

'I might have overlooked it, but Charles is very firm, and I suppose the best thing I can do is to drop them. I sent a tactful message about May being ill, and asked them to postpone dinner with us.'

'I should think they'll have the grace to leave Chenwood, now,' said the Admiral.

'I feel a little sorry about it, for Mrs. Manstone's sake,' said Mrs. Furnaby. 'She's a great friend of mine. I don't want to be the cause of harming Terry. I daresay she's been punished enough as it is.'

'*I* shan't say anything to anybody,' said Mrs. Stanson. 'But of course if people down here ask me why I'm avoiding the local doctor and his wife, what *can* I say?'

'Yes, it's so *awkward*, isn't it?' said Mrs. Furnaby.

'The man ought to be struck off the medical register,' said the Admiral. 'If he'd been in the Service he'd have been asked to resign. That's what's the matter with England today. Too much licence. Too many people running after other people's husbands and wives. Makes for a decadent race.'

Mrs. Stanson, with a momentary vision of Terry's slim, childish figure and sun-browned face, felt a sudden motherly pang.

'I'm so *grieved*,' she said again. 'They aren't the sort of couple one would expect would do such things. I suppose they were terribly in love.'

'Love!' exploded the Admiral, pink in the face. 'Damme, Aggie, are you going to uphold all this stuff and nonsense that they talk about *love* these days? It's only another word for lust.'

'Charles!' gasped his wife. 'Remember — Rita — '

The Admiral coughed, glanced at his wife's niece; told himself that she wouldn't know what the word meant; apologised, and took his cigar into the smoking-room.

4

Chenwood was a very small village. In such places big news travels rapidly. The pseudo-sympathetic whisperings of the more charitable are as dangerous as the loud blaring of those who seem ever anxious to reform the world.

Admiral Stanson, having had his say in his own home circle, said no more, as is often the nature of man. But Mrs. Stanson, after her sister and niece had returned to London, found it, as she had said, 'awkward' — difficult not to explain when asked why Mrs. Farlong was off her visiting-list.

She explained to her best friend.

'Don't say anything,' was her final word. 'I'm rather sorry for the poor girl, and the doctor really is a dear.'

The best friend hastened to her best friend.

'I oughtn't really to tell you, but it's

most *peculiar* about the Farlongs — have you heard . . . ?'

From mouth to mouth the news travelled. Finally, somewhat distorted, the story was breathed into the ears of a certain Miss Pilbeam, a maiden lady with plenty of money and nothing to do but to play Bridge and talk. It was a jest in the village that if one wanted to circulate a piece of news Miss Pilbeam was more efficient than a telephone or telegram. She was a genius at the art of publicity.

From Mrs. Parker, the dentist's wife, who shared a stall with her at a Women's Institute Bazaar, Miss Pilbeam first heard the exciting rumour.

'My husband said that I wasn't to say anything, and of course I wouldn't tell anybody but *you*, Dora, but do you know that those two, Dr. and Mrs. Farlong, *aren't married?*'

Miss Pilbeam, who had no chin, and the profile of a parrot, opened her beak wide.

'NOT MARRIED! My *dear*, tell me more.'

Mrs. Parker told her more. That was about a fortnight after the Furnabys had left Chenwood. Within twenty-four hours the story had been flashed, as though by radio, from one end to the other of Chenwood, Little Chenwood, Mercoombe, and one or two other outlying districts which were in Dr. Farlong's radius.

Half the village firmly believed that the doctor and his young wife were still unmarried and living in sin. A few had it that *she* had been a kept woman before this. Others said that *he* had had the most vile reputation in Sussex, and was a most dangerous man for young girls to associate with.

The other half of Chenwood credited the fact that the Farlongs were now man and wife, but were shocked to think that such had not been the case when they first came to Chenwood. Moreover, the divorce case had been of an unsavoury kind. It was altogether shocking that such a man should come, like a whited sepulchre, and bluff decent, respectable people into believing him a reputable physician.

Of course, as in most of these cases, the victims of such scandal were always the last to hear of it, and it was quite a month before Blaise and Terry became conscious of the wild rumours that were flying around concerning them.

Perhaps both of them had cherished a forlorn hope that the story would not go beyond the Manor House. At any rate, Blaise went on with his work, and for the time being Terry made no difference in her method of existence. It was with the arrival of March, with its blustering winds and fitful sunshine, that the first real consequences of the Furnabys' visit to Chenwood were brought home to the Farlongs.

They had tried to forget about that postponed dinner at the Manor House, and Mrs. Stanson had subsequently avoided coming face to face with Terry

447

and so had saved herself any awkwardness of that kind.

Since then Terry had been out to tea, and two or three callers had come to Thornbank. People of no importance, and who had not yet come within the radius of Miss Pilbeam's broadcasting.

Then, one cold but fair morning of the second week in March, Terry awoke with a shock to the full realisation of the extensive damage that had been done.

Blaise was on his rounds — a not too happy Blaise, because, although the panel kept him busy, there had been a distinct falling off in his private practice. It might have been that there was no illness at the moment, but the telephone-bell was strangely quiet. And he knew for a certainty that one patient to whom he had given gas had forsaken him for another anaesthetist. But he was carrying on doggedly, and the pin-pricks, up to date, had not been sharp enough to hurt him badly.

Terry strolled down the High Street

in a tweed coat and skirt and jumper, with a little green wool cap on her bobbed head which made her look absurdly young.

In the Chenwood stores she met a certain Mrs. Asbury — a lady very much County and mother of a large family. One of her sons was up at Cambridge now. Mrs. Asbury had called on Terry, and a link had been established between them because Blaise had been up at the same college as her son.

Early in February, Mrs. Asbury's sixteen-year-old daughter had come home from boarding-school with tonsilitis, and Blaise had operated on her with great success. Mrs. Asbury, pretty and young for her years, had been extremely nice to the Farlongs since they came to Chenwood. Without thinking twice, Terry hailed her in the stores:

'Hallo, Mrs. Asbury.'

Mrs. Asbury turned and looked at Terry. Then, with an icy nod, she walked straight past her out of the stores. She left Terry standing there, scarlet to the roots of her hair. Mrs. Asbury as a rule always stopped for a long conversation.

So she had heard — and she had no further use for her.

Feeling rather sick, Terry turned her attention to the young man with the white apron who was asking what he could do for her this morning.

Mrs. Asbury walked out to her waiting car.

'I felt frightfully awkward, but I simply cannot continue my friendship with those people,' she confided to the friend who was shopping with her. 'If Mrs. Farlong is that sort of girl, I don't particularly want my John hanging round her when he comes back from Cambridge, and as for my little Pamela — I'm horrified to think that I ever let that man touch her — a man who could commit adultery with a young girl under his own roof!'

Terry, with a queer, set look on her

brown face, completed her purchases and walked down the street, wondering what Blaise would say when he heard about Mrs. Asbury. It undoubtedly meant that he would not be asked to attend Pamela again. Reaching the end of the High Street, she heard somebody hail her by her name.

'Mrs. Farlong!'

Terry stopped and looked round. A woman in a scarlet jumper-suit, with a very much powdered face and unnaturally yellow hair, came hurrying after her and fastened eager eyes upon her.

'Hello — how are you? I want you to come and have a cup of tea and a chat this afternoon,' she said effusively.

For the second time that morning Terry flushed red. This was Mrs. Lemmon, who did not live in the village all the year round, but had rented for the summer one of the new bungalows which threatened to spoil the rustic beauty of Chenwood.

Blaise had attended her professionally, and she had been trying ever since to cultivate an acquaintanceship with them. Terry liked neither her painted face nor her common voice. She was a vulgarian of the worst type, and her reputation was not good. Nobody who was 'anybody' in Chenwood knew her.

This morning she fastened upon Terry like a clam.

'But you simply *must* come — I've got a cocktail-party at six and a few boys motoring down from town for the week-end. I'd love you to join us, dear.'

The 'dear' made Terry writhe.

'I'm terribly sorry, Mrs. Lemmon. I'm engaged.'

'Oh, well, come along tomorrow.'

'I'm sorry, I'm frightfully busy.'

'Sunday evening, then.'

'I'm sorry,' said Terry again, feeling horribly uncomfortable.

An unpleasant look then crossed the features of Mrs. Lemmon, known to her friends as Trixie.

'You don't want to come,' she said resentfully.

'I — it isn't that — but I — ' Terry

stopped, stammering.

Then Mrs. Lemmon looked her up and down and laughed.

'You needn't be hoity-toity with me, my dear. *I'm* not one to mind what other people choose to do. I've been divorced myself. I think you're rather a sport, and — '

She got no further. Terry, as white now as she had been red, turned and fled from her. She almost ran up the hill towards Thornbank, her heart beating so fast that she thought it would burst. Her eyelids pricked with furious tears.

So that was how it was — Mrs. Lemmon was hailing her as a friend, calling her a sport. She, too, had heard . . .

Humiliated, horribly jarred by those two revealing episodes, Terry went home.

Blaise came back to lunch to find her weeding a flower-bed with a frozen look on her face and red-rimmed eyes. He looked at her in astonishment.

'Sweetheart, what on earth's the matter?'

Terry walked with him into the house and flung off her gardening things.

'Nothing much.'

In the consulting-room, Blaise took a look at his pad for telephone messages, found none, and turned back to Terry.

He had never seen her with quite that expression on her face before.

'Tell me,' he said quietly, 'You've been crying.'

'I'm a fool to upset myself,' she said, 'but I just couldn't help shedding a few tears — sheer rage, darling.'

He sat down in his big chair and pulled her on to the arm of it. Lighting a cigarette, he blew a cloud of smoke through his nostrils and looked up at her.

'Out with it.'

She told him, still raw with resentment. Grimly he listened to the tale of the frigid reception accorded her by Mrs. Asbury — who, Terry said, more or less cut her dead. Then to the sordid incident with Mrs. Lemmon.

'Calling me a sport!' Terry said in a

choked voice. 'Saying she's been divorced herself. You see, it must be common knowledge; we've been rather deaf or blind, haven't we, Blaise? I expect everybody knows, and quite possibly they've heard an absolutely distorted version of the whole thing.'

Blaise pressed Terry's fingers so tightly that she winced, then dropped them and covered his eyes with his hand.

'Oh, *God!*' he said softly.

Terry stared over his head out of the window. The grass was so green today, the sky so blue, rather lovely with the little white fleecy clouds scudding across it in the wind. March and spring, and the vivid yellow and striped purple of crocuses round the trees and along the borders. The tulips they'd planted were just coming up, and next week they had planned to bed out the delphinium seedlings. They had been happy. Why, why should this have happened to crush all the beauty and ecstasy out of everything?

Then Blaise got up and began to walk up and down his room. She noticed that he was losing flesh again, and his face was getting back that gaunt look.

'Damn and blast the whole damnable crowd of them!' he said through his teeth. 'Why in God's name can't they keep their mouths shut? Why must they take the first opportunity of tearing somebody's character to shreds? Why couldn't that wretched woman at the Manor House have kept things to herself?'

'And why should a friend of my mother's have come down here and started the ball rolling?' added Terry miserably.

'I hoped we stood a chance,' said Blaise. He stared at her, his eyes brilliant with anger and disgust. 'But it doesn't look as though we do.'

Terry locked two cold little hands together. 'It rather struck home this morning, Blaise.'

'I knew about the Asburys,' he said. 'I

didn't want to tell you and worry you. But I heard that Mrs. Asbury called in Grant from Barnstaple to look at Pamela's throat the other day.'

'And *you* took out her tonsils and saved her — you were up there all night with her — scarcely ate any food for days because you were so worried about her! It's iniquitous that they should shelve you for Dr. Grant.'

'Dr. Grant hasn't been mixed up in a shoddy divorce,' said Blaise.

Terry burst into tears.

Immediately he was at her side, arms around her, cheek pressed to her hair.

'Oh, my darling, don't cry. They can all go to hell — but I'm not going to have you crying. My sweet, what does it matter? We're together, let the cats yowl — they can't separate us.'

'They certainly can't,' she said, checking her sobs. 'Sorry to be such a little idiot, Blaise. That final business with that horrible Lemmon woman upset me.'

'I don't wonder, but forget it.'

'What are we going to do next?'

'I don't know. We'll have to think. We can't do anything at the moment. This is my living, and here I'm going to stick for the time being, anyhow. We're not going to be pushed out by the first cat-call.'

Terry raised a wet, defiant little face, took a big handkerchief from Blaise's pocket, and blew her nose.

'No; why should we? We'll show them that we don't care.'

'And we'll have a good afternoon in the garden,' he said, trying to be cheerful, although his spirits were sinking.

'Haven't you got to go out?'

'No. No patients this afternoon.'

Terry pressed the big handkerchief to her lips, and her eyes stared mournfully over it at her husband. That didn't sound too good. It wasn't the best thing in the world for a doctor to have no patients to see. But, having recovered from her fit of weeping, she was anxious now to cheer him. She joked with him as they walked into the dining-room for lunch.

When the little meal was over, Edith, the young general, approached Terry.

'Can I speak to you a minute, please, Mrs. Farlong?' she said.

Terry raised her eyebrows. Edith generally called her Madam.

In the kitchen, Edith, avoiding her eye, gave her a week's notice.

'You pay my wages weekly, and father says I can go at the end of the week,' she said.

'That's quite true,' said Terry slowly, 'but why do you want to leave? I thought you were settling down so well. When I bought your new uniform last month you said you loved the place.'

Edith, a red-cheeked Devon girl, pretty in a milk-maid fashion, looked at her mistress out of the corners of her eyes.

'I quite like my place,' she said.

'Then why are you leaving, Edith?'

'My father says I've got to.'

'But *why*?'

Edith licked her lips and sniggered.

'Well, you see, I didn't know when I took this place about you and the doctor.'

Terry's cheeks went scarlet. Her heart jerked unpleasantly.

'What do you mean?' she asked in a suffocated voice.

'Father says,' mumbled Edith, twisting a corner of her apron, 'that he don't like the thought of me, a young girl, sleeping under the roof of a gentleman who did what the doctor did.'

Terry, ashen now, trembling with rage, gave Edith a speechless look, then walked to the kitchen door. Somehow she managed to preserve her control sufficiently to turn back and say:

'You will go today. At once. You can pack now.'

'I can claim my wages,' began Edith.

'You will get your wages,' said Terry. 'Go! You needn't clear away the lunch. Pack now. I give you an hour to get out.'

She shut the kitchen door. She was so furious, so humiliated, she hardly knew what she was doing. She walked blindly into the consulting-room. Blaise was seated at his desk writing a letter.

'I say, darling,' he began, 'I forgot to tell you I had a chit this morning from a great pal of mine who was at Bart's with me — John Herringford. One of the best, and done awfully well — made a big name for himself. He knows all about us, and his sympathies are with me. I knew they would be — that he'd understand. He's coming down this way, passing through to Cornwall, and he's going to look us up — ' He broke off abruptly. He had seen Terry's face. 'Anything wrong? Why, you're trembling, darling.'

He rose and went toward her. She gave a hard little laugh and pulled his arm with both her hands.

'This is a red-letter day. Edith has given notice.'

'Why? I thought she was rather a nice girl.'

'Her father thinks her too nice to sleep under *this* roof.'

Blaise stared. The red blood crept up under his tan.

'What do you mean, Terry?'

'Just that. Her father told her to leave because of you — of us — '

'Oh,' said Blaise in a deadly voice. 'She told you that, did she?'

'I told her she could go now — within an hour. I won't have her here for another week, smiling out of the corners of her eyes.'

'I'll go and knock her father's head off.'

Terry caught his hand.

'No, Blaise, you can't do that — how can you? What's the use, anyhow? They're only acting according to their lights. They've heard with the rest of Chenwood. It isn't their fault.'

Blaise clenched his hands.

'So I'm not even safe with a servant-girl under my own roof, and with my wife here. It's too much, Terry. I can't and won't stand for that.'

'Darling, I know — it's abominable — ' She wound her arms about his waist. 'But I don't see what you can do or say. We've no defence — we never have had any.'

For a moment Blaise stood still, fighting with himself; then he relaxed and dropped back into his chair.

'You're right, Terry. We haven't any defence. Well — let her go. I daresay you can find a decrepit old woman who'll feel herself immune from my charms.'

Terry tried to laugh.

'I daresay. Poor darling, it's too pathetic — labelling you a sort of hungry spider waiting to inveigle the young flies into your web.'

He echoed her laugh grimly.

'We're only just beginning this sort of thing, Terry. It's rather got me down. It isn't going to help the practice when people hear our maid has left us for some mysterious reason. I don't know whether you realize it, my dear, but the money isn't coming in as it used to.'

She was frightened, but she wouldn't show it now. She felt that she must shoulder this burden sensibly and courageously. She must not let Blaise give way to his black moods. His health would suffer. It was up to her to keep the flag of hope flying, no matter how hopeless she felt.

'We said before lunch that we weren't going to be pushed out at the first set-back,' she reminded him. 'Don't despair, darling. This may be a temporary storm which will blow over.'

He knit his brows fiercely and lit another cigarette.

'What I cannot get over is the damnable injustice of it.'

'Yes, I know,' said Terry in a low voice, 'but don't fret about it. It's no use. After all, we knew what we were in for when that divorce went through.'

The hardness suddenly left his thin, tired face. He put out a hand and touched Terry's hair.

'Always brave — always marvellous to me,' he said. 'I love you so much,

Terry, that it's going to break me up if you're made to suffer too badly through this sort of thing.'

She put her arm around his neck and drew his head against her breast.

'You know I don't mind,' she whispered. 'And I never will mind so long as you go on loving me. It only hurts for the moment when beastly things like this happen.'

She wooed him back to peace, to content again. They joked together as they worked in their garden, and once Edith had walked righteously and for ever out of the house.

The news that the Farlongs' maid had left her place very suddenly soon leaked round the village. It was accompanied by raised eyebrows and dark insinuations.

'Perhaps the doctor has been trying his old tricks — he seems to like young girls,' one estimable resident of Chenwood remarked.

Ere another twenty-four hours had elapsed there was an ugly rumour in circulation that Dr. Farlong *had* cast an eye upon the ripe charms of Edith, and that her father had taken her away just in time.

5

There came a morning early in May when Blaise and Terry faced the fact that unless they left Chenwood, Chenwood would make it so unpleasant for them that they would be forced out of it.

Day after day some fresh humiliation was heaped upon Terry. Somebody else cut her. Bazaars were held and she was not asked to take a stall, which was the custom for the local doctor's wife. Parties were given and she was conspicuous by her absence. Even the local tradesmen looked at her queerly when she entered the shops.

So far as Blaise was concerned, he was heading for complete disaster. His private practice was almost nil. Only one or two of the most broad-minded and charitable had some use for his services. But one by one the patients on his list faded away, until it was common knowledge that Grant from Barnstaple, and a certain Dr. Fuller from a village just outside Blaise's radius, were now doing most of the private practice in Chenwood.

The ugly and persistent rumours which had spread and thrived in the village had so seriously affected Blaise's reputation that even his panel practice was dwindling. This girl's mother refused to let her go to Dr. Farlong's surgery, and that woman's husband warned her to keep away from him, and so on, until one thing was apparent to Blaise: he could no longer make a living in Chenwood.

The final blow was struck through the stupid behaviour of an hysterical girl, the daughter of the local fishmonger.

The girl, aged eighteen, more thoughtless, perhaps, than harmful, was one of those foolish, neurotic creatures to be dreaded and avoided by such public men as Blaise.

He had attended her early in the spring for glands. He had met her kind before, and knew that he had to behave with the utmost care and discretion. She was pretty in a fluffy way, and man-mad. She began by using her large blue eyes upon him with a desperate effort to turn the cool, prosaic physician into a man of flesh and blood.

Her complete and utter failure only fanned the flame. She called repeatedly at the surgery just to see Blaise and make him take notice of her. She affected complaints which she had not got and never had had. She pretended to turn faint when he touched her hand in order to take her pulse, and on one occasion flopped into his arms while he was sounding her heart.

Blaise dealt with her firmly, even brutally, and told her that she need not come again, as she was perfectly well and he could not waste his time.

She then waylaid him; hung round his gate when it was time for him to come home, and openly declared her passion for him.

Blaise was annoyed. Terry laughed, unable to treat it seriously. But the thing had more serious results once the story of the Farlong divorce was thoroughly in circulation.

The girl, Dolly Pilchard, in a hysterical moment, tried to take poison, and was only stopped in time by her mother. Moaning and weeping, she confessed to an undying passion for Dr. Farlong.

Pilchard, the fishmonger, a worthy and respectable tradesman, and a devout member of the Plymouth Brethren, worked himself up into a towering rage, came round to Blaise's surgery, and accused him of trying to seduce his daughter.

The row between the two men was brief and fierce. Blaise, half mad with indignation and fury, almost lost control of himself and struck Dolly's enraged parent, but Terry saved the situation. She had been standing outside the surgery door, white and trembling, listening to the filthy accusations against her husband until, unable to endure it, she walked in. Holding on to Blaise's arm, she, herself, answered Pilchard's attack.

'How dare you come here and accuse my husband of making advances to your daughter! It's a rotten lie. He has only attended her professionally, and to my certain knowledge he's done his level best to get rid of her because she was behaving in such a stupid fashion. I, myself, have seen her loitering around our gate — she is the sort of girl to ruin a doctor's reputation. It's vile — unjust!'

Blaise, shivering with fury, tried to stop her.

'Leave this man to me.'

The fishmonger gave Terry a sullen look, picked up his cap, and went to the door.

'I'm not taking any high-handed talk from you, mam,' he said in a sneering voice. 'From what I hear, *you're* no better than you ought to be.'

Blaise uttered a roar like a wounded animal, and would have flung himself bodily on the man, but fortunately he escaped in time and slammed the door after him. Terry rushed to it, put her back against it, and warded Blaise off.

'No, no,' she panted. 'Don't go after him — don't. He'll only have you up for assault — it'll make things much worse. Blaise darling, don't — please let him go. He didn't know what he was saying. I don't mind, anyhow.'

Blaise breathed quickly, nostrils widening, eyes bloodshot in a face which had grown a shade thinner these last few weeks.

'But I do mind,' he stammered. 'By God! it's too much — to have you insulted in front of my very face.'

She shut her eyes.

'Let the man go — to please me.'

Blaise fumbled in a pocket for his pipe.

'Very well.'

Terry's tense little body relaxed. With a deep sigh she followed Blaise back into the consulting-room. She felt a little sick and faint as she bent down to put some coal on the fire. It was a mild May night, and they had been working in the garden until they were both cold. They had just finished supper. They had had no maid since the departure of Edith. Nobody in the village had answered Terry's advertisement in the local paper.

These had been wretched, depressing days, and neither of them looked well on it.

Lack of finance was crushing them. When the next quarter came, unless things had improved they were going to find it hard to pay their bills. That knowledge, combined with the general boycott to which they were submitted, made it hard for both of them to look on the humorous side of things.

Herringford, Blaise's friend, had come down to see them as he had promised, motoring through to Cornwall. He had been extraordinarily charming to them. Terry had found him a most delightful person; a man who had never married because of an unhappy affair in his youth, but one who could appreciate, perhaps more than most, what a woman like Terry would mean to the man who loved her.

He had never cared for Ruth Farlong, and he found it very easy indeed to sympathise with Blaise for letting that divorce go through. Despite their efforts not to let him see, he had been quick to discover that these two were up against things in Chenwood. He had said nothing, but he had seen a lot — signs of rigid economy, of a frugal existence, and of nothing but their absorbing love for each other, and their garden to make life worth living for them.

He had wanted to lend Blaise money, but of course Blaise would not hear of it. So he had gone his way, admiring their fortitude and perhaps envying them their love for each other.

Once or twice Terry had been tempted to write to her mother and accept the offer she had once made to finance her should she ever be in need. But the temptation had not been very strong, and she had never given way to it. No — she was too proud, and it would hurt Blaise terribly to accept a penny from her family.

Somehow or other they must hang on and hope for the best, but tonight's episode had sounded the knell of doom.

They sat opposite each other by the fire in the consulting-room, considered the situation, and found it utterly without hope.

'We can see,' Blaise said, 'by the attitude of that swine Pilchard, what the general feeling is in the village. I haven't any practice left, Terry. Before long I shall be asked to leave. We'd better go before that happens.'

She clasped her hands over her knees, the flickering firelight showing up the shadows which were like dark bruises under her eyes. Her lips quivered.

'Give up our home — our garden

— when we've only just made it! Four months' work.'

'I know,' he said. 'I know!'

'And we did so want to see the flowers come out — especially the delphiniums and the roses.'

He drew a hand wearily across his forehead. He was exhausted, no longer with hard work, but by lack of it, and the strain of repeated failure.

'I'm almost at the stage where I don't care about the garden. But I do care that this should happen to you. When we came here, I wanted to make a success of things for you. I meant you to be so happy once we were married.'

She slid on to the rug before the fire, sat at his feet with her arms clasped about his knees and bowed her head upon them.

'But I have been happy — terribly so. You know that.'

'How can you have been happy these last two months?' he asked bitterly.

'It's been unpleasant at times, but I've been able to bear it — gladly

476

— because of you.'

He made no answer. She looked up at him, anxious and unhappy. His face was drawn and bitter.

'Blaise!' she cried suddenly, panic-stricken, 'hasn't it been worth while to you? Are you tired of me? Are you sorry we started life together? Would it have been better for you if I had never come away with you in the beginning?'

The pain in her voice and her eyes wrenched his heart. He put his arms about her, stooped, and pressed his lips passionately to her head.

'God, no! It would have been ten thousand times worse if I hadn't had you, Terry. I haven't regretted it — and I could never grow tired of you. I love you with every drop of blood in my body! But it shatters me — to think that we should have reached this *impasse* and that it should involve you. God! I nearly killed that swine when he insulted you in that surgery just now.'

Terry hugged his knees.

'Don't think about it, darling.'

'I can't bear it to have happened to you.'

'And what about you?' she cried, lifting her face. 'Do you think I've liked hearing you insulted and seeing you shelved by one patient after another? It's nearly broken my heart.'

He hid his face in her hair and shut his eyes.

'It's broken us both, darling. They've defeated us. We're beat. I must sell the practice. We must go.'

'Yes,' she whispered. 'I suppose we must.'

'The practice isn't worth very much,' he added. 'We shan't be so well off as we were when we came down here. And it will mean starting all over again, and perhaps having to face the same sort of thing.'

'No,' she said in a scared voice. 'We can't go on paying all our lives.'

'We can, easily,' he said with a mirthless laugh.

He reached out a hand and picked up

The Times from his desk.

'Some people don't pay. They're generally the guilty ones. I meant to show you this this morning. Here is an announcement of my former wife's engagement.'

Terry froze. Her small face was stony as she took the paper from her husband and read the paragraph he had marked with a blue pencil:

'The engagement is announced between Lieut.-Commander Hugh Spalderson, R.N., of Wynch House, Dartmouth, and Ruth Christabel Farlong, of 97 Link Street, Lancaster Gate, W. The marriage is expected to take place early in June.'

Terry handed the paper back.

'God help the man,' she said.

Blaise had to smile at that. It was so deliciously feminine. He bent down and kissed the top of Terry's head.

'I can't say I envy him.'

'She isn't long in consoling herself,'

said Terry. 'Did you know him?'

'Not personally, but I vaguely remember Ruth mentioning his name.'

'Well,' said Terry, 'I don't care whether she marries a Naval Commander or the Emperor of Japan. I don't call her lucky — she must sometimes be ashamed of what she did to you, and sorry that she lost you, too.'

'I'm quite sure she isn't sorry about that. We never got on.'

Terry lifted a passionate face.

'But we do, don't we? Whatever we have to go through, Blaise, we do love each other, don't we?'

'God knows we do, dear,' he said, and sealed her eyelids with his kisses. Some of the misery, the degradation, the hopeless failure faded into the background while he held her thus.

Terry held on to one of his hands with both of hers and pressed her lips to the palm.

'It's rather a rotten moment to tell you, Blaise — just when we're down and out — but you know, don't you, that one of my ambitions has been to give you a child.'

His cheeks flushed. He looked down at the bowed brown head in dismay.

'Terry — you're not — '

'I am,' she whispered. 'I'm quite sure. I would have told you before, but I thought it would worry you so under the circumstances. Darling, don't think I'm afraid, or that I mind about the money or anything else — I'm so frightfully proud; it will be just the touch of perfection in my happiness. Perhaps it will be a son — would you like to have a son, Blaise?'

He could not speak. Her courage, her unswerving devotion, her beautiful generosity, were things before which a man must uncover his head and remain still. Since Priscilla's death he had always wanted another child, and to have one who would be Terry's flesh and blood as well as his would mean so much. He knew it. He had hoped for it, but not yet — not while their living was so precarious, and mud was still being flung at them. It was not fair on Terry or the child.

'Darling, darling thing,' he said huskily. 'It's marvellous, in a way — and you know as well as I do that I'd adore to have a son. Your son, Terry. My God, what a fine man he ought to be if he's like you! But I oughtn't to have let it happen just now. It will drive me mad to think I can't give you what you need — or put you in the position in which you ought to be.'

'Don't worry about that, Blaise. I shall manage.'

'On what?'

'We aren't altogether penniless, are we?' she said with her brave smile.

'No — not altogether. There's always my three hundred a year. But that's not enough.'

'We'll sell this practice and buy another.'

'Yes, but, Terry' — he drew her up on to his knee and cradled her there like a child — 'this isn't the time for you to be having an infant — with all this worry and suspense and the moving. My sweet, I do feel so remorseful — '

He broke off. She covered his lips with her hand.

'Don't dare say it. I want my son.'

He gave a deep sigh and hid his tired and troubled face against her hair.

'What a woman you are, Terry. I do adore you.'

'That's good,' she said happily, and put her arm about his neck and lay there in his arms, drowsily, watching the firelight.

Blaise Farlong marvelled at the wonder of such women as this one who had been given to him as a wife. Facing disgrace, poverty, every kind of difficulty, she lay there in his arms, smiling and content — because she had her man and her unborn child, and for her they were fulfilment of all her dearest needs.

But he, man-like, could not share her brooding peace. He was tortured with worry because of her and their coming child; infinitely troubled because he was responsible for her, for whatever happened to her, and he loved her more than anybody or anything on God's earth.

The injustice of Pilchard's foul accusations and the humiliation of the position in which he had found himself these last few weeks in Chenwood had left a mark on Blaise. It was like a festering sore in the man's very soul. He could not see that the future would bring anything better. In spite of all Terry's sweetness and seeming content, he could not still the voice of his conscience which asked him if he had had the right to take her away; to act in such a fashion as had branded her for all time as his partner in crime. God knew they were innocent of that crime, but Ruth Farlong's accusations had had such far-reaching effect as to damage his reputation here, months afterwards.

Loving Terry so much, it was intolerable to him to contemplate that she should go on suffering for and through him. Yet in the beginning the thing had not been his fault. Fate — circumstances — had been too strong for them both.

With passionate tenderness he pressed Terry's brown head closer to his shoulders and smoothed a strand of hair back from her eyes. She stirred in his arms.

'It's going to be all right, Blaise darling . . .'

He whispered huskily, against her ear:

'With you — anything must be all right — angel!'

'What shall we call our son? — if it isn't too previous!'

'Blessed one, if it is a son, you shall call him what you wish.'

'What was your father's name?'

'Adrian.'

'That's a beautiful name. Shall we call our boy Adrian Blaise Farlong?'

'Do you want to?'

'Yes. I'm sure your father must have been nice.'

'He was rather a grand old chap, Terry.'

'Tell me about him.'

'He was a doctor. He spent twenty-five years in cancer research. He gave his life for it. I was just going up to the 'Varsity when he died. My mother died very soon afterwards. They had had thirty-two years together. It was an unusually perfect marriage, and it seemed that she could not live without him. She just faded out six months later.'

'Blaise, what a lovely story!' Terry hugged him close. Her lashes were wet. 'It's the first time you've ever told me about them. Blaise, your father must have been like you. You are capable of making a woman perfectly happy for thirty years — and more.'

'Sweetheart, don't be so nice to me.'

'Yes, and we shall call our son Adrian Farlong.'

'That's dear of you,' he said. 'I should like that. But if it's a girl it's going to be Teresa Mary.'

Terry's eyes sparkled at him.

'But that's the name of your new delphinium.'

'The delphinium must share it — with my daughter.'

'All the same, I want it to be Adrian.'

He kissed her softly all over her sweet brown face. Then he stood up, lifting her in his arms.

'I'm going to carry you up to bed. It's getting late, and you're tired. And look here, my child, no more digging in the garden. You've got to take care of yourself now. Go easy.'

'Course I shall, silly.'

He carried her slowly and carefully up to their room, and in the darkness laid her on the bed, sat beside her, and held her close for a moment.

'Are you coming up too, Blaise?'

'Not just yet, dear. I have work to do.'

'Don't sit down there worrying.'

'I'll try not to.'

Her hands caressed his thick hair and touched his cheeks.

'And don't get thin again. I can't

bear it. You were looking so well.'

'I shall be all right — so long as you are.'

He put his lips against her hand, and then lit the gas-jet for her and went downstairs.

Something rattled in the letter-box. He saw a piece of white paper lying on the fibre mat, stooped, and picked it up. He drew a sharp breath as he read the few words on the soiled sheet of paper scrawled in an illiterate hand.

'If you and your kep-woman, don't clear out of Chenwood you'll find yourself in the duck-pond.

'(*Signed*) FATHER OF A YOUNG GIRL.'

Blaise drew a deep breath and crumpled the note in his hands. There were two white lines on either side of his mouth, as he walked into his consulting-room. He and his 'kept-woman.' He thought of the clean, sweet, fine creature whom he had just left upstairs; his wife, and mother of his unborn child. That they should sling mud ... filthy, rotten mud ... at her! ...

He sat down at his desk and put his head between his hands. And he knew that now the ugly rumours, started by the whisperings of a gossiping woman, had reached this preposterous pitch, Terry must leave Chenwood at once, and he would follow.

6

One fine, warm morning in August, Mrs. Manstone and her faithful maid, Davis, turned out the three box-rooms at the Cedars.

The Cedars was up for sale. Mrs. Manstone had decided that the place was too big for her now that she was living alone. Her income had been somewhat reduced by the falling stock-markets, and she had made up her mind to move; to leave Wimbledon after all these years and take a flat in south-west London. She meant to find a place near Barbara, who was not going into the country after all. Barbara had been very ill for the last two months, and had only recently emerged from a nursing-home. Her hopes of motherhood had been shattered. Mrs. Manstone was the only one who regretted that fact. Francis seemed indifferent, and Barbara was relieved that she would not have to bear the worry and responsibility of a child. But Mrs. Manstone was distinctly disappointed. She had reached a stage in her life when she wanted grand-children to play about her knees.

She was altogether a disappointed woman these days. Barbara's marriage had been such a failure. She did nothing but quarrel with Francis, and they were even contemplating a separation. But both Mrs. Manstone and Mrs. Colroyd had rushed into the breach and prevented the disaster — temporarily, anyhow.

This morning, Mrs. Manstone felt depressed while she searched through boxes and hampers which were full of those useless articles which somehow collect through the years, accumulate, and are treasured only to be thrown away finally on the rubbish-heap.

She was ageing, and, as Davis remarked in the kitchen last night: 'Not so full of herself.' A little less authoritative and managing. And it was quite certain that she had begun to worry about Miss Terry.

Mrs. Manstone had just discovered some old notebooks covered with the big scrawly handwriting of a child, and had put on her reading-glasses and glanced through them.

'Good gracious,' she said. 'Fancy finding these! They're the fairy-stories Miss Terry used to write when she was a little thing of ten. Do you remember how she loved scribbling, Davis?'

'That I do, madam. She was a quaint little girl, wasn't she? Full of fancies. I often wonder what's happened to Miss Terry. I can't help it, madam.'

Mrs. Manstone put down the book, took off her glasses, and stared a moment past Davis into the shadowy corner of the box-room. The gloom which had been weighing her down since she got up this morning increased. She had a disturbing memory of Terry, aged ten, with her determined little face and unruly brown hair — it had been curly then — and she had been brown as a berry — always sunburnt — so different from Barbara, who had such a milk-white skin. She could see Terry, bending earnestly over her notebook, holding the stump of a pencil tightly in grubby fingers, and refusing to abandon her job for the less congenial one of darning stockings.

'I want to finish my story!' she had argued with her mother. 'I must make the prince and princess live happy ever after. I *can't* stop till they do!'

So like Terry. Determined to create a happy romance; certain that it was of more account in life than needlework. That was where Mrs. Manstone had failed to understand her.

She began to wonder if she had been horribly hard and unfeeling to cut Terry right out of her life in the way that she had done. It was almost a year since she had set eyes on the girl. And she had never answered that letter from Devon. She had wanted to, but she had been too proud, still too angry because of the disgrace Terry had brought upon the family name.

She had heard news of Terry from the Furnabys. They had come back to Wimbledon full of talk about Terry. May Furnaby had wasted no time in telling her friend about her unexpected meeting with both the girl and the husband. A very good-looking, distinguished sort of man, she had described Dr. Farlong, and Terry looked wonderfully well and happy, and far from penitent.

Of course, Mrs. Furnaby had left no doubt in Mrs. Manstone's mind that the unpleasant story of the Farlong divorce case had been spread about Chenwood. She had felt quite angry with May for starting it. It was really uncharitable not to have left them alone.

Since then she had found her thoughts frequently recurring to Terry; wondered how she was; what was happening to her; whether May's gossiping had done her any damage.

Mrs. Manstone finished her sorting and clearing for the morning and went downstairs to wash for lunch. Her mind was still strangely full of Terry.

She began to contemplate writing a letter to her — telling her that she would like to see her, although nothing would induce her to meet her *husband*. But she really would like to see the child again. Perhaps she had been too hard on her. She might discuss it with Barbara. But Mrs. Manstone felt uneasy when she thought of her elder daughter. Barbara would be all against starting communication with Terry. The Colroyds would not like it. In her heart of hearts Mrs. Manstone was a little weary of the Colroyds.

During lunch Davis brought the post. Mrs. Manstone sighed, and sought distraction from her thoughts of Terry in her letters. One was an invitation to an 'at home'; one, a bulky letter, written on cheap mauve paper in a small, not very educated hand.

Mrs. Manstone opened the mauve letter, frowning. From whom could it possibly be? Then, as she began to read it, her cheeks became crimson and her breath quickened. She read the letter rapidly, and with absorbing interest, to its conclusion. The address was from a hospital in Hammersmith.

'DEAR MADAM, — I am sending you this letter because I don't know where to find your dorter who went away with Dr. Farlong from Rossdown. You may have heard my name. I am Mrs. Clarke, who was housekeeper to Dr. and Mrs. Farlong at Rossdown where all the trouble started. Madam I know where to find you because your dorter told me she come from Wimbledon and I found it in the telephone book. Madam I am not long for this world and want to put things right so far as I can before I die. I have an incurable disease, and my boy Willy died of the flu in December and I've nothing more to live for but I feel I done a very wicked thing and I want it to be known.

'Madam your dorter did not sleep that night with the doctor. She was innocent and so was he and I can't rest at nights for worrying over the wicked thing I done. I did it for money for my boy and Mrs. Farlong tempted me. Madam, Mrs. Farlong wanted a divorce and she offered me money if I would swear your dorter and the doctor slept together. So I did, but I haven't known any peace since. Madam I done an awful wrong to your dorter and the doctor who was a good respectable man. I heard the divorce was over and the doctor married to your dorter but if I helped ruin them I sincerely regret it and ask your pardon and want the present Mrs. Farlong to forgive me before I die as I haven't long.

'I am truly sorry, Madam,
        'Your obedient servant,
                'ADA CLARKE.'

497

When Mrs. Manstone came to the end of this long and amazing epistle, her face was almost purple and her breath came so rapidly that it nearly choked her. She started to read the long, badly written letter all over again. Then, swallowing hard, she rose from the table and stared blindly out of the window. Her eyes were suffused.

So Terry had not lied. She *had* been innocent that night. She *had* told the truth when she had sworn that the whole thing was an iniquitous conspiracy on Ruth Farlong's part ... a plot to enable the woman to get her divorce.

The housekeeper who signed herself Ada Clarke had perjured herself in the divorce court — had accepted a bribe to swear that Blaise Farlong had committed misconduct under his roof, that night, with Terry.

For a few moments Mrs. Manstone could scarcely analyse the whole thing to its full extent. Her thoughts were chaotic. It was all too horrible; too incredible. But here it was, in black and white: the confession of a dying woman from hospital; indisputably true.

Then gradually the whole significance was made clear to Mrs. Manstone. She realised what had happened — what she had done. Through her disbelief in Terry, her readiness to accuse, to condemn, she had driven Terry into the arms of that man. Yes, driven her own daughter to sin. And the doctor himself, whom Mrs. Clarke had described as 'a good, respectable man,' had been driven to sin, too. All through that wicked creature, Ruth Farlong.

Mrs. Manstone's high colour faded. She grew pale. Her heart-beats hurt her. She put both hands to her ample bosom and held them there, trembling. She was stricken with remorse; with the awful feeling that she had blundered badly; and that was not a very agreeable thought to such a woman as Clara Manstone. She was, according to her lights, a good woman, and she was appalled by the thought that she had helped to ruin her own child.

'How was I to know?' she asked herself. 'How was I to know?'

How could anybody have dreamed Ruth Farlong had invented such a monstrous story in order to rid herself of her husband? Mrs. Manstone had a sudden vision of Terry sitting on the edge of her bed in that little room upstairs which had been empty and locked for a whole year, saying:

'I didn't sleep with him ... I didn't ... I would have thought that you, my mother, would have defended me ... '

Mrs. Manstone sat down heavily, dropped the mauve letter in her lap, and hid her face in her hands.

'God forgive me,' she said aloud.

Then suddenly she sprang up and pressed the bell. She was still pale and shaking when Davis entered the room.

'Davis,' she said, 'I have just had — very peculiar news — concerning Miss Terry.'

'Indeed, madam?' said Davis eagerly.

'Yes. I — I hope we may see her again — quite shortly.'

'I hope so, indeed, madam.'

'Bring me my hat — my coat — my gloves — quickly. And telephone to the cab-rank for a taxi. I must go out at once.'

Davis stared. The mistress looked 'properly upset'. As though she had seen a ghost. She hastened to do her bidding.

Five minutes later Mrs. Manstone sat in a taxi speeding to the West London Hospital, Hammersmith. She was going to see Mrs. Clarke. And, *en route*, she had sent a telegram to 'Mrs. Farlong, Thornbank, Chenwood.' It said:

'I know everything must see you immediately come home. Mother.'

Later that same day, Mrs. Manstone, unusually extravagant, took another taxi from the Cedars to South Kensington. She had important news for Barbara.

Barbara came back from tea and Bridge to find her mother, in a state of nervous excitement, awaiting her in the drawing-room of her flat.

'Hello,' Barbara said, without enthusiasm. 'I didn't know you were coming. Have you been here long?'

'Yes, but that doesn't matter. I had to see you.'

'Why, what's happened?'

Barbara, who looked thin and white and had lost all pretensions to good looks since her recent illness, took off her hat and stared at her mother. She seemed very upset about something. Barbara had never seen her so moved from her usual poise and dignity.

'It's about Terry,' said Mrs. Manstone breathlessly.

'Terry! What has she done now?'

'It isn't that. It's what have *we* done?'

Mrs. Manstone seated herself on the chesterfield and drew Barbara down beside her. She took a mauve letter from her bag and handed it to the girl.

'First of all — read that.'

Barbara read it. When she had finished, she looked up, and her own cheeks were a deep shade of pink.

'Good heavens — but is it true? Do you believe it?'

'I know it's true,' said Mrs. Manstone in a solemn voice. 'I went to the West London Hospital this afternoon and saw the woman myself. A wretched creature — with only a few days to live. She repeated everything that she said in this letter, and a bit more beside. I heard all the details of the story. Barbara, that woman, Ruth Farlong, ought to be — to be *hanged*!' finished Mrs. Manstone fervidly.

Barbara stared at her mother.

'But it's incredible — that she could have bribed a servant to back her up in such a rotten story.'

'Such is the case. That miserable Mrs. Clarke had a son — he's dead now — and she was willing to be bribed for his sake. She confessed to me with her own lips that a better man than Dr. Farlong never lived. She said he had done his best to be a decent, faithful husband, and that his wife nagged until it was hard for him to be even civil to her. Our poor Terry was caught in a thunderstorm that night. She asked for shelter at the doctor's house, and Mrs. Clarke gave it to her. The doctor came home unexpectedly, but they were both *absolutely* innocent. Mrs. Farlong invented the whole terrible story. Mrs. Clarke even hinted that Ruth Farlong wanted to go to this man in the Navy whom she married a few months ago . . . and that was one of her reasons for wanting the doctor out of the way.'

'But it was preposterous!'

'Monstrous is the word. Ruining Terry's reputation — and that man's career — '

Barbara pulled her wedding ring off and on her thin finger, an uneasy look in her eyes. She had been only too ready to join in the general accusation against her young sister. She felt suddenly ashamed.

'I'm frightfully sorry about it, mother. It's rotten luck on Terry.'

'We helped to drive her to that man.'

'Well, he seems to be quite nice, anyhow, from what this housekeeper says.'

'Yes. Thank God. But nothing can undo the fact that Terry ran away with him — and that the divorce went through.'

'I can't think *why* she ran away with him — if they were just strangers — not in love.'

'They were thrown together — and you know how impulsive Terry always was.'

'Yes,' said Barbara slowly.

'Thank heavens,' added Mrs. Manstone, 'from what Mrs. Furnaby said, Terry seemed happily married. But what worries me is this: I wired this afternoon to Terry, at Chenwood, telling her I want her to come home and see me at once. I've had the wire sent back. They said it was undelivered.'

'What does that mean?'

'Only that this doctor and Terry have left Chenwood. I suppose May Furnaby started a lot of gossip and made it unpleasant for them. Well, now I've had to content myself with a letter. I wrote to Terry and asked that it should be forwarded — which no doubt the post-office will see to.'

'So perhaps we shall see Terry again quite soon,' said Barbara in a low voice.

'Yes.' Mrs. Manstone's pince-nez became misty. For the first time for many years her cold, blue eyes were full of tears. 'I've had the child on my mind for days — and particularly this morning, Baa. My dear, I've not been as good a mother as I ought to have been to her — and I regret it from the bottom of my heart.'

Barbara bit her lip. This — from mother — who had never been known to admit herself in the wrong! Then suddenly her face brightened. Her head shot up.

'One thing, Francis and his precious mother won't be able to sneer at me or my sister any longer. My God! I'll see they know about Ruth Farlong — or — or Mrs. Spalderson, or whoever she is now! They shall hear of the disgraceful way that the marvellous niece got her divorce. I'll see to that!'

'Yes,' said Mrs. Manstone, staring in front of her. 'And I shall see that everybody else — Lady Carisdon included — hears that Terry was most *unjustly* accused.'

Mother and daughter looked at each other, the light of battle dawning hopefully in two pairs of hard blue eyes.

7

Not far from the Cromwell Road there is a tall, narrow house with the usual ugly basement and area, but which has clean net curtains over the windows and a general atmosphere of gentility. A certain widow lady, by name Mrs. Fraser, once occupied the house in comfort, but, having fallen upon bad times, it ceased to be a private house and became, very quietly and decorously, a private hotel. Mrs. Fraser took in people by recommendation only.

It was to this same house that Blaise and Terry came after the degradation of their enforced exodus from Chenwood.

One of the few loyal patients remaining to Blaise was distantly related to Mrs. Fraser, and, having heard that the doctor and his wife wanted quiet and inexpensive accommodation in town, had sent him to the place, which was by way of being a Godsend. Not only was it cheap, but it was clean, and they had one large double bedroom right at the top of the house, which was as airy as one could expect in such a congested area. The windows looked right over the ugly roofs and chimney-tops and gave them a sense of space and freedom which they both badly needed. They felt stifled in London.

These last twelve weeks had been a severe strain upon the affections of these two who shared an undeserved disgrace. But their love had not faltered under the test.

It had not been easy for either of them to pack up and leave a place in which they had settled so happily, and with every confidence of making a success of things. Flight seemed an admission of guilt, and yet they had had no choice. Ill-feeling against Blaise in Chenwood had become too rife, and he refused to allow Terry to remain where she might at any moment be subjected to insult.

They had the first real argument of their lives together that morning after the wretched episode of Pilchard the fishmonger.

The nasty warning note shoved through their letter-box had decided Blaise that he would not allow Terry to stay in Chenwood another day. He had told her that she must go — and go immediately — and that he would follow almost at once.

Terry had been appalled by the thought of leaving him, even for a week or two. She protested hotly that she preferred to stay with him, no matter what happened in Chenwood.

But Blaise, grimmer than she had ever known him, had put his hands on her shoulders, looked down at her, and said:

'No, Terry. For more reasons than one I am not prepared to let you stay here. God knows I don't want you to go — I shall loathe it without you — but you're going to be the mother of my child, and I'm not going to risk worse things happening to you than happened last night.'

'I don't mind — I can't leave you alone,' she had argued, and ended up in tears in his arms.

But Blaise had been quite firm. Deeply depressed, she found herself in Mrs. Fraser's house off the Cromwell Road. It was a full fortnight before Blaise could join her, and the longest two weeks of her life. Her usually brave, bright spirits had flagged with the heat and by reason of the fact that she was not feeling particularly well. Every day Blaise had written. Every day she wrote to him. But their separation seemed interminable.

She could only guess at the bitterness and loneliness which he must be enduring down there in the little home they had made together. He refrained from telling her about any further difficulties and unpleasantness to which he was subjected, but Terry knew that he had had to put up with a lot.

In one of his letters he had said:

'This morning I went out into the garden, and the delphinium seedlings are growing quite big. It seems so tragic, darling, that we shall never see them flower.'

She had wept passionately over that paragraph. Yes, it did seem tragic that they would never reap the benefit of all their work in their garden. It might seem a little thing as compared to the world's big tragedies, but it was symbolic of all the failure and misfortune that they had shared, and that they would face in the future.

There were times during those two solitary weeks in town when Terry was afraid. Not only were there Blaise and herself to think of now; there was the coming child. So many awful things might happen. Blaise might not find another suitable practice. As it was, they were in a tight position financially. Then there was the practice at

Chenwood which had yet to be sold, and she knew from Blaise's letters that business transactions were going to be difficult down there.

She was immensely relieved when finally he joined her. It was so much easier to bear the burden of things together. They were both looking pale and harassed and not too well. And, while they smiled and kissed, fear knocked at their hearts, each for the other.

'You're losing all your sunburn, my sweet,' he told her when he first held her in his arms.

'I shall have to buy a bottle of it.' She tried to jest, and, outlining his gaunt cheek-bones with her fingers, added: 'Oh, darling, don't get any thinner!'

'I'll fatten up when all this worry is over,' he comforted her. 'It's you I'm worrying about most, my dearest. This isn't the time for you to be going through such an ordeal.'

But she only laughed and told him that nothing mattered so long as he was with her, and that he must never send her away from him again.

Sitting beside him on one of the twin beds in their top room, her hand locked in his, she heard the story of his departure from Chenwood. Thornbank was empty. Their furniture had come up to London and gone into store. The agents were trying hard to sell the practice for Blaise. Dr. Fuller, meanwhile, had taken over Blaise's panel practice.

His last few moments at Chenwood had been unpleasant. He had come up against Admiral Stanson at Barnstaple Station when he was catching his train to town. The Admiral, with whom he had so often played billiards and exchanged a cigar and a joke, had turned his back and cut Blaise dead.

The hideous injustice of the whole thing had gnawed at Blaise's very soul all the way up from Devon. But much of it diminished at the first touch of Terry's hand, and the sweet, passionate fervour of her welcome.

Then had followed the dreary weeks of looking out for another practice. It was so difficult to find the right one. Money was so scarce. He dared not take a definite step until he had sold the practice at Chenwood.

The sale was completed at the end of June, but he found himself poorer than when he had taken it.

Terry was strong and healthy, which fact was a big comfort to him. In spite of her condition, the trying heat, and the monotony of the existence they led in Cromwell Road, she managed to keep the flag flying. It was Blaise who suffered most. London had never suited his health, and he was labouring under a terrific strain — obsessed by the feeling that he had no right to let this thing happen to Terry. She was so plucky; so full of gay courage and humour; so utterly uncomplaining. But he knew that she hated every day and every night in London, and that she was as worried as he was about their future.

If the Thorntons had been in

England, he would have insisted upon her going down to stay at Frog's Hall, and knew that Gage would welcome her. But unfortunately Gage and Tony were in America. A big offer had taken Tony over to New York, and of course Gage had gone with him.

Again and again Blaise tried to make Terry agree to leave town and go into the country. But she would not stir without him. And he could not afford to come up and down from town. London was the centre of everything, and he could not afford to miss any opportunity.

Several times Terry turned her thoughts to her mother. It was only natural that now, when she was to be a mother herself, she would like to have seen and talked to Mrs. Manstone about everything. But nothing would have induced her to go to Wimbledon or make any overtures, since her mother had never replied to the letter she had sent her from Devonshire months ago.

Two or three times a week Blaise suddenly left town and travelled to various parts of England to investigate some practice which was for sale. But nothing seemed to come within his limits, either where his capabilities or his finances were concerned.

Many were the nights when he returned to Terry weary and dispirited — so much more anxious for her than for himself. Sometimes when it was really hot, and there seemed not a breath of air, they would sit together by the open window, he with his pipe, she with her last cigarette, smoking and talking before bedtime. It wrenched his heart to see the shadows of fatigue under Terry's eyes, and that slight thickening of her childish figure.

'Why can't I tuck you up in that big bed at Victoria's Cottage again?' he once asked her. 'Why can't I go out into the garden and pick a delphinium for your jug?'

''Fraid there's only a hot and cold basin and no jug in here,' she answered, with her head against his shoulder.

'We both loathe this,' he said wearily, and looked round the room which was stacked with their luggage and so unlike home, despite all Terry's efforts to add a touch of comfort. On the table beside her bed there were some roses in a vase. He had bought them for her from a woman outside the Underground. She pointed to them, smiling.

'Look how sweet they are — '

But he looked at her.

'I can only think how sweet *you* are!'

She rubbed her cheek against his arm.

'I hate chimney-tops — don't you?' he added with a wry smile.

Terry tilted her head and gazed upwards, dreamily.

'But there are still stars — look at them instead, Blaise.'

He kissed each of her hands and folded them in his long fingers.

'Any man who lives with you will always find the stars in the darkness, Terry. Sometimes I wish you weren't so

brave. It makes me feel rotten —
because I can do nothing that I want to
do for you.'

'I'll start complaining bitterly if it will
make you happier, darling. Complaint
number one is that you aren't eating
enough and aren't sleeping enough. You
were terribly restless last night.'

'Did I disturb you?'

'No, I didn't find it very easy to sleep
myself. It was so close. But you weren't
feeling well, were you?'

He knocked the ash from his pipe,
laughed, and laid it down on the table.

'I've got one of my attacks coming
on, I think.'

She did not feel brave then. With eyes
darkly anxious she looked at his thin,
worn face and shook her head at him.

'Go easy, darling. Don't worry.'

'I feel rather good tonight, as a
matter of fact.' He lied at once because
he had seen the change in her face at
the mention of his ill-health. 'Hop into
bed, sweetness, and I'll read to you.'

And later he sat beside her, reading

while she lay in the bed with her eyes shut and her arms behind her head, listening. He read her something that made her laugh, because he loved to watch her open her eyes and show the old mischievous sparkle. They were still laughing when they turned out their light. But long afterwards they lay awake in the darkness, worrying about each other, until finally from Terry's bed came a small apologetic voice:

'You awake, darling?'

'Yes, just going to light a cigarette.'

'Come over here and smoke it. Hate twin beds, don't you?'

'Despise them,' he said.

And the next moment he was there beside her in the darkness with his arms about her, and she, more content, watched the red point of his cigarette glow and fade until she slept. He did not move for fear of waking her.

There were other nights like these — some harassing, exhausting days and some moments of bitterness. Terry, like any other woman, had her spells of irritability brought on by sheer weariness and the *malaise* which accompanied her prospective motherhood. Once, when they were both worn out, Blaise spoke to her shortly and she snapped back. But the next moment she was crying passionately in his arms, and everything was forgotten except their love for each other.

But of course it could not go on. Blaise's health went first. Terry awoke one morning early in August to find that he had a high temperature and one of the worst attacks which he had experienced since she had lived with him.

In a panic she rushed to the telephone in Mrs. Fraser's lounge and called up Blaise's friend, Herringford.

Herringford had seen them once or twice since they had come to London, and had grown almost as fond of Terry as he was of his friend. He came round from Harley Street within half an hour. One look at Blaise, a brief examination, and he told Terry that he was going to send an ambulance round and have Blaise taken to his own private nursing-home off Bentinck Street.

When Terry raised a white, distraught little face, with eyes that asked a question her lips dared not frame, Herringford added gently:

'It's all right. Don't look like that. He isn't going to die or anything of that sort. But he's a sick man, and the strain of this damn show has been about as much as he can stand. I'm just going to have him round in my home and nurse him up. Now what about you, my child? Isn't there anybody you can go to?'

'No,' said Terry. 'But I shall be all right here. In fact, I shall be much happier now that I know Blaise is to have every attention. I've been terribly worried about him lately.'

'It's time things took a turn for the better for you two,' said John Herringford.

Terry smiled up at the kindly, clever face of her husband's friend.

'As long as Blaise gets well, it'll be all

right. I expect we'll hit on the right practice soon.'

'I shall have to see what can be done,' said Herringford.

He drove away from the house in Cromwell Road, profoundly disturbed by the thought of those two who were struggling against misfortune which they had never deserved. On his way to the nursing-home he stopped at a florist's and ordered a huge bunch of flowers to be sent round to Terry. He thought, whimsically, that he would have liked to have seen her face while she unpacked them and arranged them in her room.

So Blaise and Terry were separated again, and this time for quite a long spell, because Blaise was a very sick man when he entered Herringford's home, and it took him longer than Herringford expected to pull up again.

Terry, however, was not left alone in the private hotel as expected. For it was about two days after Blaise went into the home that she received her mother's letter, forwarded by the postal authorities from Chenwood.

She was conscious of real excitement when she had read that remorseful and apologetic letter from Mrs. Manstone.

It seemed too good to be true that Mrs. Clarke had taken it into her head to confess to the truth. Terry rushed to the telephone and called up the old familiar number at Wimbledon — a number which had not passed her lips for over a year.

When she heard Davis's familiar voice answer her, Terry's excitement increased. She had never realised until now what the old home meant, in spite of all the unhappiness and misunderstanding.

'It's Mrs. Farlong — Miss Terry,' she said with a catch in her voice.

'Goodness gracious alive!' came Davis's voice. 'Fancy it being you, Miss Terry.'

'Is my mother in?'

'No, Miss Terry. She's out playing Bridge.'

'She would be!' said Terry, and began to weep stupidly. She gave Davis her address, and added: 'Perhaps my mother will ring me up.'

'I know she will, miss — I mean madam. It's so hard to think of you married, Miss Terry.'

'Well I am, Davis, and listen — you're the first person to know it — I'm going to have a baby, Davis.'

'Goodness gracious alive!' Davis repeated. 'The mistress *will* be pleased. Miss Barbara — Mrs. Francis — was going to have one and didn't, and the mistress was very disappointed.'

Terry, wiping her eyes, said:

'Where is Miss Barbara?'

'She lives in Alfred Place, miss.'

'Why, that's only a short way from here,' exclaimed Terry, 'and I've been here all these weeks and haven't dreamt it.'

'I'll let the mistress know as soon as she comes in,' said Davis.

That same evening, soon after half-past six, Mrs. Manstone drove up to the private hotel wherein her youngest daughter had been living all these weeks. The meeting between them took place in Terry's bedroom at the top of the house. They looked at each other and found little difference. Perhaps Mrs. Manstone had aged a trifle and grown a trifle stouter, and of course Terry looked more mature. But it seemed hard to believe that a whole year had elapsed since they had set eyes upon one another.

Mrs. Manstone, trying not to show how the meeting upset her, opened both arms and received Terry in a close embrace.

'You must try and forgive me, my dear. I didn't understand — I didn't know.'

'That's all right, Mummy. It really is nice to see you.'

Mrs. Manstone gave her a searching look, removed her pince-nez, and wiped them on her handkerchief.

'We all make mistakes,' she said, in an attempt to restore her dignity.

Terry, half laughing, half weeping, thought:

'Mummy's the same as ever — but a little more understanding.'

Then Mrs. Manstone looked round the room. All Herringford's expensive carnations and roses could not disguise the genteel poverty of it.

'But why are you here in this place?'

'Sit down and I'll tell you everything.'

There was so much to be said — so much to tell each other. They talked until it was late and Mrs. Manstone realised that it was long past the hour for dinner. But she had by this time firmly made up her mind that Terry was going back to Wimbledon with her at once.

'It's still your home — and I did you a great wrong, Terry,' she said. 'You've got to let me make up for it a little. I can't have you living in this wretched place alone. You must come home with me, my dear.'

Terry gave a faint smile and glanced

at the photograph of Blaise which stood beside her bed.

'It hasn't been so wretched as all that,' she said softly.

'But, my dear, in your condition you want every care. You know, I can't believe that you're going to have a baby — you still look and seem such a child.'

'I'm not such a child now. I've been through a lot.'

'Too much,' said Mrs. Manstone, and blew her nose violently. 'I really don't think I shall ever speak to May Furnaby again. She was responsible for all that wretched business in Chenwood.'

'Appearances were rather against us, weren't they, Mummy?'

'Yes, I'm afraid they were,' said Mrs. Manstone, and winced when she thought of her own injustice towards her girl.

'I'll only come home on one condition,' said Terry, 'and that is, if you'll be friends with my husband.'

Mrs. Manstone blew her nose again. 'Very well, Terry.'

'He really is the dearest thing in the world, and he's been frightfully ill. You've got to like him, Mummy.'

'I daresay I will, my dear. But you must give me time to readjust my thoughts. After all, he ought not really to have taken you away, even under those peculiar circumstances.'

Then Terry shook her head and laughed.

'Thank God he did take me. The happiness we've had has far outweighed the trouble.'

'You always were a queer child.'

'Shall I stay where I am?' asked Terry.

But Mrs. Manstone put an arm about her and said huskily:

'No, come home, and Davis and I will look after you, darling.'

It was the first time in her life Terry had ever heard that word from her mother's lips. They went back to Wimbledon together. It seemed strange and rather nice when she got there, to be fussed over by Davis and petted by a mother who had never shown this side to her before. And it was even nicer when Barbara came round, added her apologies, and spent the evening with them.

Terry was sorry to see Barbara looking very miserable and discontented, and still sorrier when Barbara confessed that her own marriage was not a happy one.

'You're lucky to be in love with your husband,' Barbara said, eyeing her sister enviously.

'When you see Blaise, you'll realise that it would be impossible for me to do anything but love him.'

'I look forward to meeting him,' said Barbara. 'Mother and I have been telling everybody the truth and showing them the housekeeper's letter. It's made my husband and my mother-in-law look up a bit. Mrs. Colroyd was horrified, and said she didn't think Ruth capable of it. But there it was — shown to her in black and white.'

'What does it matter now?' said Terry.

'It matters a lot,' said Mrs. Manstone. 'You see how your husband's reputation has suffered in Devonshire. The worst of it is, we have no redress because you went away with Dr. Farlong.'

Terry gave her a faint smile.

'Don't ask me to regret that, Mummy, because I can't.'

'Oh, well,' said Barbara. 'It's all very difficult. Ruth married this Commander Spalderson and they've gone to Malta. The decree can't be rescinded now, can it?'

'I sincerely hope not!' exclaimed Terry. 'Consider my poor child! I've no wish to find myself unmarried.'

Barbara gave a feeble laugh.

'You haven't changed, Terry. All the same I do envy you.'

'So long as Blaise gets better, and we can find another practice and have another garden, I'm the luckiest woman in creation,' said Terry.

And then Davis came in with a cup of Ovaltine for Terry and Mrs. Manstone sent her firmly to bed. Feeling that she was right back in the past, Terry found herself in her old bedroom, strangely at peace. But she lay awake for a long while thinking of Blaise in the nursing-home. She dwelt wistfully on the memory of his thin, haggard face as it had looked on the pillow when she had gone to see him this morning.

'I'm feeling tons better,' he had said. 'The nurses here and old Herringford are being perfectly splendid. I only wish you were with me, darling.'

She had laughed and kissed him.

'I'm afraid this is a respectable home, darling,' she had said in her jesting way. 'We can't start having our temperatures taken lying side by side.'

That night, in Wimbledon, Terry longed for his presence, and knew that it would always be so. Only when she was with him could she feel whole and entire. Even like this, back in the bosom of her family and with the unborn child quickening within her, she was incomplete. Blaise was so much part of her life — of herself.

It was rather wonderful to know that up to a point Blaise could now uphold his reputation. The dying confession of the housekeeper might go a long way toward clearing the horizon for them in the future. But she felt, too, that had she never shared disgrace with him, she would never have known how absolutely and entirely she loved him or how much he cared for her.

She slept peacefully that night, looking forward to the morning when she was going to take her mother with her to the nursing-home to meet Blaise and show him the vindicating letter.

8

A nursing-home, more often than not, is the scene of pain and weary endurance, sometimes of bitter loss and more bitter tears. But it can also be a place of rejoicing, and, so far as the lives of Terry and Blaise Farlong were concerned, John Herringford's beautiful home off Bentinck Street was an amazingly happy memory on two very big occasions.

The first big occasion was when Blaise rose from his bed, convalescent, and was led by his wife down to a big Daimler limousine wherein, looking strangely shy for her, sat Mrs. Manstone.

Mrs. Manstone, for the first time in her life, was thoroughly enjoying the rôle of Lady Bountiful to her daughter and her son-in-law. With a great flourish of trumpets she had closed her house, sent the maids on holiday, gone to the unheard-of extravagance of hiring this Daimler and a chauffeur, and had arranged a tour through Cornwall with these two who had so remarkably endeared themselves to her during the last three weeks.

It seemed to Terry that her mother was trying to make up for all the years when she had misunderstood her and given the major portion of her affections to Barbara.

She had been strangely soft and understanding with Terry all the time she was at Wimbledon. And although she had felt, secretly, that the thing was rather a jar to her pride and dignity, she had made herself agreeable to Terry's husband.

When she had first accompanied Terry to the nursing-home and seen him lying there, a thin, tired man whose keen and clever eyes looked with such adoration upon Terry, Mrs. Manstone had lost much of her early prejudice. Blaise had taken her hand, looked up at her with one of his wide smiles, and said:

'I know I had no right to take Terry away, but, under the circumstances, try and forgive us. We're awfully happy.'

It had been difficult, then, for Mrs. Manstone to resist his charm. After all, she was heartily sick of Francis Colroyd and the continual bickering and dissatisfaction between that other pair. It was refreshing to come across these married lovers who had ridden so triumphantly over the stormy sea of failure and disgrace.

She had felt quite a warm satisfaction in being able to show Blaise Mrs. Clarke's letter and offer him an apology. But after she and Terry and Blaise had discussed the thing thoroughly, there had seemed nothing for them to do but to leave matters where they were. It was impossible for there to be a public clearance of Blaise's name. Nobody wanted any more publicity. A copy of this letter would be sent to everybody who had known Blaise or

Terry — including some of the principal scandalmongers down in Chenwood. Mrs. Manstone was more insistent upon that than anybody. As for Ruth Spalderson — let her stay in Malta with her husband.

'Good luck to them,' Blaise had said grimly. 'But frankly I should hate to wake up and find there had never been a divorce, and that I was not married to Terry.'

Later on — in September, when it was finer and warmer than it had been all the summer — Mrs. Manstone took Blaise and Terry for that motor-tour, and enjoyed herself more than she thought possible.

There were times, while she watched Blaise and Terry together, when she felt she had missed something in life. For never, even as a girl, when she had first loved and married Terry's father, had she been quite so ridiculously happy as these two.

She had insisted upon paying all expenses, which, she had assured her son-in-law, she could well afford, and Terry reasoned that he owed it to himself to cast off worry and get quite well again. Only then could he settle down to hard work, which he wanted to do, and ensure against another break-down.

It may truly be said that days of lying on a warm beach on the Cornish coast, sunny days of bathing in a glorious sea while Mrs. Manstone watched them benevolently like a mother with two children, did them both a world of good.

At the end of the fortnight Terry looked upon her husband and, as she told him, 'felt bursting with pride.' He was positively fat, brown as an Indian, and amazingly young again.

'You're quite handsome, darling,' she told him one day. 'I think I shall be quite satisfied with you for life after all.'

When the jesting was finished, he had told her just how satisfied he was with her. And of course there were hours and hours of happy conversation about

Adrian. Terry was quite convinced that it would be Adrian, and spoke of her son as though he were already in existence, which made Blaise laugh and Mrs. Manstone feel a trifle embarrassed.

'The young modern girl really hasn't any reserve,' she complained to Blaise one evening when Terry had firmly announced that she and her son were going to take a nap.

'But you wouldn't have her any different, would you, mater?' Blaise asked her, smiling.

'Well,' said Mrs. Manstone with a sigh, 'I suppose not. You've made a great difference to Terry, my dear boy. She's developed into a splendid little woman.'

Blaise repeated this to Terry, who giggled delightedly.

'Poor old mother! She doesn't realise that I haven't changed at all, and that it's she who's developed into rather a splendid old woman.'

The happy holiday came to an end,

and the search for a suitable practice began again.

And then quite suddenly the fortunes of Blaise and Terry completely changed.

The change, agreeable though it was for their future, was shadowed by grief and a sense of real loss to them both. For John Herringford died very suddenly one day toward the end of September. Unknown to anybody but himself, he had, for the last two years, been suffering from angina pectoris. The end came suddenly; and as suddenly and unexpectedly came the news to Blaise that Herringford had left him everything. With the exception of a few small legacies to a nephew and a niece and an old servant, John Herringford had recently made his will entirely in the favour of Blaise.

Blaise, who had been a great friend of his since they were at Bart's together, had always known that he was John Herringford's executor and trustee. But, so far as he had been aware, the bulk of Herringford's money was going to hospital charities. Blaise was astounded to find himself with a capital sum which would bring him in at least £4,000 a year and Herringford's beautiful house.

The day before he received the news from Herringford's solicitors, he had attended his friend's funeral and felt that the loss was a personal disaster. Terry had wept with him. Herringford had been so very kind to them both.

They were bewildered as well as deeply touched when they heard of his last great kindness to them.

They discussed it, walking together in the garden at the Cedars, which Mrs. Manstone had insisted should be their home until Blaise had found a job.

'This means a terrific difference to us, darling,' Blaise told her. 'I can hardly credit it, and I can't think why John should have been so thundering good to me.'

Terry squeezed his arm against her side.

'That doesn't surprise me — he was

devoted to you, darling. But it's all frightfully unexpected.'

'It isn't that I want a lot of money and an idle life, but I am more relieved than I can tell you to think that I'm going to be able to do what I want for you.'

'And for Adrian!' she reminded him, with tears in her eyes.

Blaise, with a lump in his throat at the thought of his friend, was rendered suddenly speechless, and walked silently through the garden with his arm round Terry's shoulders.

That was in September. In December, just after Christmas Day, the second very big and memorably happy occasion took place in the nursing-home, which, with the rest of Herringford's possessions, had passed into Blaise's hands.

It was a cold afternoon, with a bitter north wind tearing down the streets and a few snowflakes drifting from a sullen sky — an unforgettable after-noon for Blaise Farlong and his mother-in-law. Knit by a strange bond of sympathy, they sat together in the waiting-room and talked about everything on earth except a certain gallant young mother who was fighting with the courage, which was an intrinsic part of her nature, in the room upstairs.

Somehow or other Terry had known all the way along that it was a son which she would bring into the world that December day. And Blaise was not really surprised when a nurse came down with a tiny bundle wrapped in a fleecy shawl, showed him a rose-crumpled face, and said:

'You've got your son, Dr. Farlong. And such a beauty — just on nine pounds.'

Blaise, looking as though he were about to die, had only one question:

'How's my wife?'

'Much too perky — I've never seen such a girl. Says she's going to take him out in the pram tomorrow herself. For goodness' sake, doctor, go up and use your authority.'

Blaise went up those stairs two at a time while Mrs. Manstone examined her grandson and congratulated herself that she made him a very youthful grandmother.

In a big, warm room, where soft lamplight and the rosy glow of an electric fire dispelled all the shadows of that bitter day, Blaise knelt beside Terry's bed and thanked her for his son.

She, weary after the long ordeal, but with starry eyes, hung on to his hand and said, weakly and proudly:

'Isn't he hideous? I did think, with two such divine-looking parents, he might have been better-looking.'

'Little idiot,' said Blaise. 'Newly born infants are all the same — he's bound to be handsome later on. Look at me!'

'Well, there are limits!' said Terry. 'Must I look at you? I've just been through a very bad time.'

'Darling,' said Blaise huskily, 'I do love you so much!'

Terry raised his hand to her lips,

rubbed her cheek against it, and shut her eyes.

'I love you a bit. Tell nurse I want Adrian Blaise Farlong. Everybody's seeing him except me.'

'You shall have him now and at once, and you must also go to sleep and be good and do what the nurses and your doctor tell you.'

'How's the practice?'

'I'm pretty busy.'

'That's not because you're a good doctor, darling; it's because you're rich enough to be in Harley Street.'

'Little beast,' said Blaise.

She opened her eyes very wide and gave him a long look for a moment. Then she said softly:

'When I'm well enough, will you take Adrian and me to Victoria's Cottage just for a night?'

He took her hand and kissed it, then pushed the brown hair back from the brown young face. She looked too ridiculously young to be the mother of a great boy.

'It's a bit cold for Victoria's Cottage now, my sweet,' he said gently, 'but when the spring comes — in June — I'll take you there — both of you.'

'I shall always love the memory of it,' she whispered, 'and this time there must be two delphiniums in my jug. One for me and one for our son.'

With that Terry Farlong shut her eyes and went to sleep.